If you were President of the United States, who would you trust?

PAUL FERRIER, CIA Director, whose power rivals your own... **FENELLA JONES,** your beautiful assistant, willing to do anything, anytime... **PETER SPENCE,** Director of the Secret Service, who has carelessly—or carefully—cleared a murderer for White House duty... **GEORGE McMILLAN,** your Vice-President, a loyalist perhaps too eager to please... **LOUIS STERN,** your brilliant Press Secretary, who bears you an ancient grudge... **JACQUES HASBROUCK,** celebrated attorney and old college chum, who knows all the right people and defends all the wrong ones... **EVERETT QUINCEY,** adviser to Presidents, a man with a golden tongue and even more expensive tastes...

Within their ranks there is at least one unknown traitor bent on destroying you...

*   *   *

"TOP LEVEL ADVENTURE."
—*Publishers Weekly*

"AN EXPERT SPINNER OF STORIES."
—*Associated Press*

Also by John Crosby

*An Affair of Strangers**
Nightfall
*The Company of Friends**
Dear Judgment
Party of the Year
Penelope Now
Men in Arms
*Take No Prisoners**

*Published by
WARNER BOOKS

CONTRACT ON THE PRESIDENT

JOHN CROSBY

WARNER BOOKS

A Warner Communications Company

Warner Books, Inc.
666 Fifth Avenue
New York, N.Y. 10103

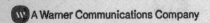 A Warner Communications Company

Printed in the United States of America

First Warner Books Printing: March, 1986

10 9 8 7 6 5 4 3 2 1

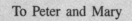
To Peter and Mary

PRINCIPAL
CHARACTERS

Harry Prentice	President of the United States
Roger Soames	Secretary of the Interior
Paul Ferrier	Director of the CIA
Fenella Jones	Secretarial assistant to the President
Miss Doll	Personal secretary to the President
Tony Canozzi	White House gardener
Louis Stern	White House Press Secretary
Peter Spence	Director of the Secret Service
Joplin	Head of CIA task force "Ozone"
Tasio	Mafia chieftain
Lamport	Crime specialist for *The New York Times*
Corbett	FBI agent
Jenkins	Treasury agent
Jacques Hasbrouck	Attorney at Law and friend of the President
Bernie Stove	Attorney General of the United States
Fred Tupper	Aide to the President
George McMillan	Vice-President of the United States
Muriel McGee	Wife of the senator from Oklahoma
Janet Blair	Wife of the senator from Florida
Agnes Costain	Wife of the senator from Vermont
Osgood Carruthers	Secretary of Defense
Roger Jackson	Secretary of State

Major General Dyke	Ordnance Chief, U.S. Army
Rosemary Prentice	The First Lady .
Jeremy Wisdom	President, British Board of Trade
Everett Quincey	Adviser to Presidents
Hanover	White House butler
Peter Battersea	Associated Press White House correspondent
Abner Dodge	Chief of the Narcotics Bureau
Jeremy Fisher	Director of the FBI
Aitken	White House correspondent, *Kansas City Star*
Whitney	Aide to the President
Peter Dewey	Secretary of the Navy
Paul Wright	Secretary of the Air Force
Tom Bakke	Secretary of the Army
Sargent	Everett Quincey's butler
Angela McMillan	Wife of the Vice-President
Atkins	
Hsu Chin	
Ed Grove	
Kyptos	
Lockheed	
Mitch	"Ozone" task force
Oscar	
Jerry Patch	
Robert	
Wenceslas	

The Time
In the very near future

CHAPTER ONE

"Tonight at the very latest. Select your own time," Prentice said, hanging up the white telephone in time to prevent the protest. It was very rough on Joplin, but then life was rough these days.

Prentice picked up the blue telephone—he was the first President to litter the desk with so many telephones, each a direct wire to various department heads, blue, green, purple, no one else permitted to pick them up—and a voice at the other end said almost immediately: "Mr. President?" A question, properly deferential.

"Roger, could you postpone our talk from 10:30 to—uh . . ."

"Of course, Mr. President."

He had no choice, of course, but Roger Soames didn't like it. He'd been pushed around quite a lot lately and he wished he knew what it meant. It showed in his voice.

"Something's come up," said Prentice, casually. He never explained what had come up to any of them, even when there was no reason not to. It was part of his technique. He was flipping through the appointments. Where could he fit Roger in? Not today certainly, or for that matter, the next day. Hell.

"Roger, you're going to be there tonight, of course. We could have a little chat before the dinner, up in my room."

"Mr. President, a few minutes will hardly..."

Because "up in my room" meant very few minutes.

"It's either that or next week."

And that was that. Prentice rang off abruptly. It was part of the system to give them a choice but not much of a choice. It worried them and he liked to worry them a little but not too much. Lately he'd worried Roger much too much. They were all entrenched in their little domains (although Interior, which took in the whole country, wasn't so little) and counted each slight as a personal affront. He'd have to be especially nice to Roger tonight.

Prentice picked up the green phone.

"Yes, Mr. President."

Not a question. A much more assured voice. He's got as much on me as I have on him, thought Prentice.

"I'd like you over here as soon as possible, Paul," said the President.

There was a pause. Paul was the only one who dared make pauses. Well, he was the head of the CIA, a different realm of power. "I'm in the middle of... something." Prentice knew instantly what the something was. There were timbres in Paul's voice that were better than code.

"Will forty-five minutes do?"

"It will have to," said Prentice pleasantly. That was part of the technique, too, being pleasant when they expected him to go through the roof, and going through the roof when they expected him to be pleasant. "Go, man!"

He hung up and picked up the blue phone again. "Roger," he said immediately, "if you can get over immediately, we can have our talk now. I've got an unexpected breather." He hung up without even waiting confirmation. He'd come.

The Oval Office was very quiet. Lights blinked on and off in the mass of telephones on the desk but were answered in other recesses of the White House. Prentice liked his telephones to get at others but he didn't like others to get at him. All his telephones were a big national joke. No other President had had this telephone mania, and he laughed along with the others at the joke. But it was no joke, really. The private lines insured a privacy no other President had wanted or needed.

Prentice had spoken to three people in the last minute and a half and none of them knew he'd spoken to the others. None of them knew what was up in other departments. If he'd had to go through his secretaries, they'd have to know at least who he was talking to—and you could infer a lot from that alone—and unavoidably a bit more. He couldn't allow that. He was the most secretive of Presidents and even his secretiveness was a secret.

He swiveled around in his great leather armchair and stared out over the green lawn and considered the loneliness of power, his special thrill. Loneliness bothered others; it stimulated Prentice.

Outside, Washington shimmered in spring sunshine. It had been an early spring, the Japanese cherry trees, already in full bloom, the air pregnant with promise. The green lawns sloped away from his vision, green as shamrocks, empty except for a gardener on his knees before a line of shrubbery in the Rose Garden.

A gardener?

Prentice opened his bottom drawer and pulled out the field glasses he kept there since the affair had started. Gardener? *What* gardener? Prentice was a nut about the White House lawns. He knew every gardener personally, had picked most of them. Through the field glasses he could see only the man's back; he didn't think he knew this one. Anyway, no gardener usually was about that bit of White House lawn at that time.

He rang the buzzer and Fenella entered at once. She was very pretty. Very new.

"Have we a new gardener, Fenella?"

She drew in a breath. Obviously she had no idea. She was scared to death—they all were. It was a damned nuisance, this fear. "Find out, will you?" he said gently. "Ask Miss Doll." Miss Doll, who was sixty-two and had been with Prentice since he was Governor of Wisconsin, knew everything.

"Yes, sir," said Fenella.

Soames was there in ten minutes. That was the nice thing about Washington; hardly anyone was more than fifteen minutes away.

"... the Oswego Preserve is one of the most popular camping sites in all of Idaho," Soames was saying. The President was staring out of the window at the lawn and specifically at that new gardener, who had hardly stirred from his bush. "Just when the season starts, and I can't get any word about when we can have it back. My God, they don't even answer the *phone* over there."

"Do you have to bother me with this, Roger?"

The voice was lazy and very friendly because Roger was an old friend and he'd put up with a lot. But Prentice wanted the idea to come through clearly. "I've got Northwest Africa and a few other rather pressing things on my mind. Really, Roger, campsites."

Roger stared back stubbornly. He was being made to look ridiculous but he mustn't be made to look *too* ridiculous. "Have you taken it up with anyone else?" asked Prentice.

"Who the hell else *is* there to take it up with? The CIA won't even answer the phone."

The President chuckled. "Well, they hardly ever answer me either. I hate to bug them over a few thousand acres of forest. What did they say they wanted it for?"

"They never tell you a damned thing, you know that."

The President sighed. "What do you want me to do, Roger?"

"I want you to ask Paul what he's doing with ten thousand acres of *my* preserve."

My preserve. Secretaries of the Interior treated the whole U.S.A. like their front lawns. Prentice said gently, "I couldn't tell you that, even if I could find out myself—and they don't always tell me things."

"Well, find out when I can get it back, will you? That preserve is used by 123,000 campers in August alone."

The President ushered him out personally. He'd try to find out, he said. He knew very well what was happening in the Oswego Preserve, although as a matter of fact, the CIA didn't know. The CIA had been just a cover for a cover. The huge intelligence outfit wasn't secretive enough for the most secretive U.S. President.

Miss Doll grabbed him with the expertise of twenty-five years' experience after he got rid of Roger and before he managed to slip back into the new office. "The new gardener's name is Tony Canozzi and he's been with us since last Wednesday."

"All right," said Prentice absently, as if he'd already forgotten he'd asked.

Miss Doll had three other things on her mind. She tried to get rid of at least one of them. "Stern has been after you for a week, Mr. President, about the press conference." Prentice loathed his Press Secretary, but where do you find good Press Secretaries these days?

"Get him on the phone," said Prentice. He did not have a direct telephone to Stern because who wanted a Press Secretary with direct access? He smiled at her. "And whatever the other two things on your mind are, forget them." He knew her as well as she knew him. Better, in fact. "Ferrier will be here in about ten minutes. Show him right in—I'm running a little late."

He vanished into his office and took up the black phone which went to the Secret Service. "Peter, do we have a security check on this new gardener, Tony Canozzi? Send it along to me right away, will you?" And he hung up. Peter Spence thought he was paranoid, of course. And wasn't he? Was anyone at the head of a huge apparatus like the U.S. Government *not* paranoid? He'd like to think that he had the problem in check because he was deeply aware of it, but wasn't even that a symptom? Paranoia was the occupational disease of U.S. Presidents. After all, four of them had been killed in office. Good thought for his memoirs. He wrote it down quickly on his memo pad and dropped it in the bottom drawer where Miss Doll collected all the stray thoughts every evening and filed them away. Some day he'd write the only good book about this marvelous and terrible job—that is, if he survived it. Paranoia...

The purple phone (Miss Doll's favorite color) lit up and Prentice lifted the receiver. "Stern is on," said Miss Doll, and put him through.

Stern launched into his complaints very rapidly. It had been three months since the last press conference. "Nixon used to go six months," said Prentice pleasantly. "Before Roosevelt they didn't have the damned things at all." A whir of malevolence came from the other end of the phone. Stern was one of the few people who talked back and hard to the President. Prentice put up with it and with Stern for one reason only; if he could talk him down—*if* he could make his point with Stern— he could make it with the country. Stern was very tough, very searching, and totally courageous. Other U.S. Presidents had had their pet poodles and drinking companions for Press Secretaries; Prentice had Stern, a schoolmate at Groton and a lifelong—what? Certainly not a friend, nor an enemy exactly. A rival perhaps? But not even that really. Always the bridesmaid—except that Stern never managed to actually *become* bridesmaid. When Prentice was Governor of Wisconsin, Stern was *not* Lieutenant-Governor—he was the Aide to the Lieutenant-Governor. It had always been that way—a string of appointive offices while Prentice was getting elected to the big ones. But brilliant. No one ever disputed that. Prentice made him his Press Secretary because Stern kept him on his toes.

Stern's voice grated on. *The Times* was asking some very hard questions about this Mafia war, if that's what it was. "Mafia war?" said Prentice. "*What* Mafia war?"

"Well, all these killings."

"Tell *The Times* the Department of Justice is where it always was. Same phone number."

"Henderson thinks it's bigger than that."

"Bigger than the Justice Department?" Prentice chuckled. "What do they want me to do? Solve a gang murder? The President of the United States?" This was a very highly developed Prentice technique. Answer a question with a question. He did it all the time, with a slight note of exasperation. It threw the questioners on the defensive—and the harder the question, the more defensive they got. He was trying it out on Stern before using it on *The Times*. If there were any holes Stern would find them.

Stern did. "Mr. President, there have been sixteen killings. Three in Detroit, four in San Francisco, six in New York, three in Chicago." (And three more in New Orleans they hadn't linked up yet, thought the President.) Aloud he said: "Sixteen? Really that many?"

"You must have read the count in the papers, Mr. President." Full of irony, was Stern.

"I don't always read the crime news, Stern." He loved to bait Stern. Such a humorless fellow.

"It's the most savage gang war since Capone's time. And Justice seems to be doing nothing about it."

"Oh, I wouldn't say that," chided the President gently. "It came up at the Cabinet meeting yesterday. Justice is doing quite a lot about it, actually. It has 112 U.S. Attorneys working on it right now."

"Doing what?"

Running around in circles like U.S. Attorneys always do when turned loose in packs, thought the President. Aloud he said: "They're fitting together the pieces about who is mad at whom in gangland. It's a very complex business—who owns which slice of San

Francisco. It takes some doing. They don't want to talk about it until the picture clears up a bit.''

Lies, all lies. And if Stern swallowed them, the country would.

Stern was having none of it. "The *St. Louis Post-Dispatch* had a very stinging editorial yesterday; it said that open gang warfare was making the U.S. Government a laughingstock in the world press. If we can't manage to prevent private wars in our cities, how can we influence the Middle East? A very good question, Mr. President. Such a good question that all the other numskulls who write editorials are going to steal it because they haven't any ideas of their own. You'll find that question being asked in all the other papers and we'd better be prepared to answer it.''

"Well, you'll just have to fend off the press until I can think of a good answer, won't you? Tell *The New York Times* some jokes, Stern. It might take some of the stuffiness out of it.'' And out of you, too, thought Prentice. "I have a guest. Good-by, Stern.'' In a mocking voice. Stern was the only one he ever said good-by to on the telephone. Usually he would just hang up. He couldn't resist a little triumphant good-by to annoy the man. But, by God, he was a good man.

Miss Doll was showing in Paul Ferrier, the dark, slender, and laconic CIA head. She had a file in her hand which she handed the President. "Sit down, Paul.'' Prentice opened the file. "Tony Canozzi, b. 1945, Chicago, ed. Chicago P.S. 129.'' Long list of places he'd worked. Twenty-two lines in all. Not enough. He handed it to Ferrier.

"Get one of your hound dogs on that, will you? And don't tell him who wants to know. Just find out a lot more and have it back as soon as possible.''

Ferrier took the envelope silently, his eyes on the President. He hadn't even said hello. The head of the CIA wasn't supposed to talk much and Ferrier talked hardly at all. Prentice wondered if he said hello to his wife, who was just as intelligent as he was. Ferrier had been born in Hell's Kitchen and brought up on the streets. He worked his way through Harvard Law School and was as tough as hammered steel. And brilliant. It wasn't easy to fool him and Prentice was never quite sure he was getting away with it. Long pause. Prentice let him wait and wonder. It was an unfair advantage the President had over the others.

"Joplin needs six helicopters. Bell X-20's, armored."

"When?" said Ferrier. He was a difficult man to faze.

"Tonight. Six P.M., at the latest."

"Where?"

"Oswego."

That fazed him. "Too far."

"Where are they now?"

Ferrier stared at him stonily. "Where does Joplin want them? He's not mounting this operation from Utah." Ferrier didn't know where, but was too smart not to know where it *didn't* come from.

Prentice stared back suavely. Two men trying to reveal nothing. Somebody had to give a little.

"If it wasn't Oswego, could you deliver?"

"To where?"

Prentice very much didn't want to say where he wanted those helicopters, even to the head of the CIA. He considered the problem. What place was three hours flying time from Detroit? What other place was three hours away from Red Bank, New Jersey?

"Could you give me three in Madison?"

Ferrier pursed his lips and thought about it. "All right. Where—the airport?"

Prentice nodded.

Where were they coming from? Prentice didn't care, as long as they got to Madison at 6:00. Now, Red Bank.

"New Rochelle?"

Again Ferrier calculated. He had to remember where his helicopters were and in what condition and how fast they flew.

"All right," he said. "Where?"

"The golf course. The tee of the fourteenth hole."

"When do we get them back?"

Everyone wanted to know when he would get his playthings back. Prentice smiled. "Tomorrow."

Silence filled the room.

"Senator Hastings is getting very inquisitive, Mr. President," said Ferrier—a long sentence for him. Hastings was chairman of the committee that was allowed some access to the CIA's bag of tricks to help mollify the Senate about where all those billions went.

"What did you tell him?"

"Surveillance." The word covered a lot of territory. "It's not going to satisfy him forever, Mr. President. He's very bright. He was in the OSS in the war and he knows a thing or two. This operation can't go on indefinitely."

"It will be over soon."

"When?"

The President smiled and rose. "Thanks, Paul," he said and shook hands.

Miss Doll came in and said that the Mothers of America delegation was outside. The CIA went out and the Mothers came in. They wore ribbons across their fronts that proclaimed them Mothers and Americans. Prentice shook hands with each one and smiled and was photographed against his desk, the American flag and the portrait of Abraham Lincoln behind him. He'd had Lincoln's portrait moved in because they'd both had Civil Wars, but Lincoln's had been easier. Prentice's war was private, though just as serious for the country at large, he felt. Had anyone ever fought a private civil war before?

The Mothers were ushered out by Prentice personally, talking and smiling with his magisterial calm to the head Mother. Then he picked up the white phone.

"Joplin," he said. "The airport at Madison and the tee of the fourteenth hole of the golf course at New Rochelle. Six P.M."

CHAPTER
TWO

The three Black Bell X-20's coughed through the blackness quietly at 150 mph—it was the least noisy of all helicopters, which was one reason Prentice loved it—heading straight out to sea, fifty feet over the water. Straight down the Jersey coast, two hundred yards of shore totally invisible in the blackness, below the radar screen. In the cockpit Joplin bent over the plans of the house.

. It was a huge place built in the flush of the twenties—twenty-five bedrooms, a ballroom, library, music room, twenty-five acres of lawn. After the crash only the Mob could afford such a place—and only the top mobsters at that. Joplin already knew the house backwards and forwards and inside and out, but a brief review could do no harm. His problem was that Tasio slept all over the house. Different rooms every night. That was one of the reasons he'd survived so long.

That, and his habit of never being on time for appointments and never following the same route twice. And in recent years, never leaving the house at all. He had the girls brought in, but recently—after all, he was seventy-two—that was pretty infrequent now and, pray God, there wouldn't be one tonight.

Joplin was a huge, craggy Latvian, straight as a poker, and his name wasn't Joplin (he'd had so many names in the last five years he often forgot his real name, which was unpronounceable). The man at the controls was named Ed Grove (was that his real name? It was so straight it must be phony—which was the way Joplin thought). Beyond the name Joplin knew nothing. He was just a whirlybird driver who had been told nothing but a compass course and didn't scare easily. At the crucial moment Joplin would steer him in vocally and the other X-20's would follow. On such a black night it wouldn't be easy—but they'd picked a black night deliberately.

When the time came the X-20's purred in silently from the sea, the offshore wind swallowing the noise of the blades. Tasio would have some men, certainly more than one, on the headland of his estate. There must have been some attempts to get at him by sea—and he was the wisest old owl of all. Better count on three men in that area alone, Joplin had said. He knew how many men were at the gatehouse—two at all hours. Intelligence had told them that, but Intelligence had not been able to dig the sea approach at all, so they had to use their brains.

Grove swiftly put the Bell down at the very tip of the headland, and just as swiftly the sixteen men poured out of it and scattered. Twelve of them melted into the ground and three into the shrubbery, one right and two left where there would probably be action. The Bell coughed back to sea to join the other two Bells hovering two hundred yards offshore and thirty feet off the water.

There was nothing to do but wait. The Jasper chopper guns were terribly silent, but no one had ever figured out how to conceal their lethal orange flash. Joplin watched for the flashes and they came very fast from the left, as he'd anticipated. There was a little wooden folly there and he had suspected the lookouts took refuge there on dark nights. Two bursts of orange light. Two men, probably. They were Jasper bursts and no one else had those guns except him.

Presently, Lockheed's voice came over the chatter box. "Got two."

"Right on," said Joplin.

Maybe there *had* only been two. The twelve men on the ground were on the move now toward the house. If they ran into anyone, well, they'd have to be dealt with and one hoped the flashes wouldn't be seen in the house.

"Oscar, move up," Joplin said into the mike.

The second Bell coughed in silently, very fast and discharged its sixteen men on the turf, which they promptly embraced. Held in reserve. Just in case. The third Bell was even more "in case." One never knew with these bastards. They were very tough indeed. Joplin remembered the Lorenzo job a week earlier in Detroit. The house had been a litter of bodies; the job was done, so they thought, when twelve more men came blasting out of a sub-sub-basement no one had suspected. It had been a near thing. Now Joplin wasn't taking any chances. He wanted an overwhelming superiority.

From the shore he saw another orange flash—a

Jasper flash. That wasn't so good. He wouldn't find out about that because Lockheed would be much too busy for radio messages. Joplin ached to know what was going on at the front gate. The front gate was very important because they had a telephone there. They also had some very fancy kind of alarm system that would flash the house immediately. The idea was to keep the house sleeping as long as possible.

How many men in the house? Who knew?

"Move up to 150," said Joplin to Grove. As the big copter silently lifted to 150 feet, Joplin turned on the infrared scope. The screen glowed awake, a square of dim light with scattered tiny orange oblongs. This was the CIA's latest pretty, and very nice, too. Joplin used it to keep track of his troops, even those at the front gate. Each orange oblong was a man, his coveralls sending back the oblong electronic beam to Joplin's scope. It wouldn't work in the house, but at least he'd know they were *in* the house.

On the scope three orange oblongs were circling in a line far to the right. That would be three men converging on the gatehouse. Twelve others were in a spreading line encircling the house. Sixteen more formed a straight line at the bottom of the scope. The reserves.

Joplin divided his gaze between the scope and the window. He was waiting for more flashes, particularly from those three closing in on the gatehouse. They must be getting very close. The oblongs were fanned out now in an isosceles triangle. Joplin looked at his watch. Three minutes until landing. A long time in this kind of operation.

The flashes came—and there were far too many of them. Three orange Jasper flashes. Then, ominously, two bright white lights. Firing back. Damn, he hoped they had silencers. It would wake the whole neighbor-hood and the house would certainly be awakened.

"Shit!" said Joplin softly. He'd hoped to wipe out the gateposts quietly. "Move up! Move up!" he yelled into the mike. But the sixteen reserves were already moving up, spreading out. Very fast, too. The twelve oblongs around the house suddenly became eight ob-longs. *Four* men were in the house now. As he watched, four more oblongs disappeared. *Eight* men in the house.

"Move in, Robert."

The third Bell whirred up to the headland and dumped its reserve manpower on Tasio's carefully and expensively manicured lawn, adding sixteen oblongs in a straight line.

"Move in fast," barked Joplin into his mike. Hell, there was no point in reserves now. "Right into the house. Speed! Speed!" The sixteen oblongs sprinted toward the center of the scope.

Joplin looked out into the blackness. The flashes had ceased around the gatepost. His eyes darted to the scope—two oblongs headed toward scope center, which would be the house. That left one oblong in the upper part of the scope, by the gate. Had he instructed them to leave a lookout by the road? No, damn it, he hadn't.

"Grove," ordered Joplin, "bring us down quick and fast at the gatehouse. Be careful. Lots of trees."

"I know," said Grove.

Into the mike Joplin barked: "Robert and Oscar, put down. Put down!" He was positioning them on the lawn for the getaway. No point in cover now. They were blown sky-high.

His Bell nosing down cautiously, both men stared out into the darkness looking for trees. There were no openings, so Grove expertly put the big copter right down on the highway—who would be on the road at 4:00 A.M.? Besides, what else could they do?

The two men broke for the gatehouse. Joplin stepped over one body on the front porch, kicked another body aside on the gravel, and found the black coveralled body he was looking for almost underneath. Bunscombe. A good man. *Had* been, anyway. Grove and Joplin picked him up head and heel and dumped him into the rear. The big copter took straight off. They'd been on the highway twenty-two seconds. A long time.

The Bell X-20's whirred down onto the center of the lawn—Robert off to the right, Oscar to the left of it. Joplin checked the time. Six minutes. Four minutes to take off, if everything went well. The house was a black mass in front of his eyes; you felt rather than saw it. Sixteen oblongs on his scope now, surrounding the house. Inside, thirty-two of his men, being very quiet about it.

The minutes ticked away. This was the worst part. It was especially hard on the sixteen in reserve surrounding the house. They were very well-trained killers in an age when killing had become the most honored of professions. All keyed-up and nowhere to go. Very hard on killers. He'd make it up to them on the next job. First in for that platoon next time.

From the upper story came the vivid orange flashes he'd been waiting for—a lot of them. And from almost every window. Nothing downstairs. They must have heard the alarm and concentrated up there. It was very sharp strategy and very bad news for him, Joplin thought, but then he'd never expected it to be easy to take Tasio. He'd lasted through three generations of gangsterdom; he'd even outlasted the perils of respectability which had done in so many of his compatriots. Respectability led them into letting down their guards. Tasio had never made that mistake.

The silent orange flashes were letting up now—except in the southern corner of the building where Tasio himself was. At least that is where Joplin had guessed Tasio was by the most thorough study of his habits. Tasio liked the sun, and while he moved from room to room night after night, on sunny days—he gravitated back to the southern exposure. Joplin had guessed that was where they would find him.

And that's where they *had* found him. And where he still was. Entrenched behind four inches of solid steel.

Lockheed's voice came through the squawk box—and it must have been very urgent for Lockheed to break silence like that. "We can't break that door, Jop. Solid steel. We'll have to go in through the window."

Cursing, Joplin pushed the D button on his mike and gave the order to the reserve platoon. On the scope an orange oblong moved away from the line and toward the house.

Joplin pushed the D button again—Tasio might have a radio in the house but he'd never get on that frequency. "No flame throwers, Burt. We want the body clearly identifiable."

That had been part of the technique. It would have been very easy to knock off these old gang czars and dump them far out to sea. No one would have missed them. So total was the *omerta*, so misleading had been those carefully rigged best-sellers from those two brain-washed authors, that the public thought these old mob-sters were long dead. Or if not dead, harmless. And rather quaint. Their disappearance would have gone totally unnoticed. Prentice (for reasons Joplin didn't fathom but didn't question) wanted them found. Messily dead. Prentice wanted their extinction spread all over the front pages. It was part of the larger plan, far too large a plan for Joplin to understand or even wish to understand. Prentice was too big for understanding. He was way, way up in the sky beyond mortal comprehension.

The oblong doing a pirouette on the scope could mean only one thing. Atkins was using a scaling ladder—and going up it very fast. Tasio now had the choice of sticking out his head to shoot him down—and getting his own head shot off—or waiting for Atkins to jump him inside. But Atkins never gave Tasio the chance to make the choice.

There was a white burst of flame from the house that lit up the lawn like daylight—the helicopters menacing black bugs on the lawn. Joplin could even see the fifteen-men reserves spread-eagled on the grass, Jaspers at the ready. Then there was blackness and the whomp of the little grenade. *Little,* hell, thought Joplin. He hoped it left enough of Tasio to identify.

The oblong on the scope did another pirouette and then disappeared. Atkins had climbed into the second-story bedroom to check the wreckage caused by his grenade, a very special weapon developed exclusively for the Ozone task force.

Joplin looked at his watch. The four minutes were up. Time to get out of there. Into the mike he called: "Bust it! Bust it! Back to the nursery! Back to the nursery!"

The scope was suddenly illuminated by orange oblongs moving back on the double to their copters. Then two blobs of orange. Bad news indeed. Two oblongs carrying a third. If he got away with just two he'd be lucky. But he didn't. There came another and

another. Four casualties. Dead or wounded, he didn't
know. Dead, probably.

Joplin saw the Atkins oblong come out of the
second story and pirouette down. "Bring the scaling
ladder," said Joplin, urgently. But of course he would.
Atkins was one of the brightest of his killers.

There were thudding noises on his Bell now—
exhausted men, breathing hard, clumping down inside
the big copter. Grove was counting them—fifteen, sixteen, seventeen...

Seventeen?

Joplin violated his own strict order—well, there
would be no one left alive in the big house to look,
would there?—and sent his little pencil flashlight probing into the copter's quiet interior, past the blacked-out
faces of the black-coveralled, exhausted men. Two blacked-
out faces, eyes staring, bullet holes in the forehead,
dead. Then came another set of staring blue eyes on a
white face.

A girl. Dead.

Joplin snapped off the flash. Hell, they'd caught
Tasio on one of his horny nights. The orders had been
quite clear about that. *No* witnesses and *no* girl corpses.
The public found all these dead mobster bodies vaguely
comic. It was very hard to feel much about dead
mobsters, although the lawyers were trying to pump up
sympathy. Girls were a different matter. You couldn't
leave a lot of dead girl bodies around. Feminists wouldn't
like that a bit—neither would the Ladies Aid societies.
And, of course, they couldn't be turned loose to talk up
a riot.

The mob was not only to be killed, but to be seen
to be killed. Conspicuous murder was part of the plan.

But not of girls. The girls had to be dealt with but never seen again by anyone.

"Up and away," commanded Joplin.

The Bell lifted off and headed straight to sea, far out to the edge of the continental shelf. There the three dead soldiers and the dead girl, shrouded in tough canvas bags with very heavy lead weights on their feet, were dropped into the sea, sinking straight down for almost a mile, where no one would ever find them.

Not during this administration, anyway, thought Joplin. Or the next two thousand.

That left only one thing. Joplin pulled the black box from under the seat, fitted the slim key into it, and lifted the cover. Inside he found the right bit of coded cardboard—a gay, blood-red card—and slipped it into the slot. If it had been the black card, it would have meant serious trouble and brought in a flotilla of those new very fast, but very noisy hovercraft that lay a mile out at sea—just in case. If it had been the white card it would have meant even worse trouble—the worst—and alarm bells would have started ringing in a forest in Utah; men would have been roused in a dozen places, code books burned, identities changed; and hundreds of people would have vanished down scores of long-planned holes.

But the gay red—for blood—card simply shrieked in its coded electronic way: Success! Success! What it actually did was to activate two recorded messages; a telephone rang in FBI headquarters in Newark—and rang and rang until the sleepy FBI slob there finally woke up and picked up the receiver—and a long recorded message said into the sleepy, resentful ear: "This is Lacey again." There was no Lacey. Lacey was a myth concocted months ago, even his voice and speech patterns carefully neutralized and untraceable. He inspired trust because he was always first with the bad news and, the FBI had discovered, very, very accurate. "Lacey here. Are you awake, man? There's been a rumble out on the headland. Tasio's place. You got that? Tasio's place—the Elms—out on Highway 26. It's finals for Tasio." And Lacey, the mythical Lacey, rang off, leaving a very wide-awake FBI man in Newark reaching for his trousers and his gun at the foot of the bed.

This had been part of the plan, too, to get the FBI on the scene ahead of the local police. Not that Prentice had anything against the local cops. Frequently, they were better and quicker than the FBI. But crime solving was not what he was after. He wanted things kept in federal—that is to say, *his*—hands. The FBI had its orders (for almost the first time in its history, under the Prentice administration it was taking orders) to get Narcotics and Treasury on the scene very fast, and to leave the place undisturbed until they had had a look around.

The other recorded message set the bedside phone at the President's head buzzing softly, so softly that his wife, Rosemary, who lay in the twin bed three feet away, never woke up. Prentice instantly awoke, as always, and lifted the phone to his ear. "Da da da da," caroled the recorded message. Beethoven's Fifth Symphony bringing the good news. "Da da da da." And rang off.

Prentice hung up the phone and looked at his sleeping wife. He was wide awake. That was the trouble with these late-night capers. Once awake he had trouble getting back to sleep—and yet he had to know. Because the whole operation was in his head. If things went wrong it meant a dozen people had to be called off, instructions had to be changed, lies had to be formulated on the spot and told with the expertise only he commanded.

Prentice grasped his robe and slipped noiselessly out of the room into his study, one of his favorite rooms in the White House. Square, low-ceilinged, and above all, small. It cut a man down to size and Presidents needed to be cut down to size once in a while. Power always corrupts. He wondered about that. Does it really? It stimulates, certainly.

Prentice was fascinated by the machinery at his command, the dozens of law enforcement agencies alone—the FBI, CIA, Treasury, Narcotics—to say nothing of the Army, Navy, and Air Force. He loved to use them, but the great trouble was that all Presidents loved to use them and frequently got the country into great trouble playing soldier in Vietnam, Laos, Cambodia, the Mediterranean, and Central America. It was very difficult not to use the great engines of destruction and he kept himself reined in. Just a few gangsters knocked off now and then. Better than knocking over a Prime Minister, wasn't it?

So now Tasio was added to the growing list. Tasio had been a legend in the Mob—the most Untouchable of Untouchables. Nothing could get at him. He had the muscle, the brain, the daring, and the caution. Plus a battery of lawyers who kept enforcement at bay. And a publicity wizard who fed the world the image of a tired old mobster from whom nobody had anything more to fear. Nothing could get at him except a fleet of deadly hummingbirds coming in from the sea on a dark night with an offshore wind.

Prentice had planned the whole operation—picked the night, the helicopters, even the Jaspers—talked to twenty-six people, none of whom knew he had talked to the other twenty-five, and broken the whole thing into a jigsaw puzzle, telling each one only his fragment. Only Joplin knew more than Prentice would have liked; Joplin *always* did. The men in the helicopters hadn't even known whose house they were invading or even what state they were in—although when they read the papers they would certainly guess.

Prentice was entranced by the sheer gadgetry of his operations—the Bells, the Jaspers, the electronic wizardry that bounced recorded telephone messages from a helicopter off a CIA satellite in space and into his bedroom. He was the first President ever to make a thorough study of all the marvelous gadgetry at his command and to use it—all of it.

Tasio was only part of a very large operation whose most dangerous operations still lay ahead. He'd wanted to erase Tasio now to shatter the legend of invulnerability. It would shake them up very badly in the upper reaches. Tasio was by no means the top rung of the ladder. Prentice didn't know who was the top of the ladder and if he didn't, nobody did. But Tasio's death would certainly shatter the serenity up there to such a degree that they might make mistakes. Or move around. Or do something that would make the upper reaches a little more visible.

CHAPTER
THREE

It was a sunny morning and Lamport of *The New York Times* sat on the bench where Tasio had once sat and stared out at the sparkling waters of the Atlantic Ocean. The story was long gone. *The Post* would skim the cream off the top. To him lay the interpretation which meant he didn't have to go grubbing around the house wallowing in sordid details. Especially since there were already seven other *Times* men in there. *The Times* was always over-covered on everything like this and the trouble with having seven men on a job is that all seven thought the other six were doing the work. Consequently nobody did it. It was amazing how much detail seven men could miss when one man would get it all.

Still, it was a nice day and it was pleasant to sit on old Tasio's bench and think what a nice life these old mobsters had had for so long. Power. And money. The same reward as popes and kings and, well, all the powerful of the world, had always wanted. And even, late in life, a sort of glory was theirs, a kind of prestige, given by romantic books like *The Godfather.* But then, hadn't that been the story of civilization? If you looked back far enough, the origin of all power and prestige was gangsterism. What were medieval kings but a bunch of murderers? A great oil baron like Rockefeller Senior, who blew up his competitors' oil wells and whose grandchild was elected Governor; from gangsterism to respectability in three generations.

Lamport had long held the theory that the only thing that was going to beat the Mob was respectability. Their kids were going to Vassar and Yale and they yearned to be Governors. Pillars of the community. Respectability licked them all in the end.

That had been his comfortably cynical (or optimistic) theory for years. But Tasio didn't follow the script. Neither did Schotz (nobody had called him "Bobo" Schotz in twenty years, but that had been his old gang sobriquet). Schotz had been found in a litter of bodies just like this only a week ago after two decades of total respectability in Detroit. The Grosse Point mansion had been a fortress with walls two-feet thick and two-inch steel doors. Just like Tasio's. But they hadn't saved old "Schotzie," as his grandchildren (several of whom had gone to Yale) called him. Retribution had come very late for Schotzie and for Tasio, but it had come.

He gave a short involuntary giggle.

"You laughing at your own jokes?" asked Corbett. The FBI man sat down next to him on the park bench and they both stared out to sea.

"I was just thinking," said Lamport, "that if I can stave off retribution until I'm seventy-two, I will be very happy. When you're seventy-two, what difference does it make—a heart attack, retribution—you got to go somehow. Did Tasio have a grin on his face?''

"He didn't have much face left. But there might have been a grin on what was left of it.''

The two men soaked up sunshine and watched the sailboats that looked like white cardboard cut-outs on the blue sea. "I've got to come up with three and a half columns of theory. Have you got any theories?'' said Lamport.

"Even if I had any I wouldn't give them to you. But I haven't any. Or rather I have so many that it amounts to not having any. You can make them up as well as I can—better, in fact. You've been at it longer.''

It was Corbett's conviction that all the theories about the Mob were fantasies and all ridiculous. He'd been the Justice Department's expert on the Mob ever since Prentice had put him there. Before his time, Bobby Kennedy had been horrified at the immunity big crime had had under J. Edgar Hoover and had done something about it (before he himself had been gunned down. By the Mob? It was a theory that had long fascinated Corbett). Corbett had read every single word of every newspaperman, to say nothing of all the best-sellers about Mafialand, and his estimate was that ninety-two percent of it was absolute hogwash and that the little bit of truth—the eight percent of truth—had crept in there entirely by accident, if for no other reason than that you could not write so many millions of words without happening on the truth in spite of yourself. But then, Corbett had very little faith (although he would never in the world admit such a thing) in his own theories about the Mob.

What little faith he had had been knocked into a cocked hat by this orgy of killings. Everything about it

contradicted every last theory he had; everything about
it contradicted everything the Mob itself had stood for
in the previous twenty years. The last thing in the world
it wanted was messy killings and horrifying headlines.
If they wanted someone removed, it was done quietly.
Blood itself was considered the height of vulgarity.

"Submarine?" said Lamport, not entirely in jest.

"Yeah," said the FBI man. "That's it. A submarine. They surfaced right over there in two feet of water
and sent these little green men to scale the walls into
Tasio's room. You want to come and have a look at it?
The photographers are finished. It's a pretty sight."

The two men walked up the manicured lawn and
Corbett's eyes never left the grass. Suddenly he leaned
down and inspected a bit of grass, his nose two inches
above it.

"Submarines?" inquired Lamport.

"Just ordinary blood," said Corbett. "Get that in
your story, will you. Whoever did it had blood."

But what was important was that whoever did it,
both men were thinking, had done a little bleeding two
hundred yards from the house toward the sea. If the
invaders had come by road they wouldn't have been two
hundred yards on the other side of the house toward the
sea.

"I thought all the blood was in the house," said
Lamport. "Why was anyone bleeding out here?"

"Well, you ought to be able to speculate for at
least a column and a half on that alone," said Corbett.
"An old romantic *New York Times* man like you."

They entered through the french windows from the
terrace. All very elegant, Tasio's pad. He had no sense
of style whatsoever, but he had been attracted to the

French château because of the stone walls. Stone walls were very bulletproof. Corbett pointed to the locks. "They got in here. Nothing simpler. A boy scout could pick that lock. But then, Tasio had relied on his muscle to keep them away from the house. Getting this far would be like walking through minefields."

"How many bodies did you find on the lawn?" asked Lamport.

"Six. Three down there in that little wooden lookout house. Three at the gatehouse."

"And blood on the lawn," murmured Lamport.

A body lay face upward in the drawing room, arms akimbo. A man was drawing his outline on the parquet floor in white chalk. The man had been stitched up from crotch to face with automatic fire. Lamport could count sixteen bullet holes from where he stood, and there were probably more. Very rapid fire. Very expert fire. Only an expert stitched longitudinally.

The two men went through the drawing room and into the hall. A litter of bodies already encircled in chalk, sheeted and waiting for the wagon. A man in a dark suit came at Corbett flashing a card. Corbett grunted. "What kept you? I think what you're looking for is downstairs. There's a sub-basement—just like in Detroit. They must have had the same builders."

The Treasury man didn't reply to this flippancy. They were only interested in money, those fellows—he just hurried down the stairs at the right of the front door.

"They're on the scene very fast—for Treasury people. It used to be six weeks before a Treasury man decided he was interested. But with these killings they've become very curious. Come on. Tasio's upstairs."

The two men went up the broad staircase where

two more of Tasio's beef squad lay face up, arms outspread, having given their all.

Down in the sub-basement the Treasury man found two of his colleagues sourly eyeing an immense safe of the type used in banks about thirty years ago. It was still formidable.

Jenkins looked at it for a long moment. "French," he said. He was an expert on safes. There was not a safe made anywhere in the world he couldn't identify in seconds. "Tasio probably brought it in—and the French workmen to install it—to keep down the talk. You couldn't install an American safe that size without there being an awful lot of gossip in the safe industry—and Tasio hated that kind of gossip."

"You suppose he killed the poor Frogs after they built him his safe—like they did in old days?" suggested the other Treasury man hopefully.

Jenkins said, "Call Clerihew. He can open any kind of tin—even French tin."

Outside the front gate a commotion was going on. Hasbrouck, the celebrated lawyer who had connections clear up to the White House—so they said—was trying to gain admittance. The FBI man at the door was being enormously polite. But very firm. He had heard of Mr. Hasbrouck, as who hadn't, but he had his orders. However, if Mr. Hasbrouck insisted, he could call Mr. Corbett. Meanwhile, would the great man like to come into the gatehouse and sit down? Hasbrouck was not going to be pressed by any FBI mick, and said how very kind and he'd be honored to step inside—over the dead bodies—but he would very much like to talk to Mr. Corbett if it was not too much trouble and, in fact, even if it was.

It was. It took quite a while to find Corbett in the

big house. He was showing Lamport the automatic steel doors which had done Tasio as much good as the Maginot Line had done the French and he hated to be torn away. But he finally came to the telephone and listened for a very long time without saying anything at all.

Hasbrouck. A very tough apple indeed. He had represented not only the top mobsters but also some very fine people as well. It was Hasbrouck's thesis that mobsters deserved the very best defense, just as non-mobsters. In fact, no mobster was a mobster unless it was proved in court and, of course, it never *was* proved in court; with Hasbrouck representing them they never got anywhere near a court or even a police station.

Hasbrouck talked very politely and at great length about the sanctity and privacy of all papers on the Tasio estate. He had come armed with a court order (Corbett permitted himself a brief grin at that) and he threw out a great many Latin legal words. Also, how soon could the house be vacated, because the family wanted to take possession as soon as possible? Would it be possible for the law enforcement officers to be off the premises by 4:00 P.M.? It would be greatly appreciated. Also, he had heard through the grapevine that Treasury officials were on the scene. He was deeply shocked to hear this because, of course, Treasury had no authority to touch any of Mr. Tasio's private papers and if they did, he was afraid he would have to serve a Federal Court injunction, which he just happened to have in his pocket having stopped by the Federal Court that very morning to get it. He would serve it right now—the moment he got into the estate. Would Mr. Corbett kindly instruct this very nice minion of the law to let him in immediately? If he didn't, of course, he was terribly afraid he

would have to make trouble, and since the Attorney
General was among his best friends. . . .

Corbett savored it all. No other word for it. For
years he had been forced to be polite to the Hasbroucks
of the law offices who seemed to wrap their clients in
total immunity against all charges. Lately there had
been a stiffening, although Corbett didn't understand
why. He just knew there would be no call from the
Attorney General in this case (as there would have been
a few years earlier).

"Mr. Hasbrouck," said Corbett when Hasbrouck
had finally run dry, "we are investigating a murder. In
fact, twenty-two murders. Everything in the house—
including Mr. Tasio's papers might contain clues as to
who killed him and the *other* twenty-one people who
are lying all over the place. I'm afraid I can't let you in
because you would just obstruct the course of justice
and I know that a lawyer of your eminence would not
want to do that."

Hasbrouck said in that case he'd very much like to
use the phone to call his great friend the Attorney
General.

"Go right ahead," said Corbett agreeably.

Within five minutes Hasbrouck was back on the
line. He had not been able to get through to the
Attorney General. Far from chastening him, this had
made him even more menacing. He wanted to warn
Corbett that keeping a lawyer from his client's private
property had been held in *Stanton* v. *Connecticut* to be
as serious an infringement of the First Amendment as
keeping an attorney from the client himself, and that
Corbett could face prosecution. Did he know that?

"Very interesting," said Corbett.

Furthermore, the federal courts had held again and

again that law enforcement officials could occupy premises only for a reasonable length of time and since the FBI had been in possession since 4:30 A.M., a reasonable length of time might quite accurately be said to expire at 4:00 P.M. that afternoon. Corbett laughed. Hasbrouck didn't like that laugh. No FBI schmuck of Corbett's relatively low status would dare to laugh at Hasbrouck unless he was very, very sure of himself.

Hasbrouck changed tactics swiftly. "When," he asked softly, "do you think you will have the job finished in order that you may vacate the premises, Mr. Corbett?"

"Twenty-two murders?" said Corbett reflectively. "I think we could clean up the work and be out of here in about two months."

While Corbett was listening to Hasbrouck's harangue, Jenkins handed him a slip of paper on which he had written that he needed at least two months in which to get into that safe and to photocopy and follow up every last scrap of paper in there all the way to those Swiss banks.

Prentice was in the East Wing conference room, smiling as far as his tight face would allow, at the International Association of Telephone Engineers. "Mr. G. M. Young has said that statesmen are not architects but gardeners working on such material as only nature can furnish. They never pull up the plants to see how the roots are doing."

There was a gasp of pleasure and a polite spatter of giggles from the engineers, who realized they had heard a *mot*, but who did not quite understand it. Prentice knew they wouldn't, but the reporters following through the White House would duly report it and a milligram would be added to his mystique.

He strode out of the room amid tumultuous applause, having given the engineers two minutes of his time, won their loyalty (and he hoped their votes), and added a tiny anecdote to what he privately called his Abraham Lincoln routine.

Back in his office, the white telephone glowed fitfully. He picked it up. Joplin's voice said, "Twenty big ones." Prentice subtracted the day of the month (the sixteenth) and came up with four dead (big ones). The phone was scrambled and theoretically bug-proof, but Prentice doubted anything was secure. It was a simple-minded code, but it made life a bit tougher for anyone listening in, if anyone was.

"How are you?" asked Prentice kindly.

Joplin hesitated. "How are you" didn't mean anything like how are you. It meant was the group ready for another punch up? and it wasn't.

"Pretty tired," said Joplin. "I didn't get to bed till all hours."

Now it was Prentice's turn to hesitate. Just as a matter of tactics, a one-two would have been stupefying. Still, if the group was exhausted—and Joplin wouldn't say such a thing unless it were truly streaked out—it was wise to hold off. Prentice was a very cautious, daring man.

"You'd better turn in early then. Tomorrow night is a full moon."

Joplin grunted. "Tomorrow? It's the maid's night out."

That meant the group wouldn't be full-strength, but then one had to balance a bit of risk against the probable return. If he left them too much time to ponder, they'd figure this caper out—or they'd go underground. Either would be disastrous.

"Someone else will have to do the dishes then," said the President. "When the weather's right, we just have to move it. What do you need?"

What Joplin really needed was men. He couldn't get those—not *that* fast anyway. "Fourteens," he said stubbornly.

Fourteens were recoilless rifles and Joplin knew he didn't have a chance in hell. Prentice laughed.

"You're out of your ever-loving mind," he said gently. "Fourteens are for children." ("Children" was both Prentice's code word and his private opinion of armies the world over. Prentice thought armies were as obsolete as the priesthood—and as useless.) "They leave crumbs all over the room."

That had been an ever-present danger from the very first—that something would get left behind which would signal access to very sophisticated hardware. The FBI would reach too many conclusions.

"I promise I won't take a single bite unless I'm starving—and then we'll clean up the mess to the last crumb."

Long pause. Even if he let Joplin play with those dangerous toys, how to get them there?

"I'll call back," he said gently. "Go sleep it off, Jop. And thanks."

He hardly ever said thanks.

Miss Doll was in the room, but not before knocking. Even after twenty-five years she knew it was as good as her job was worth to catch the President by surprise. *Ever*.

"The Attorney General is on the phone," she said, hitting every syllable like a little hammer.

Prentice permitted himself a large guffaw. Miss Doll's little vocal tricks amused him immensely. Her little hammer blows meant *this is very large trouble indeed*. She might have said the same thing dragging each syllable, which would have meant *that old bore is on the phone, shall I tell him to get lost?* Or she might have given each syllable a little lilt, which would have meant *we've got him exactly where we want him*.

Prentice picked up the black phone and Miss Doll quickly said, "You're due in the East Dining Room in just ten minutes—the Senate wives."

"With or without husbands?"

"Without."

Prentice nodded. Into the phone he said, "Bernie, how are you? Sorry to keep you waiting."

The Attorney General, Bernie Stove, who had known Prentice for thirty years and was aware he knew almost nothing, was razor-sharp, full of Jewish jokes and geniality, his eyes twinkling behind gold-rimmed spectacles—but a headache when he got tough. He was in one of his tough moods.

"Mr. President," he began.

Still the title after thirty years, thought Prentice. Oh, Stove was very shrewd. "I've had Hasbrouck on my ass for two hours. He says the FBI is out at Tasio's place."

"Whose place?" asked Prentice innocently.

The Attorney General made a face which the President fortunately didn't see. He knew damned well Prentice was too smart not to know who Tasio was and what had happened.

"A big mobster who got erased last night along with twenty-one of his henchmen."

Prentice gave a gasp of horror. "Twenty-two men!

Murdered! Mr. Attorney General . . .'' When he used the title with a mister in front of it, it meant a dressing down. Attorney General Stove closed his eyes and listened for a full three minutes as Prentice told him these gang murders were a disgrace to the American flag, a black spot on American justice, and a shame on the American people. Prentice was a master of political cliché. He used it to stun, muddle, and blunt attack by counterattack. Stove just had to wait it out.

"What is the Justice Department doing about this horrifying affair? This is a day that will live in infamy, Mr. Attorney General.''

Stove had almost, but not quite, forgotten what he had called about by the time the flow of Presidential horseshit paused long enough for him to leap in:

"Mr. President, Hasbrouck—and don't ask me who he is. He's one of your closest friends—has been out at Tasio's place for two hours. The FBI won't let him in. He says Corbett is violating the First, the Sixth, the Eighth, and the Twelfth Amendments and he's going to take every last violation all the way to the United States Supreme Court.''

"We can't have that,'' said Prentice. "Mr. Hasbrouck is a very eminent attorney as well as a close friend. Why is the FBI doing this to him?''

Stove made a face at the phone. "Because, Mr. President, the White House—over my head—has ordered them to and ordered me to lay off.''

"The White House?'' asked Prentice in polite horror.

Stove strongly suspected this was play-acting, but he didn't know for sure. He couldn't prove it. And as a lawyer he knew if he couldn't prove it it wasn't true.

"Your brilliant young assistant, Tupper, has issued

these orders with the clear implication that they came from the very top.''

"Tupper?" said Prentice, pretending to grope. "Oh yes, Tupper. Oh yes, indeed. Well, you see, Bernie, Tup is doing some very important, very secret work on the heroin situation. I don't know *what* exactly (like hell he didn't), but if he wants Hasbrouck off the FBI's turf, then there must be a very important reason. On the other hand, we must not allow the FBI to violate the First, the Sixth and—what were those other Amendments?''

"The Eighth and the Twelfth.''

"Well, we can't have the Constitution pushed around like that. I'll tell you what I'll do. I'll have a talk with Tupper and we'll straighten this out. If Hasbrouck calls again, tell him I am personally very sorry for this and I am personally looking into it, and believe me, something will be done.''

He rang off smiling.

On the other end Stove was left with a telephone in his hand and a look of very civilized exasperation on his face.

He called Hasbrouck at the Tasio gatehouse where the lion of a thousand courtrooms was pacing up and down, increasingly furious.

"I talked to the President—" said Stove to Hasbrouck in little mouthfuls—"at great length. He talked to me. At great length. He was furious. That Tasio was murdered. That you were inconvenienced. That the constitution was being ravished. He promised heads would roll. He's looking into it personally. He wanted me to tell you personally how personally angry he was that you personally had been treated in such a way. And, if you want my advice, Jacques, you had better stop wasting your time out there because no one is going to let you in until they are good and ready which, as Corbett says, may not be for two months.''

Miss Doll came into the Oval Office, lips pursed as only she could purse them. Enunciating with wry precision, she said: "*The* Vice-President of *the* United States is on the purple phone." She picked up the purple phone on the President's desk and handed it to him. The President put his hand over the receiver.

"Really, Miss Doll," said Prentice, "you shouldn't speak of the Vice-President of the United States in that tone of voice."

"What tone of voice?"

"You say it as if you're saying *that pain in the ass*. Where is that pain in the ass right now?"

"Ethiopa—where you sent him—to look into the relief situation."

Prentice puffed out his cheeks in resignation. Where he'd sent him, eh? Where hadn't he sent him to get him out from underfoot? Southeast Asia, Northwest Africa, central South America, northern Europe. Where could he send him next time? He was runnning out of earth.

Into the phone with a great show of heartiness, Prentice said: "George, how are things in Northwest Africa?"

It was a smallish luncheon. Only the wives of the Senate Committee chairmen, some very bright, some very stupid. Miss Doll had put the brightest of the lot, Muriel McGee, wife of old Senator McGee of Oklahoma, chairman of the Senate Foreign Relations Committee, on his right. They were joking about Mariner 26, which had now passed out of the earth galaxy altogether and was headed toward the Peondonnis galaxy, still bleeping back information that couldn't be of any earthly use to earthlings, but might conceivably be of interest to their own galaxy—if there were people there capable of unscrambling the earth code, which was highly unlikely.

"Three billion dollars, Mr. President," said Muriel. "Just to send that thing out to hell and gone, making those bleeping sounds I can't even get on my radio. We could have built a whole new school system in Oklahoma."

"You know we couldn't spend Federal money on your schools, Muriel," said the President genially. "That would be a violation of state's rights. We can build schools in Ghana—not in Oklahoma."

"Just what are we doing out there in outer space, Mr. President? Looking for little green men with pointy heads?"

"Trying to avoid them," said the President. "They might very well be one hundred million years ahead of us in development. *Homo sapiens* is, after all, only about two and a half million years old. You wouldn't really enjoy running into anyone who ranked you by ninety-eight million years, Muriel. Not *you*."

"I'd be *thrilled*," protested Muriel McGee.

"No, you wouldn't. They'd regard you as you regard a mosquito—just a nuisance. And squash you like that." He snapped his fingers.

That was as far as they got because Janet Blair—wife of Senator Blair, chairman of Armed Services and Very Important, gushed in with what Prentice had kept at bay so far. "Mr. President—" Janet Blair knew just how to bore through and make contact in a conversation. "Aren't these gang killings *horrible*—in a *marvelous* sort of way?" She tinkled with laughter.

All conversation at the table dried up instantly. It

was what they all really wanted to talk about—or listen
to. No one had had the temerity to bring it up. That was
one of the things Prentice noted about being President—
topics of conversation that were on every tongue at
every other dinner table were frequently not brought up
at the President's dinner table unless he brought them
up himself. People discussed events of great public
moment like a death in the family at the President's
table. Or some other scandal. Something unmentionable—
unless the President himself introduced it.

"All I know is what I read in the papers," said the
President agreeably. That he was the last to find out
things was a myth that he fostered with only indifferent
success.

"Oh, come off it," said Muriel McGee. "Not a
pin drops in Washington that you don't know about."

"Oh, but this wasn't Washington. It was Red
Bank, New Jersey, wasn't it? Wasn't it Red Bank? You
know, I haven't even read the papers, I've been so
busy."

Agnes Costain, wife of the Senator from Vermont—
there since her husband had just become Chairman of
Rivers and Harbors and it was thus her first White
House luncheon—fell into that trap with great enthusiasm. "The *Washington Star* says—" she shrilled. The
others stared stonily. They had not come here to hear
what the *Washington Star* had said: they had all read
what the *Star* said. They had come to hear what the
President of the United States said, the Horse's Mouth.

But the President had turned his attention to Agnes,
and listened with intense interest to every silly word.

"The *Star* says," said Agnes Costain, "that there
is only one mob sufficiently organized and powerful
enough to take on Tasio. That is the Chicago crowd—

the Stein mob—which is really the old Capone mob re-organized. They have both the muscle—'' You could almost hear her putting it in quotes, ''and the manpower and the motive.'' Nice alliteration there, thought the President. She must be quoting the *Star* verbatim.

''. . . the motive is the important thing. Why? Well, the *Star* says the Chicago crowd wants to take over the eastern ports because it needs them for its cocaine operations.''

''The *Star* said that?'' asked the President, innocently. So Stern had managed to plant that big lie—on *who* over at the *Star*? He, Prentice, had planted it on Paul Ferrier with instructions to plant it on Stern (with strict orders to conceal where it came from, of course). Prentice, who amused himself in the shower every morning thinking up new and wilder rumors about what the Mob was up to in these bloody affairs, had doubted that Stern would swallow such nonsense. Maybe he hadn't. He had dutifully planted it anyway.

''Do you believe that, Mr. President? That these killings are just one mob trying to move in on another one? It does seem very stupid. And the one thing the Mob has never been in matters like this is stupid.''

Damn the woman, thought Prentice. Aloud he said, ''It's just possible that we have been overestimating the intelligence of the syndicate (using an old, old term to show how out of touch he was) all along. Lately, there have been several books suggesting that the younger Mafia generation is not nearly as bright as their fathers.''

In fact the Mafia was getting very bright at public relations, thought Prentice.

''The one thing you should bear in mind in reading all these newspaper stories,'' said the President gravely, ''is that they are merely speculation. The Mafia, you must know, is renowned for its secrecy. Nobody has really been able to penetrate it, and when someone reports that he has, believe me, he is kidding himself. He hasn't.''

This had been the great strength of the Mafia, *omerta*—secrecy to death—and it was Prentice himself who had perceived what a great weakness it was. For if they were all that secret they couldn't fight back. Any sort of implausibility, like that rubbish in the *Star*, could pass for true currency, since no one knew what the facts were. Like the CIA, you could accuse them of anything at all, and they simply had to take it in silence. It was only since the cocaine scandal had become so horrifying in the last ten years that the Mob had got around to public relations, planting a whole host of best-sellers which in varying guises told the same story: that the Old Families were no longer in heroin or, in fact, had never been in it and were simply a bunch of doddering old men soaking up sunshine surrounded by their adoring grandchildren and had never done anything worse than run a little harmless gambling.

But this facade had not concealed from Prentice the tremendous weakness of their position, shrouded in secrecy, unable to break the habits of decades. Say nothing. And as long as they said nothing, you could plant any number of cover stories. And he did. A different one every day.

"Some day," said the President, "we'll know the real secret of the Mafia. And what a story it'll be! Who killed who—and how and why? If only I live long enough to be able to read it."

He rose. They all rose.

"Ladies, it has been, as always, a great pleasure to play host to you once again. I can't think of any party I look forward to year after year with such enormous pleasure. I return to my heavy burden with a light tread and an even lighter heart.'' He himself led the laughter at his old world courtesy. He said good-by to each and every one, asked after each and every husband and each and every child.

He actually did return to the Oval Office with a light tread and a lighter heart. The dear girls would spread that *omerta* slush all over Washington. One social affair out of the way. That left only dinner tonight, which wouldn't be so easy. Hasbrouck would be there and he'd be in a driving mood.

CHAPTER FOUR

The Cabinet meeting was at three o'clock and every last man—Treasury, State, Interior, Health, Welfare and so on—was interested in one thing only, the Tasio killings. "Bernie," said the President genially, "you're on. This is your baby all the way."

Bernie pursed his humorous mouth in a little *moue*. It was not his baby all the way, not at all. Lately, initiatives he had undertaken had disappeared in the general direction of the White House and were never seen again. But how could one say this in a Cabinet meeting? One couldn't.

Aloud he said, "We are still investigating. We have put top priority on an instruction to every FBI office in the country to find out and report instantly about any large movement of hit men in their areas. If twenty-two men were gunned down in what amounts to a fortress, it was a very large operation. I don't think that kind of muscle could be transported from even such big cities as Chicago or Detroit without being noticed. All our undercover people have their ears open and are being asked to report by tomorrow at the latest.''

There was silence. Before someone else got in ahead of him Prentice put in mildly, ''Bernie, this is exactly what you did in the other affrays—put out feelers. And came up with nothing much. You say they can't move all this muscle without causing commotion, but obviously they have. Is it possible this operation is being staged from some other country—Canada perhaps?''

Red herrings. He was the world's greatest expert on red herrings.

Stove spent ten minutes explaining how this was impossible. The Coast Guard would spot them before they got anywhere near New Jersey.

Osgood Carruthers, the Defense Secretary, broke in finally: ''Army intelligence is very concerned about the explosion that blew up Tasio. As I understand it, there was—apart from his face—hardly a wound on him. He died from sheer blast, and that usually blows an arm off or something. This means they have some very advanced explosives, even more advanced than Ordnance. This might suggest a foreign country.''

The President said nothing. He didn't like this line of talk at all. But any further exploration of this avenue was cut off when Roger Soames burst in to ask the question on everyone's mind.

''Has the FBI any idea *how* this assault was accomplished? The place is a fortress, walls twenty-two feet high. Twenty-two guns inside. That would give pause even to an Army Assault Group.''

Soames had been a lieutenant in the Green Berets in Vietnam. These gang killings had fascinated him from the very outset as exercises in sheer combat tactics. "I'd hate to take on Tasio with anything less than company strength, with mortars to knock out the strong points. But there *were* no mortars."

"Army Intelligence thinks it was helicopters," said Carruthers. "But it would take a *lot* of helicopters—and they would have woken up half of New Jersey. No one heard anything."

That was just about enough of that. Prentice coughed the warning cough which ended all the speculation. "Gentlemen, the situation in Southwest Africa has deteriorated even further with this latest outburst from the Prime Minister of Ruanda. Roger, would you please fill us in."

Roger Jackson, the first black Secretary of State in U.S. history, took center stage and expertly filled them in on affairs four thousand miles away—in another part of the forest, as Shakespeare used to say. There was nothing like another part of the forest to take men's minds off suspicions more close at hand.

Prentice strode from the Cabinet Room to the Oval Office at the half run he'd developed since he'd been in office, eyes straight ahead. There were always people in the Appointments Office, much as he cut the numbers down; a moment's hesitation meant he'd be grabbed. He missed nothing though. Out of the corner of his eye—an eye that everyone tried and failed to catch—he saw Major General Dyke, head of Ordnance (what in hell did he want?), Stern (Prentice knew what *he* wanted), and Tupper, all in a row like little indians.

Inside the office waiting for him—the only man in the world accorded that privilege—was Paul Ferrier, wrapped as always in his special brand of cool imperturbability. Without a word, he handed the President a folder. Prentice sat down with a little sigh and opened it.

C A N O Z Z I. Just like that, capitalized, double-spaced and mind grabbing. It began without preamble:

> His real name is James Fitts. b. Brooklyn 1938 or thereabouts. Served apprenticeship in old Eighth Avenue gang, later Murder, Inc. Indicted murder of seaman, 1956; indictment quashed for lack of evidence; indicted Sullivan Law 1960, indictment quashed. No other arrests. Pretty well known hit man for the Brooklyn harbor gang for ten years, 1956-66. No one knows what he's been up to since then, at least on quick sniff around. Very bad man for White House gardener.

The President looked at Ferrier. Ferrier looked back, totally at ease. Prentice wondered if anything would ever ruffle Ferrier's aplomb, short of a bullet. Not even that. Well, he wasn't going to speak first. He swung around in the massive black leather chair and stared out at the lawn and did some thinking.

Who the devil had let the man in? How had the Secret Service missed this magnificently inappropriate hiring? Who had put the man there? Did it have anything to do with the Affair? But of course it did—what else? But above all—and this intrigued Prentice more than anything else—why, oh why, had they called the man Canozzi? Why give a man an Italian mob-style name to cover the perfectly ordinary name of Fitts? Much more understandable to hire a hitman named Canozzi and give him a cover name of Fitts. Wasn't it?

It sounded—and the thought sent a thrill of fear right through him—as if someone had a sense of humor. Was this just someone's way of saying, We're on to you, Prentice—and with humor? Prentice didn't like the humor a bit. He was trying to shatter someone's cool up there. If they were playing jokes, obviously he wasn't getting through to them. Pity.

Prentice swung around to face his CIA chief. "What are you doing about it?"

"I was going to ask you what *you* wanted done about it?"

Prentice gritted his teeth. Imperceptibly. Sometimes Ferrier's cool got him down, but he'd never, never admit it. "I mean right now. What *have* you done about it?" With the implied rebuke that a great deal should have been done instantly.

It had been. "You have a new gardener. One of our best Italian gardeners."

Prentice was amused. "I didn't know you had Italian gardeners."

"The CIA has everything. Already he has spotted a very bad fungus on your roses that should have been attended to—by the other guy. He's keeping an eye on him. Never letting Canozzi more than six feet out of his sight. Also, Canozzi has been assigned duties on the other side of the lawn—down by Pennsylvania Avenue."

"What else?"

"We went through his room. Nothing. Tapped his phone. Nothing yet. We've also got a day and night tail on him. If you want him picked up someone else will have to do it. You know we're way out of our territory."

The CIA had no business operating in the U.S.A. at all, a regulation widely honored in the breach. The FBI was theoretically not supposed to leave home shores or invade CIA territory—also widely honored in the breach long before Prentice came to the office. He was the first President to use the two agencies to the fullest extent in their illegal capacities. One way to insure secrecy.

"I don't want him picked up," said Prentice quickly. "I want him watched—just as you're doing. I want to find out who put him there—and why. You haven't told Spence any of this."

"Certainly not."

"Good man." The President stared at Ferrier thoughtfully. The ramifications were breath-taking—and, of course, he couldn't tell Ferrier any of it. How much did he guess? "I know it's difficult—without tipping Spence— but is it at all possible to find out what numskull in the Secret Service cleared this man? And why?"

The "why" was explosive. It implied that someone had done it deliberately.

"We're already on it, Chief." Ferrier was really letting down his hair with the word "Chief." Usually, it was the other way around—Prentice called *him* Chief. It meant he was just a tiny bit alarmed. Fancy Ferrier being alarmed by anything! "We're especially interested in the why. Especially *why Canozzi*?"

"Is there anything special about the selection of that particular name?" asked the President.

Ferrier said, "Maybe it's just an accident. But Canozzi was a famous Sicilian leader—famous in Sicily anyway—for shooting down Very Important People, the Mayor and the Governor, among others. It's almost as if someone was trying to tell you something, Chief."

It almost seemed as if he was supposed to spot this hit man, didn't it? As if Canozzi had been planted there for the sole purpose of being spotted. By someone with a sense of humor. Oh, I'm scaring the hell out of them, thought Prentice. And to whom could he complain? Nobody. Nobody at all. Not even Ferrier, really. Certainly not Spence, whose job it was to keep him alive. *Omerta*. He himself had so skillfully exploited the Mob's use of silence; now the weapon had been turned against him. He'd kept the wires so firmly in his own hands, letting no one into the whole plan (well, Joplin knew an awful lot), that now he had no one at all to turn to. He was being trapped by his own secretiveness. Delicious irony.

The light on the purple phone had been glowing angrily for some time. He picked up the receiver. "The natives are getting restless," said Miss Doll.

"I want to see Tupper ahead of the rest of them," said Prentice. "And what the hell is General Dyke doing there. He hasn't got an appointment, has he?"

"He made it a month ago."

"Tell him to—oh hell, I better see him, I suppose. But tell him he has got to make it very fast."

Prentice faced his CIA chief. "Keep in touch, Paul. I've got a small dinner tonight—just a few friends. Don't hesitate to break right in—if you have anything worth breaking in for."

He rose. Ferrier didn't rise. He just looked at his Chief. Then he opened his black attaché case, brought out a little toy-like hand gun. All of four inches. When he closed his hands over it, it all but disappeared. Ferrier rose and opened his hand again, showing the tiny thing once more, then slipped it into his side pocket. He patted the pocket. "No bulges at all," he said. "I have always been opposed to shoulder holsters or any kind of holster for this kind of protection because you have to make a characteristic gesture." He made it shooting his right hand under his armpit. "A dead giveaway. Whereas with this—" He slipped his hand into his pocket, came out with the fist folded over the little gun, then in another almost imperceptible movement, it was pointed at the President. He kept it pointed there for a moment to make his point.

"Or," said Ferrier gravely, "you could handle it like this." The tiny gun disappeared into Ferrier's sleeve. Then he extended his hand as if shaking hands with Prentice; suddenly with a double jerk of the arm, the little gun flashed into his palm, and the gun was right in Prentice's face, two inches from his forehead.

After a moment, Ferrier put his arm down and extended the gun to the President, who picked it out of Ferrier's palm with thumb and forefinger.

"That's the way—if you need it—it should be used, Chief," said Ferrier gently. "Arm extended right into the guy's face and pull the trigger. Otherwise it's not much use. It has a new explosive—not gunpowder at all—which gives it a muzzle velocity of almost six thousand feet a second. Very deadly. But the bullet is only three millimeters across, so lay it right on the fellow's forehead."

The thing dangled from Prentice's thumb and forefinger.

"Are you suggesting *I* carry this thing?"

"Everywhere."

"Ferrier, you're out of your skull. I've got one hundred twenty-two Secret Service men in the White House." He stopped. He had one hundred twenty-two Secret Service men and they had allowed him to hire a member of Murder, Inc., as a White House gardener.

"They didn't do President Kennedy much good, did they?" asked Ferrier dryly. He had a low opinion of the whole Secret Service. It was his opinion that the Secret Service was enormously effective only as long as no one wanted to kill the President.

Ferrier brought out a tiny box of cartridges. "There's fifty in there, which is more than you'll ever need. Six in the gun. It loads the usual way—and I know you know how to load a revolver. I'll get right on it and be in touch—maybe by tonight."

He paused at the door. "It makes a muffled crack—just like a drawer slamming."

He left swiftly and without invitation. Prentice dropped the gun and cartridge box into his side pocket as Tupper came in. Tupper was another laconic one—bald as an oyster, the nearest that Prentice had to a Harry Hopkins. Presidential aide. Has dinner jacket, will travel, anywhere, do anything, say nothing. They were very old friends.

"Tup, I can't talk now. Go down to the White House pool, put on a swimsuit, and get a little exercise." He patted the bulge on Tupper's stomach. "You could use it. I'll be down in twenty minutes, after I get rid of these other idiots."

Tupper turned on his heel and left without a word. That's what he liked in men, thought Prentice. Instant reflexes, without a lot of chatter. Tupper could get more done than his twelve other aides put together, and with one-fifteenth the amount of talk.

General Dyke was summoned in. He was formidable, old Army, a bulldog, and a pain in the ass to Prentice. "General, you've got ten minutes," snapped Prentice, using the General's own methods on his own subordinates.

The tough old General (Ordnance was a celebrated mausoleum for the aging, but not quite retired old Army

boots) beetled his fierce eyebrows. "I don't like the
implications of this last gang killing, Mr. President.
There were at least three kinds of material used at that
Tasio killing which are better than anything we at
Ordnance have got, starting with that little hand grenade."

That was as far as Prentice would let him go. He
exploded. "You too, Brutus! My God, everyone in this
goddamned administration from top to bottom is on my
ass about this ridiculous gang war when their minds
should be on higher things! Might I remind you,
General—" And he reminded him in staccato order of
the new anti-tank weapon that didn't work, of the rocket
that burst at the wrong altitudes, and of six other
weapons that were not working up to the President's
expectations. This was known as putting the ball in the
other man's court. Prentice had other fish to fry. "I'm
bored with these damned gang killings. This is the
concern of the Justice Department. If gangsters want to
kill each other, let them. Meanwhile I want the rest of
my family to get back to their own work."

In six more minutes the General was out of his
office, having first stammered out a few explanations
concerning what strides his department had made in
confusing Russian anti-tank missiles by some kind of
electronic wizardry, announcing encouraging news about
the rocket warhead, etc.

Prentice knew he would carry the whole outburst
back to the Pentagon, where it would be luncheon
conversation on the highest level: that the President was
bored with the Tasio affair, that he considered gang wars
beneath Chief Executive contempt, and of no very great
importance even on the lower rungs of the administra-
tive leader. This point of view would radiate outwards
and by the next morning would be in Joseph Kraft's

column, possibly in Scotty Reston's, and certainly in Jack Anderson's. There might even be an editorial here and there within the next few days chiding the President for not taking gangland seriously—and that wouldn't do any harm either.

With Stern the President used exactly the opposite tactics. He leaned back in the black leather armchair, totally relaxed, and watched with vast interior amusement while his ferocious press chief poured forth fury. His subject: the foreign press. *Aftonbladet* said the U.S. was a nation of gangsters, and *Isvestia* had crowed that the imperialist lackeys were sinking into a morass of gangsterism which was its normal ethical level. *Le Monde* had been the most stinging of all: the U.S. gang warfare had demonstrated, as if it needed further demonstration, that the moral leadership of the world still rested, as it had always rested, in France, where if public morality was not always practiced at the highest levels, it was at least understood. And the *Daily Express* in London had trumpeted that America was still a frontier society where justice was pursued privately— which provoked Prentice to a bleat of laughter.

"Stern—calm down! Calm down!" said Prentice. "One of the first qualifications of a press chief is never, never under any circumstances be riled by the *Daily Expresses* of the world."

"It's not just the *Daily Express*," said Stern, spitting like a cobra. "It's *Aftonbladet, Le Monde, The Guardian,* some of the greatest papers in the world. They deride us."

"Well, let them," said Prentice, smiling. "One of the most important functions of the world's richest and strongest power is to provide amusement and, above all, a feeling of moral superiority, to the rest of the world—

to compensate them for their hunger, their poverty, their powerlessness. An Italian peasant taking a moment off from his sixteen-hour day, during his meager ration of bread and cheese, hears the news about our gang war on his cheap transistor radio and says to himself: 'Well, thank God we don't have *that* sort of thing here.' Just think what pleasure, conceivably his *only* pleasure, he gets from the scorn of *La Stampa* about the terrible gang war in the U.S.A.''

Five minutes later he was in the White House pool, doing a fast five lengths—he'd been a swimmer at Harvard—while Tupper watched from poolside. He bore down hard on the last two laps, swinging his arms close to the water as they did now (fourteen-year-old girls were swimming faster now than the fastest male swimmers in his day, he thought ruefully), blowing like a porpoise every time he turned his head sideways for a breath, feeling himself relax. Best exercise in the world for Presidents.

Later, he and Tupper stretched out on the poolside chaise longues and went over the drug scene. "Narcotics," grunted Tupper, "captured over a billion dollars worth of the white stuff last year. They say that's a quarter of what came in. They're full of shit. More likely about five percent. That part of the operation is a spectacular success—for the Mob. By getting all those headlines they lull everyone into thinking the problem is solved. It's not even scratching the surface."

The President listened, eyes closed. Tupper was his conscience, his goad. On the rare occasions—usually only in the few minutes after he awoke late at night—when he was troubled by the blatant illegalities of his private civil war, he would calm himself by remembering Tup, his old school chum and his fiercely repressed, never-above-the-surface indignation about cocaine.

He opened his eyes and sat up. "Did you bring all that stuff from Schotz's safe?"

Tupper opened the briefcase beside him. "We're still going through it. The lawyers are raising hell, bringing injunctions, the whole works, to get all the papers out of our hands."

"You're photocopying everything?"

"Oh yes, but if you're building a court case, a photocopied document isn't worth a damn. You need the originals."

Prentice wasn't interested in court cases against gangsters. He was using shorter, more decisive, measures.

The two men bent over the legal-sized brief.

"Names," said the President, "I want names." He was seeking those upper levels which had never been really explored by anyone. The Tasios of gangland were well known, too old, too publicized; they were important, all right; but they weren't the ones running things obviously. Who was?

"Plenty of names," grunted Tupper. "You won't like some of them. The President of General Motors. Do you want his name?"

"I know his name," said Prentice. "Is he in there?"

"They're all in there—General Electric, IBM, Union Carbide, all of 'em. That's the trouble—you want names. There are hundreds, including some of the most respectable names in U.S. industry. Schotz's operation was about half-straight, half-bent, and perfectly legal—and the question is who's crooked and who isn't."

That was the trouble with the respectability of gangsterism in America. The businessman thought that if his connection with a mobster was straight, as far as he could see, there was no harm in it. The legal and the illegal were coiled like an underground cable system of a city and you had to trace a wire to the very end of the line before you found out who was who, who was straight, who wasn't. Schotz's safe, and before that the safes in Detroit and Chicago, had contained enormous amounts of paper, which must have been secret or why were they hidden? The FBI had grabbed it all—on the grounds of murder investigation. Treasury and Narcotics had moved in right after the FBI, to take its own look and make its own judgments and after them came Tup—and nobody knew that the President of the United States was now looking over everyone's shoulder by the White House pool. The killings had got him into the gang's files—the first ever to get in there—but there was too much, much too much, for one man to digest. Prentice rifled through the fat bundle of papers. "That has been sifted down from over two thousand documents. Have you time to read it?" asked Tupper drily.

"Have you read it?"

Tupper nodded.

"Any ideas?"

"Too many. I'll keep trying—but I won't swear that I'm right. This stuff is for a financial expert—and that I'm not. You're still adamant about not bringing in some extra talent?"

There was far too much talent already on the scene. He'd have to do it himself.

"Which lawyers are giving you trouble?" asked the President idly, eyes on the paper.

"Murray and Weiskopf in Chicago, Harms and Wentworth in Detroit, Amery in St. Louis." All very prominent legal lights.

The President nodded absently.

CHAPTER
FIVE

Prentice lay back on the pillows, fully dressed except for his black tie and dinner jacket, and watched his wife bent over her dressing table, a permanent line of worry etched around her mouth. First Lady. What an awful job. Opening schools and saying hello to the wife of the party secretary of Utah and being terribly interested in what the Presidents of small black states had to say about their poverty-stricken countries, which was exactly what the President of the last black poverty-stricken country had said, and pretending it wasn't. The President himself was surrounded by a preposterous amount of awe that prevented the dinner guests, if not from being boring, at least from being too long-winded. Rosemary had no such protection. She was just the President's wife, and as such was expected to listen and listen and smile and smile. She had to suffer fools gladly—and that was the nature of the job, for which, alas, she was totally suited.

He'd met her in high school, married her just after he left the University of Wisconsin—the perfect prescription for a White House marriage. Being First Lady was the absolute pinnacle of a girl's hopes—at least a girl like Rosemary—and once in the job she had found (although she would rather die than admit such a thing) that it was the most boring, exasperating, unrewarding, anxiety-making, unfulfilling position in the world. She longed to be free of it; she longed—and this she *did* admit to Prentice—to be an *ex*-First Lady, to have all the honor and prestige of having had the job, without any of the horrible strain of actually being *in* it. She dreamed of retiring back to Madison as Bess Truman had retired back to Independence, knowing full well that her restless driving husband would never settle for Madison, not after retirement, not if he lived to be a hundred, not ever.

"Who is Jeremy Wisdom again?" she asked.

"British," said Prentice. "President of the Board of Trade and quite conceivably the next but one Conservative Prime Minister. Or quite conceivably *not* the next but one Conservative Prime Minister. Politics doesn't always run on rails in Britain. Ask him about Ireland— that should keep him in full cry for half an hour."

"Ireland," said Rosemary, the line of worry deepening. "What sort of point of view should I take?"

"Sympathy," said Prentice. "Profound sympathy."

He looked around the room in the lamplight. He had always felt safe up in the private chambers of the White House, but he didn't now. The Secret Service blunder had come as a great shock. He was just beginning to appreciate its full enormity. He looked at the french window beyond Rosemary's bent head. He'd had them filled with bulletproof glass quietly—the Secret Service thought him obsessed with security to the point of lunacy, but then they knew very little about Prentice's problems—and he wondered what else he could do. Steel doors painted white, locked by remote control? They would *really* think he'd taken leave of his senses. He let his gaze roam around the big, comfortable, very American room. Too bland for his taste, too chintzy, too early American walnut, pine-paneled and too white. He smiled. That was his own private joke about the White House, which would cost him the election if he ever dared make it aloud—that the White House was much too white, much too clean, too virginal. White was all very well when the place was built, when the country was itself virginal. Since World War II, the United States had lost its virginity—in Korea, in Vietnam, in Central America. Prentice liked to envision a White House painted Vermont barn red, with black shutters— red, the color of experience, the color of dried blood.

His wife was smiling: "Thank God for Hasbrouck," she said. She liked Hasbrouck—as didn't everyone? The Hasbrouck charmer of countless juries and countless women. Another Madison boy who'd gone far.

They were eight at dinner in the President's dining room, one of the nicest dining rooms in the whole world, and Hasbrouck was at his most perversely, exasperatingly brilliant. All about the Tasio killings. Prentice knew that it would be Topic A at dinner that night and he didn't fight it because he couldn't. It was Topic A at a *thousand* parties that night across the country—and probably abroad, too. Nothing to be done. Ride it out.

Hasbrouck, of the leonine Gallic face—like a French fox, thought Prentice—was being outrageously anti-law to the British visitor. "You see," he was saying to Jeremy Wisdom, "you British don't understand the nature of American crime or our deep need of it. We haven't got the West anymore, so we have the Mob, the Syndicate, ever changing but ever the same. They must ride into the center of town and shoot up the place or what would we do for amusement? In the last few years they have been most disappointingly quiet. They have been conducting their affairs like bankers and this is not at all what they're for. So we have had to wade in and stir them up, shoot a few of them, get their minds on their proper business again."

"Who is *we*?" asked the British Board of Trade.

"Why, the Government, of course," said Hasbrouck. "Didn't you know? You British don't understand our customs. We have a Department of Justice which has absolutely nothing to do with justice as we know it; its main job is to prosecute big business, break up trusts, harass unions, that sort of thing. Then we have the Department of *Real* Justice; they shoot up mobsters like Tasio who are far too protected by your awful English legal system ever to be prosecuted legally. The purpose of the Department of Real Justice is to give the average citizen some feeling he's getting something for his taxes. The average voter has an ambivalent feeling about the Mob—he admires the mobster enormously and wishes he could get away with it himself. At the same time he likes to see the Mob get it in the neck once in a while because it makes him feel a little less insignificant, a little less trodden upon."

The Briton blinked a bland British blink. His leg

was being pulled, wasn't it? "You're a *lawyer,* Mr. Hasbrouck?" he said, or rather, asked.

"A very rich lawyer," said the President, smiling his lazy smile. "He was once a very good lawyer but not anymore. He has, alas, become very rich—which means someone else does all the work in his office—and he has all the fun and makes all the money."

Bernie Stove took over from there. "He doesn't talk that way in court, Mr. Wisdom. It's enough to make a man throw up to listen to him defend the rights of some of these mobsters."

"Mobster?" said Hasbrouck. "Are you accusing me—in front of all these witnesses—of having a single client who has ever been convicted of a felony, Mr. Stove?"

"No, I'm not," said Stove genially. "I know the laws of libel as well as you do. I'm not saying they're criminals. I'm just saying they're mobsters, which has been held twice by the United States Supreme Court—in the case of *Sylvio* v. *The New York Herald* and of *Rowland* v. *Carney*—to be *not* libelous. As for Tasio, who was your client, he was both a mobster and a criminal. You can't libel the dead, Jacques, and you know it."

"But you are libeling *me,*" said Hasbrouck, his face breaking into his widest smile, a smile that could fill a courtroom.

"Nobody could libel you, Jacques," said the President. "It's not possible. Have some wine, Mr. Wisdom." He took the bottle from the silver decanter and poured it for him, still talking. "All Hasbrouck's clients are the biggest crooks in America—because he enjoys the gamesmanship of keeping them out of jail. They are all guilty. If they weren't, they wouldn't be his clients.

He likes the difficulty of white-washing the guilty. He's bored to death by innocence.''

"Oh, come now," shouted Hasbrouck, merrily. "The most difficult of courtroom tasks is proving the innocence of the innocent. It is the very nature of the innocence that it looks, when charged, always guilty. Just look at that poor, eternally innocent Mrs. Pritchett."

That brought down the house. They screamed with laughter, while Hasbrouck pretended to be affronted. Mrs. Pritchett was a vivacious, hopelessly depraved, enormously rich woman who had shot her last two husbands when she tired of them and had been caught red-handed each time. Hasbrouck had got her off both times.

"If I were a juror on any case you were the defending counsel, Jacques, I would automatically bring in a verdict of guilty," said the President.

"Aah," said Hasbrouck. "That's what you would do if you were the *juror*—but supposing you were the *defendant*—who would you call in?"

"You," said the President. "Immediately. Especially if I were guilty."

Prentice looked down the table, anxious to get rid of the ball. That was the trouble with being President; once you picked up the conversational ball, no one would let you get rid of it until you threw it at someone. He threw it at Everett Quincey, white-haired old Everett Quincey, stuffed with the wisdom of the ages, a professional adviser of Presidents who rarely took his advice. Quincey was a sort of parody of Bernard Baruch; Presidents used him to put the stamp of public approval on acts that would otherwise have been very unpopular. He filled the function that the Delphic Oracle filled in ancient Greece; you couldn't argue with an ancient sage

like Quincey, any more than you could argue with the
Oracle. Quincey was the final word. Prentice used
Quincey to publicly recommend unpopular politics he
himself had already privately decided on. Quincey was
such a saintlike figure that it would be considered
unpatriotic, almost heretical, to oppose any policy he
recommended.

"Everett," said the President playfully, "you've
been very quiet. What's your explanation of these
bloodlettings which are defaming our fair land?"

Everett beamed his broad, universally wise smile
(which bore, Prentice had always thought, a remarkable
resemblance to total fatuity) and said, "In the third
century A.D. the Emperor Tantullus had almost exactly
the same trouble with the Purturion mobs that we are
experiencing with the Mafia. So did Alcibiades with the
Aggutinae rebels—and at the root of all these civil
disturbances lies the same philosophical dilemma. . . ."
And so on.

Everett could always be counted to start his disqui-
sitions fifteen hundred years earlier—when he didn't
plunge into Egyptian antiquity of five thousand years
ago. Prentice wondered if he made it all up. It sounded
marvelously erudite and he was a superb performer. The
dinner guests would hang on every word of this sludge,
trying to preserve a bit for future dinner parties, quoting
what little they could remember and getting it wrong,
but getting away with it because Everett Quincey had
said it.

It got Prentice off the hook, and in the middle of
this instant philosophy, Hanover the butler leaned over
his shoulder and whispered a single word: "Ferrier." It
was the only name that could have so magic an effect.

Prentice stood up, looking enigmatic. (Always leave them puzzled was one of his rules).

"I'll be back in a moment," he said. "Carry on, Everett. I'm sorry I have to interrupt so splendid a discourse." He slipped out—leaving a vast silence. Only a momentary one. Quincey plunged on explaining just what Tacitus had said about Quintillian, which was almost exactly relevant to this current explosion of violence.

The President found Ferrier in the Blue Room, gazing at the painting of George Washington. "Sorry, Chief," he murmured. "It couldn't wait. Two things: first, Spence never heard of Canozzi—or Fitts. Neither has anyone in his office."

Prentice digested this latest enormity instantly, as was his habit. In this job one didn't have time for conventional dismay. "How about that clearance?"

"A forgery."

Prentice shot out: "The paper it's written on?"

Ferrier hesitated only a microsecond, but it showed how worried he was to hesitate even that long: "It's the real thing—at least we think it is. It's not always possible to check paper with a hundred percent certainty, but it looks as if someone had access to Secret Service paper or stole it, which amounts to the same thing."

He didn't spell out the implications because he knew Prentice was quite capable of spelling them out without his help. It meant the whole vast security apparatus of the White House was suspect. If someone could plant a killer on the White House staff who could walk almost up to the President's window. . . . The President's mind had already raced far ahead to confront and grapple with the even more sinister implications—the man who planted the killer, a man or woman with access to Secret Service stationery and. . . .

"How about the typewriter it was typed on?"

"We don't know yet," said Ferrier. "It's not a Secret Service machine—at least none of the obvious ones. We're still looking."

"How much does Spence know about this?

"As little as possible. I had to tell him a few things—otherwise he wouldn't talk to me."

"How did he take it?"

"Belligerently. Says it never happened. Says it *couldn't* happen—not with his security set-up. Says there never was any such man. Whole thing's a figment of the CIA's imagination."

The two men stared at each other in silence. Prentice couldn't suppress a chuckle.

"You have a grisly sense of humor," muttered Ferrier.

Prentice smiled: "In this job it helps." He ran his fingers through the world famous grizzled forelock. "Spence suffers from delusions of infallibility, a familiar symptom of high office," said the President, who tried hard to avoid it but wasn't always sure that he did.

"How does he explain that piece of paper?"

"He doesn't even try. I think he suspects *me* of forging it." Ferrier twisted his lips savagely.

"I want you to check them all out, Paul, every last Secret Service man."

Ferrier said, thin-lipped: "There are eleven hundred of them."

"Take the ones nearest to me first."

"They're all near to you at some time. Or responsible for you in some way. Mr. President, it might not *be* the Secret Service. Who put that piece of paper in your in-basket?''

The implications of that had not escaped the President either. It threw the whole White House staff under suspicion starting with Miss Doll, who had in fact put the piece of paper in his hand, not in his basket (because she knew from long experience that the in-basket had a low priority in getting Presidential attention).

"I don't know," said Prentice.

The slender, laconic CIA chief radiated suspicion like heat waves. "I could put someone in here tonight."

Prentice shook his head. "It would attract attention—and we mustn't."

"You can't trust anyone here until we run a check. What are you going to do?"

Prentice said, "What any citizen does these days of the trouble—lock the doors." He smiled. "I've got to get back to the party, Paul. You said two things. What's the second?"

He could tell that Ferrier hated even to mention the second.

"Canozzi—or Fitts—has disappeared. Vanished like smoke. We had three men watching him—and suddenly he wasn't there. We haven't the foggiest idea how he got away or where he is."

The party was breaking up when Prentice got back. Washington was an early-to-bed and early-to-rise town and dinner parties broke up early, one of the few blessings to Prentice. He did some of his most agonizing work after the party guests had left and before the visitors arrived in the morning. Prentice shook hands with each of them, smiled, joked, and looked Presidential. Hasbrouck had slipped away, as he usually did. After parties he had the run of the place.

The President found him in the Yellow Room helping himself to the Irish whiskey. "What was it this time?" asked Hasbrouck.

"The Middle East," said the President. It was a marvelous all-purpose excuse, the Middle East. It had been in ferment thousands of years and would remain yeasty for at least another five hundred. Prentice never revealed anything even to Hasbrouck, his oldest friend.

The President poured himself a thimblefull of cognac (of which he would drink only a half-thimblefull) and said, "You were in great form, Jacques—lighting into the profession that pays you so well, pouring scorn onto the sacred tenets of Anglo-Saxon law. I'm surprised at you."

Hasbrouck flashed his courtroom smile, all impish charm. "I was just trying it out. I am trying to put myself in my adversary's place."

"Your adversary? What adversary, Jacques?"

Hasbrouck sat bolt upright in the Queen Anne chair: "I don't know. Someone. Someone pretty high up. I can't seem to get through to people as I used to."

The President smiled at him lazily. "It's high time you can't get through to the right people, Jacques. I'm delighted to hear you have to stand in line like the rest of the poor mortals. What's bothering you?"

Hasbrouck dropped the charm act instantly: "Dozens of your men—Treasury, Narcotics, FBI—are out tearing my client's house to bits looking for evidence that has nothing to do with his murder, looking instead for evidence of *his* violations. This is against the law. The law says that the police are allowed a *reasonable* amount of time to examine private premises in which they have reason to suspect.''

Prentice cut in like a knife: "Jacques, you don't really expect the President of the United States to get involved in that sordid affair.'' That changed the tone of the dialogue for a moment and left Hasbrouck with nothing to say. He'd spent a little of his capital bringing the subject up—and Prentice wondered why. He and Hasbrouck almost never discussed their affairs with one another. Having assumed the mantle of office in a twinkling, Prentice divested himself of it as quickly.

"Why are you so damned interested in this bloody mobster, Jacques?''

Hasbrouck threw down his Irish whiskey and stood up. "Because I'm totally and absolutely mystified by this Tasio killing. I have never in my whole legal career been as far at sea as this. I can't explain it. All I can say with absolute certainty is that this is *not* a gang killing. There is nobody in the mob who has the motive, or for that matter, the muscle, to erase Tasio like that. Nobody.''

The President drank his half-thimblefull of brandy and took Hasbrouck's arm. "Come on, Jacques. I'll show you out.''

He led him down the main staircase into the great hall under the eighteenth-century English chandeliers, past the Blue Room with the two Marine guards standing at attention, and right out to the North Portico. Two Secret Service men would be skulking out on the lawn and there would be dozens more at the various gates, any one of whom might have....But he was letting his imagination run wild. The President must never allow that to happen.

He walked Jacques right down the North Portico steps, opened the door and put him personally into the car in an excess of solicitude caused partly by his desire to make amends for cutting his legs off so abruptly and partly as pure bravado. These days Prentice didn't poke his nose out of the White House very often. The outdoors were fraught with unimaginable perils.

Prentice pushed his head through the window to deliver a parting shot. (Always leave them puzzled.)

"Jacques, did you know that your dear client, Tasio, had once personally hung a man on a meat hook and then clubbed his brains out with a baseball bat? Really, Jacques, you must get more respectable clients."

Prentice walked back up the White House steps, smiling. Besides providing himself with an exit line, he had shown Jacques that he had *some* interest in the Tasio affair. To feign total indifference to an affair that the whole country was talking about was in itself suspicious and Prentice was far too smart for that. So, just to baffle and temporarily stun his old friend, he had demonstrated that he had an interest in the Tasio case. But he had done more. He had given Jacques a fragment of information which even Jacques with all his knowledge of the Mob and its legends couldn't possibly know—a fragment of especially grisly information that Prentice might have gotten from any one of a dozen top secret agencies available to him and to few other men. Prentice had *not* got that information from any of them, he had made it up altogether. He had done this for a reason. It was too much a piece of gossip to remain dormant in Jacques's skull. It would come back to him, Prentice knew, and just from which avenue it came would tell him a lot about who his old friend was talking to these days. And with any luck it might even provide a clue as to why the great lawyer, whose clients included three of the biggest corporations in the world, was so interested in the private papers of a dead mobster.

CHAPTER
SIX

The Chinese students of the new exchange agreement were crowded into the Oval Office, which was far too small for them.

"I am proud and happy to welcome you as some of the most brilliant representatives of your great country to our great country. You are a symbol of the Long March our two great countries are now making—hand in hand—together." Prentice did not hesitate to use pure parody in addressing delegations like this. He claimed (very privately, of course) that it was impossible to parody Presidential oratory. "I have the greatest pleasure on behalf of the American people, and especially on behalf of the students of my country, to welcome you as part of the mingling of our two great cultures. We throw open to you our matchless facilities in space research and you will join us in the great adventure— the probing of outer space."

In the private recesses of his mind, which never ceased bubbling with thought as he beamed at them, he was thinking: Meanwhile sizing up you brilliant kids to figure just how far the Chinese have got into outer space weaponry.

Seated to one side trying to keep the exasperation off his handsome black face was the Secretary of State, who could not understand why Prentice, in many ways the most private of all U.S. Presidents, threw open his office to delegations like this. Prentice would not dream of explaining, of course, that he engaged in this delegation oratory partly because it reduced the accusation often leveled at him of being *too* private; because it brought him immense prestige in China, where photographs of him shaking hands with these Chinese students would be in every paper; because you had to telescope activities in his job; and lastly, because he enjoyed—for the sheer razzle-dazzle of the thing—doing about twelve things at once, jumping from one role to another.

He shook hands with the leader and bowed them out, instantly resuming his monologue where he had left off. "Roger, you must stop hoping that Marcos will either resign or die. He has no intention of doing either. But you must talk very tough reality to him tomorrow because no one else does. Tell him he must push military and political reform or he'll wind up hanging by the neck from his own balcony. That's the only kind of talk he'll listen to."

The door opened and Miss Doll ushered in a group of elderly ladies. "The Daffodil Society of America, Mr. President."

The President shook hands with the chairman. "Mrs. Throckmorton" (it was writ large on a pin on her substantial bosom), "I cannot tell you what a pleasure it is to welcome you and your fair companions to my simple abode. I, too, am a devotee of the daffodil." A sweep of his hand in the direction of the Rose Garden and its brave display of daffodils. "When the burdens of this office have weighed too heavily I have—with a glance at the White House daffodils—restored my serenity and my high purpose. Thank you so much for having the kindness to pay me a visit."

Miss Doll firmly led out the Daffodil Society. They had been there less than twenty seconds.

Without a break in stride, the President went on: "The power of the purse is a very great persuader with Marcos. He has asked for twenty-two more F-18's—no more F-18's until they are willing at least publicly to *discuss* democracy in the Philippines. Anyone who expects that is out of his mind, but I just want a *discussion* of democracy, which is not asking very much."

The light on the white phone blinked. All the other phones had been blinking steadily. Prentice ignored them, but when the white phone blinked he picked it up instantly and said, "Yes," which meant simply get on with it.

In a far off Utah forest hut, Joplin said, "I got the message. If you want those shamuses done, can we get B-52's? We need speed."

"Yes," said the President.

"It must be tonight?"

"Yes," said the President.

"Public viewing?" said Joplin, an editorial concern stealing into his voice for the first time since

Prentice had dealt with him. He didn't like it and it showed in his voice.

"Absolutely," said Prentice.

Joplin's Latvian lips formed a thin line of stubbornness. "There'll be a commotion."

"Drive carefully," said the President and hung up.

To his Secretary of State he said, "Gorbachev is threatening peace again which you and I know is the most fearsome word in the Soviet lexicon. They have always claimed credit for that word peace, clear back to Picasso and his damned dove, and we must counter with some sort of semantic ploy of our very own. It is my thought that when the Soviets use the word peace they mean the graveyard which is the only peace they recognize. But since Gorbachev and I are toying with summitry, I can't say it so you must." Prentice frequently put words in the mouth of his Black Secretary of State, such good words that the man now thought of them as his own and, in fact, was already writing his memoirs explaining how he'd come to reach decisions which had been planted in his head by the President.

In another part of the White House, Fred Tupper, surrounded and almost buried, by two thousand legal-sized documents, was carefully adding a paper to a small but growing pile at his elbow. Each of these papers contained one common denominator: a name. Tupper stared at it, unable to believe his eyes. Then he put in a call to his old rival Corbett at the FBI.

"Corbett," said Tupper crisply, "that gadget you people have at the Criminal Information Center, does it know everything?"

"Everything," agreed Corbette equably. "Absolutely every known fact about crime since Cain killed Abel."

"Would it know—" Tupper hesitated. He didn't know quite how to put this without giving away information to the enemy. "Would it know, for instance, fluctuations in the hot money supply. Not little fluctuations—*big* fluctuations."

Corbett's face creased with reluctant admiration. "Dear boy, you are on to something big, aren't you? Where on earth did you learn such expressions— fluctuations in the hot money supply?"

"Night school," grunted Tupper. "I'm trying to better myself."

"Actually," said Corbett, "you have just stumbled onto our latest and, we thought, biggest secret. We have just begun to program fluctuations in the money supply— both hot and cold—in our Big Daddy. Someone upstairs has been reading Milton Friedman and suddenly realized that money is an important commodity in big crime. Funny it took us so long to find that out."

"Look," said Tupper urgently, "can I come play on Big Daddy in strictest privacy—which means that I don't want you looking over my shoulder."

"No, you certainly cannot. In five minutes you could fuck up twenty million dollars worth of programming so that we would never get it straight again."

Tupper argued. Corbett was adamant. Twenty minutes passed. Tupper yielded grudgingly. "All right, *you* can look over my shoulder but nobody else. Can you operate the damned thing?"

"Yes," said Corbett.

Half an hour later Tupper and Corbett were alone with Big Daddy. Getting the three regular operatives out of the room had been no easy task. Tupper had had to flash White House credentials of imposing dimensions before they would abandon their posts.

The machine filled a room with its elegant gleaming dials; its immense tapes on the whole world. Only State Department and the Pentagon had bigger computers.

"Now what do you want to know?"

Tupper had almost to force the question out, so conditioned had Prentice made him to security. "I wish to know about the rise and fall in the money supply of a certain individual and the various banking houses at his disposal on certain dates." They were the dates following some immense cocaine shipments that had arrived in the country. He'd got the arrivals from Schotz's safe, and since he knew shipper and receiver were not the same person or even the same nationality, someone had to pay for the stuff—enormous quantities of cash. Cash of that quantity—some payments must have been more than thirty million dollars—could not have come out of a safe deposit box. Somewhere, a bank account must have dwindled. And later, if only for a moment, swelled before it was legitimized by investment. You can't carry thirty million around in your trouser pockets.

"What's the name of this individual?"

Tupper had never hated anything so much in his whole life as parting with that name. He showed Corbett the name written on a slip of paper.

"You must be joking."

"I'm just trying it on for size. Shall we ask Big Daddy?"

The two men spent two hours on the machine tracing the rise and fall in investment capital of a certain individual, unexpected sharp fluctuations in the Wall Street money supply, especially on certain dates, affluence unexplained and otherwise unexplainable than by huge injections of hot, illicit money. When it was over they carefully put all the immense quantity of paper through the shredding machine, some of it twice to be very sure. Only one piece of paper, with long lists of numbers and dates on it in Tupper's handwriting rather than the mechanical footprints of Big Daddy on it, was tucked away in Tupper's wallet.

"Just forget everything your feeble brain took in," said Tupper.

"I don't believe it," said Corbett stubbornly. "I'll never believe it."

"Just keep it that way," said Tupper.

Out in a forest in Utah, Joplin was briefing the troops. "It's a three-pronged operation. Jerry will take Detroit, I'll take St. Louis, and Mitch gets Chicago." He showed a group of battered handguns on the table in front of him. "Now this is the most interesting part. We have to use these antiques as some sort of cover operation about which we are not supposed to ask questions. All of them are *known* guns—that is, they can be traced to certain individuals—and we are to *leave* them on the scene after we finish the job—God knows why, but ours is not to reason."

He held up a card on which two words were crayoned.

"We are to leave this calling card on each and every corpse."

In the Oval Office, Prentice was locked in disputation with his Secret Service Chief. "Spence," said Prentice wearily (it had been a trying morning), "you seem to think I'm trying to undermine your authority. I have no such idea. The fact is that *I* am the central figure in all this elaborate security operation, not you. I am not questioning your ability or the ability of your men or even Secret Service procedures in case of atomic attack. I am just saying that the object of the whole exercise is to keep this carcass out of harm's way and that therefore this carcass has a right to find out how the system works—all of it. Now no more arguments. I want you to show me where every last button is, where every last steel door is, and I want duplicates in my private possession of every last key to every last door. Do you understand?''

"Yes," said Spence. What else could he say?

Miss Doll came in.

"You'll have to put all the visitors off," said the President. "Mr. Spence and I have security precautions to look into. Spence, would you wait outside a moment."

When he left, Prentice looked at Miss Doll's face, lacerated with worry. "What have you found out?"

She shook her head, an almost incredible movement from her: "I can't remember," she said. "You know these security checks come in all the time and I think . . ." She trailed off. No, she couldn't remember. "Normally I don't even bother you with them. But because you're so interested in the lawns, I thought you'd like to know about the new gardener."

"Who has access to your desk?"

"Oh, my God," cried Miss Doll, "the whole wide world gets in there at some time or other."

The President and Spence were in the bowels of the earth directly underneath the White House and Spence was looking through a sheaf of keys. They were otherwise alone and the thought struck Prentice that if Spence was the One, he would never have a better moment to strike. He felt the little handgun in his pocket for reassurance. He'd taken to carrying it everywhere—like his fountain pen.

The two men were fifty feet below ground level on what was known as the Q level, which meant safe but not quite that safe. They were about to take another elevator, locked, as were the others, even farther down. Spence found the key with some difficulty and showed it to the President. It had an identifying Q and was longer and more elaborately perforated and filigreed than any key he'd ever seen before. That was the thing about the Secret Service: a detail like elevator keys would be handled so expertly no one could fault them; but then they'd forget to put a canopy on John Kennedy's car or to speed up the car so it wasn't a sitting duck or to check the tall buildings, and blooie. But then, he supposed assassination was an impossible business to forestall; the security forces always foresaw the foreseeable, when it was in the thickets of the unforeseeable that the danger lurked.

The steel doors of the elevator opened silently and the President and Spence went even deeper into the earth. The low-ceilinged corridor lit up automatically when they got there and the two men went down it, stooping slightly to avoid the blue light bulbs. Stark, thought the President. "It has its own generating equipment separate from the Q level," said Spence. "Just in case. Also separate water and oxygen supply."

The President suppressed a grin. "What level is this?"

"P," said Spence. "It doesn't follow any sequential logic—the letters."

"What does that door lead to?"

It looked innocuous enough, that door. Spence's

Ivy League face looked annoyed. He didn't know and he hated to be caught out this way.

"Some broom closet or other," he muttered. "It can't be important—or it would be in the plan."

The President tried it. Locked. "There must be a key," he said gently.

It took Spence five minutes to find it and when they opened it, it was, as Spence had said, a broom closet supplied with brand new brooms that had never been used, new pails, and piles of unopened soap powders. "Well," murmured the President. "We're all ready for a spot of housekeeping—in case of World War III."

Spence closed and locked the broom closet door. "You won't be alone down here, Mr. President."

You never know, thought the President. The loneliness of power was assaulting him savagely. Usually he enjoyed it. Lately, no. The job was a jail, had always been a jail, but lately, the dimensions of the jail had narrowed.

Spence was showing him the Presidential office—just in case the unthinkable happened. Stark. And small. Telephones. Squawk box, buttons, communicating with whatever might be left on earth.

Spence pointed to the telephone: "That can't be cut or tapped by any method now known. It's encased in solid steel and the steel conduit is encased in twelve feet of cement."

"Who built all this?" said the President absently. (He was always at his most absent when he really wanted to know something.)

"The CIA," said Spence. "They have their own corps of engineers now and since secrecy is their bag, all this top secret construction is their baby. We—and the armed services intelligence, of course—are the only ones who know exactly what's down here.''

The President nodded absently. Already he was planning a little construction that even the Army, Navy, and the Secret Service—especially the Secret Service—didn't know about.

Back in the Oval Office, the President said, ''Would you just leave those plans behind, Spence?''

Spence didn't like it. Like all security chiefs everywhere in the world, he didn't like to admit his inner secrets even to the object of all the secrecy. The plans, he said, should be kept in the most secure of all lockaways and by that he meant his own. The President promised wryly to be careful.

The moment he got rid of Spence Prentice picked up the green phone. ''Ferrier,'' he said, ''I had no idea you had a corps of engineers! Why have you been keeping this from me? Like all Heads of State, I adore building things! I want the head of your engineer corps in my office in ten minutes. All right, fifteen then.''

He hung up the green phone, stood up, and stretched his long legs. Then he prowled his office, wearing a smile of secret contentment. He inspected his desk, got on the floor and looked under it, backed away from it, measuring its contours in his head. Then he inspected the floors, looking at Spence's plans and beaming inwardly and outwardly. Every man, he thought, is secretly an architect in his inmost soul.

Miss Doll entered five minutes later to find him contemplating the gently curving walls with enormous satisfaction. ''Miss Doll,'' said the President, ''when was this room painted last—and who picked out this color?''

''Jacqueline Kennedy,'' said Miss Doll. ''In 1961.''

"We're going to repaint it," said the President with enormous gusto, "Vermont barn red."

Miss Doll shuddered almost visibly. "You're *joking!*"

"What's the matter with Vermont barn red?" asked Prentice. "It's almost the original color of the country. It couldn't be more patriotic, more traditional, or more old American. I knew there was something that had been bothering me. It's the psychic need to have an office painted Vermont barn red. It will give me a tremendous psychic lift."

"What is the color of Vermont barn red exactly?"

"The color of dried blood." Miss Doll closed her eyes in horror. "We're going to do it immediately," pursued the President. "So get ready for a move. We'll move back to the old office. Oh, my God, I forgot—it's awash with Presidential aides, isn't it? All right, we'll move upstairs to the private quarters—just you and me, Miss Doll. Won't that be cozy. It'll only be for a few days." He hoped they could do it by then.

Miss Doll let him run on before she sprang her little surprise.

"I have remembered who brought me that security clearance for that gardener," she said. "It was Mr. Spence personally. He was coming to see you about the plans for your trip to Chicago and he dropped it in my basket on the way in."

The President's euphoria vanished. "Are you sure?"

"Positive," said Miss Doll. "He just said 'security' —nothing more—and went into your office. I didn't look at it for three days because you kept me on the hop with that Chicago trip and when I did, I noticed only that we had a new gardener. I thought you'd be pleased. Otherwise, I'd just have filed it."

"Well, well," said the President.

Spence had denied any knowledge of Canozzi, denied that any security clearance had come from his office, or had, in fact, ever existed.

CHAPTER
SEVEN

That night in St. Louis, Hector Amery, a WASP pillar of respectability—president of the St. Louis Bar Association, member of the board of the St. Louis Cardinals, trustee of the St. Louis Club—stepped out of his car parked, as was his habit, in an alley just behind his office. It was nine o'clock and he'd been summoned back to the office by a most unusual phone call from one of his richest clients. Amery didn't like to work at night and if it had been anyone else, he would have let Rogers handle it. But Rogers couldn't handle Frankie Main. Only Amery could handle Frankie Main, probably the most important mobster west of the Mississippi. He had sounded very upset about something and Amery wondered what it was. He never found out.

He got only two steps from his car when Mitch shot him twice in the chest, both shots lodging expertly in the heart. The ancient gun made an enormous racket which made Mitch wince. He couldn't understand why when they had all this marvelously silent hardware, they had these ungainly weapons inflicted upon them. He left the thing, as he'd been instructed, at the man's side. In the breast pocket of the dead man he thrust a white card—its edge sticking out noticeably—with the words crayoned in big letters: COCAINE KILLS.

Then he strode off down the alley, onto the quiet downtown street walking at his usual pace, his heartbeat not one whit faster than if he'd been eating breakfast. Two blocks further on, he boarded a bus which took him to East St. Louis, where he took a taxi to the Air Force base and the waiting B-52. He was back in Utah by midnight.

That same night almost identical misfortunes overtook Murray and Weiskopf who, if not quite as Waspish as Amery, were still pillars of the law and the upper classes in Chicago, and Harms and Wentworth, who were not only legal eagles of great prestige in Detroit, but part-owners of the Detroit Red Wings. In Detroit as in St. Louis one had to be sports-minded if one wanted to make the very best connections. All these tremendously respectable legal lights were found shot dead—which was shocking enough and each was found with a weapon of inescapably gangster antecedents lying next to him with a white card in the breast pocket bearing the legend: COCAINE KILLS.

Corbett of the FBI and Lamport of *The New York Times* sat in adjoining seats in the airplane to St. Louis. Corbett was reading the *St. Louis Post-Dispatch*'s version of the killings while Lamport was buried in the *Detroit Free Press*'s story of the same. When they finished they traded papers. Then they both read the Chicago paper.

"Let's get a drink," said Lamport, signaling the hostess. "*The Times* is buying. Do you believe any of that crud?"

The papers had been rife with speculation about new aspects of gang warfare, the Purple gang, fighting the Stranozzi mob, and the Profucci mob fighting the Tigers (which were the criminal offshoots of the Panthers). All very lurid stuff.

"Not a syllable," said Corbett. "Don't tell me you are covering the whole Midwest alone, Lamport?"

Lamport laughed. "My dear man, you are talking to *The New York Times*. We've had stringers on the scene since ten P.M. writing some perfectly marvelous fiction. We have eight men digging up the history of the Mob and another eight writing a twelve-column feature on the history of crime since Nero. I'm just going along to make sure the improbable speculations of one man don't contradict those of another. I write the final finished speculation."

Corbett grunted: "By the time anyone finishes *The Times* he's more confused than ever."

"Nobody finishes reading *The Times,* not even the editor," said Lamport. "Don't tell me *you're* handling this job alone?"

The FBI man grinned. He couldn't even begin to estimate how many hundreds of FBI men were burrowing away, filling out forms, taking dust samples, poring over immense card catalogues.

Corbett sipped his drink appreciatively. "No doubt about it, you and I work for the two most overstaffed institutions in the whole world."

"Hell," said Lamport, "the State Department has

us both lashed to the mast. For every *Times* man or FBI man at this very moment duplicating the work of six other guys, State has one hundred.''

They bickered pleasantly all the way to St. Louis about whose outfit could waste more time and spend more money doing it. It was a lovely discussion.

"MASSACRE OF THE LAWYERS" was the headline on the *Times* editorial which Prentice read at the pleasant breakfast niche he'd put in the upstairs private quarters.

"With the brutal slaying of five of the country's most respected attorneys, the gang war—if that's what it is—has taken a new and sinister turn," said the *Times* editorial writer, brandishing the obvious in a *Times*-like way. Let the other papers experiment with subtlety. The *Times* editorial page remained totally committed to painful certainties. It found earthquakes deplorable, crime unforgiveable, death inevitable—rediscovering these large simplicities every day.

But Prentice didn't like "if that's what it is." If the *Times* editorial writers were being permitted to speculate on an explanation for the wave of killings other than gang warfare, then this idea might be said to be filtering down through the levels of public consciousness lower than he'd planned. At least at this time.

Prentice looked across to Rosemary, who was buried in the style section of *The Washington Post*. Rosemary was his barometer. When she began vocalizing about a social issue it had truly reached bedrock. She hadn't yet mentioned the gang warfare.

Prentice read on: "In each case the murders had been done with known gang weapons, as if to emphasize these highly respected lawyers' connections with the underworld, which their law firms were quick to deny. Hector Amery, it is true, was the attorney for a real estate company which is allegedly controlled by Frankie Main, the gangster, but this is strictly conjecture. Similarly, Murray and Weiskopf were involved as attorneys in waterfront real estate deals which had peripheral gang associations, but all five lawyers were as far removed from actual mob involvement as a Senator who had perhaps been helped into office by gang votes over which he had no control. Or were they?''

Aaah, thought Prentice, they had taken the bait. ''Or were they?'' That was not as good as saying that they indeed were as deeply involved as Frankie Main himself in gang matters—but at least *The Times* had asked the question and perhaps planted it in a few influential skulls. That was as much as he could ask for. At this time.

He turned to Lamport's think piece on Page one, spilling over for three columns on Page sixteen. Lamport had taken the wide view that encompassed all conceivable points of view, and in fact a couple that were to Prentice inconceivable. It might be the Tigers trying to wrest control of the St. Louis waterfront from the Profucci gang. Or it might not. It might be an internal dispute within the Profucci gang, which was known to be rent with dissension. Or it might not. And so on, through all permutations of might not and might until at the very end, with the utmost diffidence, Lamport suggested that it might not be gang warfare at all; it might be something more disquieting. (Great *Times* word—''disquieting.'')

''The cards bearing the word 'Cocaine Kills' on all the bodies, also the use of known gang guns, an incredible blunder if indeed it is a blunder, links all five murders. However, the words 'Cocaine Kills' has an editorial connotation, an aura of moral disapproval, never before known in gang warfare.''

Aha, thought Prentice, they took that bait too.

''It is known that higher mob councils have been rent with dissension over narcotics, some complaining that public revulsion against cocaine has grown to such a degree that the syndicate should drop it altogether, while the older elements are so wedded to the sheer profitability of cocaine—greater than loan sharking and gambling put together—as to be immovable. However, quarrels on this subject, or on any subject, have always been confined to the inner councils. Never has the Mob brought the public into its moral dilemmas like this. In fact, this is so totally uncharacteristic of mob philosophy that students of organized crime say these cannot possibly be gang killings of the ordinary sort.''

Lamport then engaged in an orgy of speculation about who might have put together such a bloodletting in three different cities on the same night. Some young group of fanatics like the Neo-Nazis? or the Christian Militia? Not likely, but was there perhaps some new group of zealots as yet unknown behind it? Because zealotry was obviously at work, etc.

Some of it was uncomfortably close.

''Darling,'' said Rosemary, ''hadn't you better do something about these gang killings?''

Prentice looked across at his wife. Still buried in the style section. ''What put that idea in your head, dear?'' asked Prentice.

''There is a whole article about it here,'' said Rosemary.

In the style section? Prentice rose and looked over

his wife's shoulder. Obviously the affair was filtering down to very different levels of public consciousness. He kissed his wife thoughtfully on the cheek, and went to shave.

His temporary office—the workmen were already tearing into the Oval Office—was his own bedroom. But he was separated from his nest of special telephones. All except the super secret line to Utah. Otherwise he had to go through the White House switchboard. Prentice didn't like that. He called Ferrier. "I'd like to see you, Paul," he said. The tone said soonest but he wouldn't put it into actual words. You never knew who was listening.

"I can't make it until after lunch," said his CIA chief. "Pressure of work."

"All right," said Prentice. Pressure of work when Ferrier said it on a telephone meant nasty business somewhere.

He summoned Tupper, who was in his office within minutes. Tupper showed him the piece of paper he had stuffed so carefully into his wallet and the President could not refrain from a low whistle of total disbelief.

"I got it from Big Daddy, that gadget they got at the FBI," said Tupper. "Do you trust machines?"

"Not always," said Prentice, who didn't trust anything very much. He looked at the piece of paper. "If that machine can come up with answers like this, let's use it some more."

"Corbett won't let me play with it unless he's on hand. And he's in St. Louis."

"He'll be back soon," said the President.

Tupper felt a ruffle of surprise. He didn't know the

President was so attuned to the movements of the lesser
FBI people

"Narcotics and the Treasury are all out in St.
Louis—and Chicago and Detroit, too—looking into things
there. They should have a mess of dates and perhaps
names when they get through their files. Could you run
those through Big Daddy?"

"Suppose it just comes up again and again with the
same name. You can't convict on that sort of evidence."

The President was not preparing court cases. "I
don't think it will," he said. The mists were beginning
to clear—opening a vista that was truly frightful.

Miss Doll came in grimly. "Stern," she said.

There was only one phone to pick up. Prentice
picked it up, and without giving Stern a chance to open
his mouth, said: "All right, let's have a press conference, Stern. Fix it up, will you? Eleven o'clock this
morning."

"This morning?" cried the startled Stern. "Good
God, Mr. President . . ."

"The big conference room at the State Department. With television. We'll shoot the works, shall
we?" said Prentice genially, enjoying the bubbling rage
at the other end of the wire.

"Two hours!" said the anguished Stern. "You
can't spring this on these guys in two hours, after
they've waited six months."

"Why not?" said the President. "If they've waited
six months, they must have their pencils sharp."

He hung up, smiling the big charisma smile he
used for re-election purposes and hardly ever for anything else.

"Do you want me to come along?" asked Tupper.

"No, Fred. I most certainly don't want you to

come along," said the President. "I want you to be—in this matter as in all others—totally invisible. I hope you have impressed on Corbett that secrecy is of the essence."

Tupper nodded. "You needn't worry about Corbett. He's a question asker, not a question answerer. He wouldn't tell his own wife the time of day."

Prentice was at his shimmering best in front of the cameras and the press that morning. Striding into the big State Department conference hall before eight hundred reporters from seventy-five countries wearing what he called his tiger smile (just after the lady rode him) he pointed to Battersea of the Associated Press, dean of the White House staff. "Fire away, Peter," he said.

"Mr. President, five lawyers have been gunned down in very peculiar circumstances—"

"I'm glad you asked," said the President genially, not even letting him finish, "a question the whole world is asking. Why are these highly respected members of the legal profession *seemingly* engaged in the despicable drug traffic?" He emphasized the word only to a microscopic degree, just enough to rid him of any charge that he had accused the lawyers of any such thing, "involved in the despicable drug traffic? This Administration, Mr. Battersea, is asking this same question to the extent that at this very moment representatives not only of the FBI, but also of the Treasury and Narcotics offices, are in St. Louis, Chicago, and Detroit asking a lot of very hard questions, trying to find the link between these thoroughly respectable attorneys and this terrifying cocaine war—if that is what it is—and that is what it looks like."

The President poured on the statistics. The federal

government had in the past year seized over a billion—repeat one billion dollars—in cocaine despite which his Administration felt they were barely scratching the surface, that they had captured perhaps only ten percent of the total. (Watching the TV screen in his office, Abner Dodge, chief of the Narcotics Bureau, exchanged a startled look with his Deputy Chief. These weren't their figures or the figures they had given the White House. The White House, of course, had many sources of information, but no government bureau liked to feel the White House had better sources of information about its own specialty.)

Prentice built up a picture of cocaine trade worth billions and he pinpointed—with a pointer and a map—just where it all was—New York, Chicago, Detroit, Los Angeles—spelling out just who got most of the lolly in each city—and who was thought to be in charge, revealing an awesome grasp of individual figures for shipments, supplies, prices, charges in each city. (In the office of the FBI, Jeremy Fisher, the man who had been made Director by Prentice, turned angrily on the six deputies surrounding him: "Which one of you told him all that?" No one answered.)

Prentice stunned his audience with his encyclopedic grasp of the whole cocaine problem from the moment the stuff left Columbia to the poor sucker freebased in his Beverly Hills kitchen. He dwelt on the social cost to the nation; the menace of these private armies mowing one another down. He pledged the whole resources of the nation to combat this total evil, if he had to call out the Army and do it.

He was on screen and on stage for one hour and then, without warning, he said "Thank you" and strode off, leaving behind a silent and stupefied press corps.

They had not had a chance to ask a single question (even Battersea's opening phrases had never been permitted to become a question because the President was pretty sure what it was and he didn't want to answer it). The fact was that the President, in the guise of holding a press conference, had gone right over their heads to the public glued to the TV screen in their own homes. To the electorate it was a superb performance.

His other object was quite simply to change—at one bound—his image in regard to the cocaine war. The image he had so carefully cultivated of a President far too obsessed with foreign and domestic affairs—the Middle East, the budget crisis, and Central America—to give more than a passing glance to organized crime. In one hour he had changed all that. Here was a President who knew all about the curse of drugs in astounding detail and what's more was taking care of it. He cared. He was committed. Three cheers for President Prentice.

He had decided to make this monumental switch because of Canozzi, the vanished gardener. If the Mob had managed to plant a gunman on the White House lawn and then equally contemptuously make him disappear, then quite clearly his cover was blown as the real mover and shaker of events—at least in the upper echelons of Mafialand. And that's where it mattered. The press conference was quite simply a declaration of war which would be understood only at the very highest mob levels, might tempt the deep thinkers in the upper crust to making some moves, to show their hand somehow. One thing that might happen could be to assassinate the President—Prentice knew that. He always knew his was a high-risk job.

The reporters pressed up the aisle in heavy silence. Aitken of the *Kansas City Star*, an enterprising youngster and the most recent addition to the Washington press corps, pushed through to Battersea. "Say, Pete," he said, "would you mind telling me what you were going to ask the President before he so rudely interrupted?"

"It seems so long ago I've forgotten," grunted Battersea. He glanced at his notes and chuckled. "Oh, yes. I was going to ask the President why Narcotics and Treasury as well as the FBI, to say nothing of the local police, are swarming all over the poor families and business associates of those dead lawyers out in the Midwest. Instead of treating them like murder victims, everyone seems to be treating them like suspects."

The *Chicago Tribune* man complained, "Even de Gaulle used to allow a *few* questions at his press conferences."

Prentice couldn't avoid the question forever. Back at the White House in the private quarters where few beside himself were ever permitted to enter, the President found Hasbrouck turning the full blast of his Gallic charm on pretty Fenella. The moment he saw Prentice, the sun went down. Hasbrouck's looks were thunderous.

"I do hope I'm not intruding," said Prentice with deep irony, taking Hasbrouck's arm and propelling him away from the pretty girl. "Jacques, I've got ten thousand things to do, I'll give you five minutes."

"That was a very polished performance which I watched on your wife's set. I hope you don't mind?"

"I *do* mind. I don't really think you should wander around the private quarters of the White House quite so freely, Jacques. I mind indeed, but the trouble is that you don't mind that I mind."

Hasbrouck shrugged it off. "You made one mistake in that magnificent act."

"Only one?"

"You forgot to express any sympathy for those poor murdered lawyers."

"Oh, I *did*," protested the President. "Shocked dismay was expressed in every lineament."

"You should have let some of it creep into your prose."

"I should have called you in to help write the speech," said the President.

"Harry," said Hasbrouck passionately. (He was the only person in Washington, except Rosemary, who still used his almost forgotten first name—and then only in moments of passion.) "These are not mobsters; they're lawyers of the highest repute. They're innocent people."

Prentice sat down and contemplated his old friend with quiet irony. "Jacques, a few weeks ago in Ireland a mother of ten got caught in a crossfire between the Army and the IRA and was killed. Last week the British Ambassador to Ecuador was kidnapped and killed. Terrorists killed two hopelessly innocent American technicians in Turkey. Urban guerrillas mowed down a journalist asking too many questions in Uruguay and let's see—oh, yes—two eleven-year-old boys were stabbed to death in playgrounds in the Bronx by youthful street gang leaders. This is the age of the massacre of the innocents—like all ages. What makes you think lawyers are exempt from this carnage? What divine right do you claim for the profession of law that it should get special treatment?"

"I'm not asking for special treatment," cried Hasbrouck. "They are already getting treatment that is far too special. At this very moment, the offices and homes of all these lawyers are swarming with federal agents examining their private papers, their bank accounts, for God's sake, their private memoranda of phone calls."

"How do you know this, Jacques?" said the President with his relaxed and exceedingly dangerous smile.

"I'm vice-president of the Bar Association," said Hasbrouck, "as you well know. Every one of the law partners of the murdered men have been on my phone since dawn asking what the hell is going on. These men are not being treated as victims; they're being treated as suspects."

"Calm down, Jacques," said the President, "you'll frighten the maids. This is a murder investigation of peculiar complexity. We're following every lead."

"You've got the FBI for that—and the police. What the hell are Treasury and Narcotics doing there—trying to pin income-tax violations on dead men, that's what."

"A little white card was left on every body which said Cocaine Kills—you read the papers, didn't you, Jacques?—and only the Narcotics Bureau is likely to know what significance this had. As for the Treasury men, the Narcotics Bureau is part of the Treasury Department, as you know, Jacques."

"These are not Narcotics men. They're income-tax men."

The President pursed his lips thoughtfully. "Are they? Those law partners must have been exceedingly anguished to track down just what department the investigators were working for. Very anguished—or maybe very guilty."

Hasbrouck pounced as if he were in court: "You're trying to pin complicity in the cocaine traffic on these poor innocent lawyers."

"My dear Jacques," said the President.

"You all but accused them of complicity on television, blackening their names before millions of TV viewers."

"I did no such thing. I stated the facts—and I cannot be held responsible for any implications they might draw. And you know and I know that everyone who reads the papers has already drawn all those implications—that these men are fronts for mobsters helping wash the dirty money clean by their very respectability."

"You can't prove one single—"

The President interrupted so swiftly that even Hasbrouck, the swiftest tongue in law, was caught with his mouth open.

"Nothing has to be proved against these men anymore, Jacques. They're dead. This is a whole new ball game. You're complaining because lawyers have been caught in the line of fire—along with the housewives, school kids, ambassadors, and the rest of us. For the first time since English law came of age in the seventeenth century the lawyers are catching bullets instead of writs of attainder, my friend. Is this why you're so angry? Because lawyers get struck down without due process? What makes you think your profession is exempt from the general assassination that is going on around the rest of us? Before you dissolve into tears for your poor profession, pray consider mine. There have only been forty Presidents and five of them have been murdered. An assassination rate of almost one in eight, the highest since the Roman Emperors in the fourth century A.D."

Hasbrouck stood silenced, a difficult feat: "How the hell am I going to reply to that?" he muttered.

The President sprang to his feet with the exaggerated courtesy he sometimes used to quell mutineers. "Don't try," he said, "your five minutes are long gone."

He escorted his old friend to the door of the Presidential bedroom: "Don't waste too much of Fenella's time on your way out, Jacques. We're very busy."

Hasbrouck snarled, "You should have been a lawyer."

"I almost was, you know," said the President, genially. "But then I decided that my gifts for deviousness would be stretched more fully by this job."

He closed the door on Hasbrouck and rubbed his hands together. He felt marvelous. He picked up the phone and called one of the swarm of Presidential assistants, Whitney, a bright young kid he'd had his eye on. "Whitney," he said without preamble when the young man arrived, "your talents for anonymity are going to be utilized to the utmost. I want you to set up a special task force to investigate this gang warfare. For that purpose I want you to borrow a few people from the FBI—about twenty of their best electronic people for a start. If you run into any road blocks from old Jeremy Fisher over there, refer him to me. I realize there are about a dozen other federal bodies looking into this gang war, which is one of the reasons I want total secrecy. Nobody is to know the thing even exists. Now, what I want you to do is..."

Whitney, a clean-limbed young man fresh from Yale Law School, listened with respectful silence, but with ever-widening eyes, to propositions he never learned in law school.

CHAPTER
EIGHT

Ferrier arrived at the most secretive of the White House entrances (none of them was totally out of the public eye, but the lower gate on the East Executive Drive was far less public than most) and met Prentice upstairs. Prentice took him immediately down the stairs through the Jefferson Colonnade and into the Oval office, blocked off by Marines from all public scrutiny except theirs. Ferrier inspected Prentice's improvements in silence. The President didn't explain them. He didn't have to. The meaning was self-evident.

The two men took a walk in the Rose Garden outside the Oval Office, Prentice voluble about his new rose—the Rosemary, named after guess who—although he thought it was much too scarlet to truly resemble his wife, whose personality was more a gentle pink.

Later, well down the lawn, the President said in

low tones, the lips moving hardly at all, "We're not even safe from directional mikes here, so keep it down."

Ferrier permitted himself the closest thing to a smile that ever crossed his thin face. "You're becoming awfully electronic, Chief," he murmured.

"I have to be," said Prentice, and told him what Miss Doll had remembered about Spence and the security clearance of the vanished gardener.

Nothing marred the total impassivity with which Ferrier received this intelligence. Both men bent over a rose bush far down the lawn.

"This," said Prentice, "is where I first spotted Canozzi, or whatever his real name is. Bent over this bush—for the longest time."

"Then," said Ferrier, "we'd better not look at it too publicly. I'll have someone look at it—and under it—later."

The two men strolled on down the lawn, the Jefferson Memorial shining in the bright sunshine ahead of them. "I don't believe it," said Ferrier, *sotto voce*. "Spence is too stupid to be in on something like this. And not stupid enough to do anything that dumb and that traceable. It's the old envelope switch."

"Of course," said the President, eyes on the horizon. "But who in the Secret Service could make a switch like that? Spence brings his little *billet doux* straight from Secret Service clutched in his sweaty security-conscious hands, and I could tell you the exact route he takes—even to the exact water cooler he always stops at for a drink on the way."

The men strolled on, hands behind their backs, enjoying the sunshine. "Well, if you know the route that well, so do other people. It could have happened on the way."

"Never," said the President. "He never lets go of that envelope. He's stupid, but conscientious."

"They are sometimes the easiest ones to fool," said Ferrier.

The President stopped to gaze at his favorite Washington view. "Should we just *ask* Spence?"

"Certainly not," said Ferrier. "He'd tell it all over Secret Service headquarters in an hour. Let me handle it."

The President nodded. "I'll need a few more little gadgets from your lovely armory, Paul." He told him what he required and where. Ferrier nodded, smiling a full smile, an exceedingly rare event.

"I'll see to that this afternoon," he said. It warmed his conspiratorial heart.

Back in his bedroom office, Prentice found Miss Doll holding the phone, which she handed to him silently. It was Tupper.

"They've got a mass of new stuff out of..." Tupper didn't want to mention Tasio's name on the phone, "the well. Lots of names."

"Bring it over," said the President.

Tupper didn't bring the documents. Only the names. "Thanks," said Prentice. And that was all. Later he called Joplin in Utah.

That night, two FBI men spent much of the evening on a roof across the street from the Union League Club with the most sensitive of directional mikes beamed across the street into the vast lounge of the club, where two men of imposing respectability sat quietly talking. A tape recorder was taking it all down. The advantage of the directional mike was that you didn't have to have a court order to allow you to use it as you did a phone tap. Of course you couldn't use the stuff in court, but the man who ordered the surveillance was not interested in court procedure.

One of the highly respectable Union League Club members was saying to the other one, quietly, though not so quietly it didn't come clearly through the headset of the FBI man on the rooftop: "The trouble is that none of the heads of these departments knows what is going on in their departments or why. Abner Dodge doesn't really know what his men are doing in St. Louis exactly, and Jeremy doesn't know what his men are looking for because they're all in special task forces. And when you ask who is running the task forces you run into a blank silence—which means only one person."

The silence after that was eloquent. Apparently, they didn't have to say who the person was. A look sufficed and no directional mike yet invented would transmit a look.

In Detroit, a couple more FBI electronics wizards were flying a kite which just happened to intrude over the air space of a certain Purple mobster who was caught in the middle of some terrible profanity to his lawyer seated with him in his garden.

"Listen, you little fucker," screeched the mobster, whose name was Traponi, and whose nickname thirty years earlier had been Trigger Lips, "you have got to get those title deeds out of Wentworth's office—if you have to shoot your way in. If my name is associated with that fucking contract the whole fucking bus franchise goes up in smoke. You little asshole, what are you doing sitting on your big fat behind while federal men are pawing over those contracts. They have no business, no right, to do this to me. Take them to court! Get an injunction! Goddamn it, get to work, you shitty little bastard.''

One FBI man grinned in delicious appreciation at the other kite-flying FBI man. They had never heard such language to a lawyer in their lives and having had defendants sprung again and again from just such a lawyer as this, they deeply appreciated it.

The lawyer's voice came down the kite string in a plaintive wail. "Mr. Traponi, be reasonable. I've tried to get an injunction, but Wentworth's office is up to its ass in federal agents. The Feds say they are investigating a murder and that any paper in Wentworth's office is a legitimate clue.''

"Mother fucking bastards,'' said Traponi. "Don't you see what they're doing, you stupid baboon? They're killing these lawyers—the Feds are *killing* these men—just to get at my records.''

"Please, Mr. Traponi,'' pleaded the lawyer, "this couldn't happen under our system. I think what has happened is—''

"Never mind what you think, you stupid shyster,'' howled Traponi. "What I want to know is what have you done with all those papers in *your* office—the union slush fund papers, the hotel deal. None of these things should be looked at by federal men.''

"They're all in my safe,'' said the lawyer, whose name was Smith and who sounded like a man named Smith.

"*All* those papers were in Wentworth's safe, you mother fucking idiot. And *now* where are they? In the hands of the Feds! Get those papers out of your safe and into a safety deposit box tonight.''

"Yes, Mr. Traponi,'' said the lawyer named Smith. He never made it. He was gunned down near his office that very night. By morning the very papers Traponi was so worried about were in federal hands. Traponi had by that time ceased worrying about them, being himself quite dead. Person or persons unknown had gained admittance by unknown means since Traponi's place, like the others, was a fortress and person or persons unknown had stitched him up so expertly that not a single bullet was wasted. Every bullet hit Traponi—a bit of automatic riflemanship much admired by the FBI who swarmed over the place the next day.

The newspapers hit the roof. "Following so closely on the President's speech, the fresh outbreak of gang warfare is total in its contempt for the machinery of the law," said *The Washington Post*. "It must not be permitted to go unpunished." Knowing full well, thought Prentice, reading it over the breakfast table, that unpunished it would go. Editorial fulminations, it occurred to him, were a good deal like dreams—a sort of emotional safety valve in which the nation released its frustrations. The nation had put up with the total powerlessness to cope with the Mafiosi for forty years. No editorial writer was so dumb as to think gangsters would ever be brought to justice by ordinary means. By writing it down, though, he felt a moment of quite phony power. So did the reader.

Prentice put down the paper and walked to his office—now only fifty feet away. Seated incongruously on the little gilt chair at the entrance to the bedroom was the Navy man with the little black box. A new man. Young. Polished to within an inch of his life. Prentice surveyed him, wondering what on earth passed through their heads—these automatons who sat bolt upright outside his various offices for hours on endless, boring hours. "Are you quite comfortable?" asked Prentice.

"Yes, sir," said the man.

That pretty well summed up all the conversation one could have. Couldn't very well say Hope we have a nice nuclear war this morning to give you a little excitement. One of the ironies of all time was the fact that a job which held the life or death of the planet in its hot hands could be so totally boring. A grape picker had more fun.

In his bedroom office on the desk by the window he saw the white phone blinking away, menacingly. Prentice started toward the phone, then stopped. Two black maids were making the bed and he didn't want to engage even in code talk with Joplin in front of them. The maids were maddeningly slow and maddeningly thorough. Prentice, hands thrust deep into his dressing gown, watched as they did meticulous hospital corners on each corner of the bed. The white phone blinked away. The maids plumped the pillows—thoroughly. Prentice stared out the window through the bulletproof glass at the spire of the Washington monument. When he turned back to the room, the girls were lovingly putting on the coverlet, a frilly pink lacy affair that was his wife's idea of unutterable luxury.

Finally, they were finished.

"That is without a shadow of doubt the most beautifully made bed I have ever seen," said the President.

Then to his utter horror, one girl wheeled out a vacuum cleaner. "No," said the President, firmly. He took it away from her and wheeled it back into the closet. "I'm terribly sorry to interfere with your household routine, girls, but we'll just have to let that go this morning,'' he said easing them out of the door into the big corridor. ''Mrs. Prentice can do it herself later.''

''The First Lady?'' said one of the girls blankly.

''Be good for her to keep her hand in,'' said the President. ''We don't have this job indefinitely.''

He closed the door on them and picked up the white telephone. ''How are you, Jop?'' said the President casually.

''Very bad.'' Joplin spoke with an unexpected harshness that jolted the President like live current. ''Rabies.''

''Oh, I *am* sorry,'' said the President coolly. Rabies? What in hell were rabies? He looked in his desk drawer. Where was the code book? In his own office he knew exactly where it would be—in the bottom drawer—underneath his memoirs. He looked in the bottom drawer, just in case, and there were his memoirs, and underneath—good old Miss Doll—was the code book. ''Hang on a moment, Jop,'' said the President. He unlocked it and flipped the pages of the little black book.

Rabies? Rabies? It had an ominous sound and so did Joplin's voice. Rabies. Rabies. There it was . . .

Mutiny.

Well.

''I'm sorry to hear that, Jop,'' said the President casually. ''I hope you're doing something about it.''

There was a silence. A long one.

''How widespread is it?'' asked Prentice.

''Just me.'' Very flat tone.

The President drew a deep breath. Joplin. The one person, the only person, in the whole operation who couldn't be replaced. And who couldn't be allowed to roam loose. Not with what he knew. He couldn't even ask on a private scrambled line what was bugging him. He'd picked the man personally and, though he hadn't laid eyes on him in months, he could summon up the face at will—the tough unblinking stare, the monosyllabic steely competence of the man. Now he was balking. Why? Moral scruples? How could one have suspected such a thing in as tough and experienced an operative? But then, one never knew where moral scruples might lie dormant, did one?

"You'll have to go to hospital," commanded the President. "Catch the 8:15." 8:15 didn't mean anything like 8:15, of course. The B-52 would leave Utah much earlier than that. Joplin understood that all right. The question was, would he come? How deep had rabies bitten him?

"Okay," said Joplin. And hung up.

On the President. Not even Brezhnev did that without saying "Good-by."

Prentice stared thoughtfully at the dead instrument in his hand and hung up very slowly, examining the implications. He was straining the loyalty of all these people to the outermost limits. He'd expected a crack somewhere, prepared for it, but he hadn't expected it to start with Joplin. Joplin was his most vulnerable point.

Joplin.

The President stroked his bristly chin, feeling terribly alone. His wife came in wearing the ancient pink dressing gown that he'd hated for thirty years but had never worked up the courage to tell her. A politician to the fingertips. One never told the voters (even if she was his wife) an unpalatable truth if one could help it.

She looked at him with her worried smile, the deep lines in her mouth. "It's not very nice for you—having to work up here," she said.

"It's only for a few days. It's harder on you than on me, actually. I had to shoo out the girls before they finished."

"Yes, they told me—that you thought it might be nice if I kept my hand in. Oh Harry, if only I could really clean this damned building from top to bottom. But the trouble is, it's not mine. It's not anybody's."

Prentice didn't feel that way at all. He felt very much that the White House was his. But, of course, it shouldn't be. The house should be her baby. How could it be with its Secret Service men, its stream of visitors, its offices, its sheer officialness? The White House, whatever else it was, was *not* a home.

"What are you doing there, anyway?" asked Rosemary.

"Repainting. Vermont barn red," said the President.

"They must be doing something else," said Rosemary. "They're making the most awful racket. Riveting. What on earth would require riveting in the Oval Office?"

Damn. Prentice hoped not too many had heard that sound. 'We're bolstering the walls," said Prentice.

"I thought Harry Truman had rebuilt the whole place from attic to cellar."

"The Oval Office got neglected somehow," said the President. "Anyway, it needs redoing." He went into the bathroom to shave and looked at his bristly face wryly. He supposed other husbands had to lie to their wives about infidelity, gambling debts, their drinking— things like that. He had to tell lies about redecorating the house. And many other things, if not *all* other things. He tried to remember the last time he had told his wife the complete truth and nothing but the truth about anything.

What a job.

He shaved and thought about what he was going to tell Joplin. It had better be good. The thing about him was that he was totally dedicated; you could trust not only his fidelity but his complete competence about any task you gave him. But once the dedicated ones came undedicated, the alienation was just as whole-hearted. That was the problem with dealing with these totally committed ones. The *un*commitment was just as total and then where were you? In the middle of the deep blue sea without a paddle. That's where.

If the unthinkable happened, who could handle Joplin's job? Mitch? No, not Mitch. Not Harry either. They didn't have the authority or the knowledge. Tupper? Well, perhaps, but he needed him where he was. Nobody really. Joplin was irreplaceable. And the worst of the dirty job lay ahead. I'd better be good, thought Prentice.

CHAPTER
NINE

The President rode in the bulletproof, bombproof Lincoln that weighed twelve tons down Pennsylvania Avenue, a smile pinned on his lips, nodding now and then to the few people who cared to stare. Washington was mighty casual about its Presidents. It had seen a lot of them. A movie star could cause more commotion. The Secret Service outriders were on the special running boards and another was in the front seat. Next to Prentice sat Tupper, his face a grimace of distaste.

"Why me?" he said. "I hate baseball."

"I know," said the President, smiling and waving at some girl who'd given him a passing glance. Well, they were all voters. "It's a grave defect in your character. You'll never be President if you say things like that."

"I outgrew wanting to be President when I was twelve," commented Tupper wearily. "Washington outgrew baseball ten years ago. What are you going to revive next—jousting?''

The President grinned. It was an old joke, not only from Tupper, but from everyone. When Washington had sold the perennially last-division Senators, Prentice had been the loudest to howl, partly because he genuinely liked baseball (though watching a team as bad as the Senators was a painful experience to a real baseball nut), but mostly to polish up his image as an old-fashioned cracker-barrel American. He was no such thing, of course. He was the most revolutionary of all Presidents, which was why it was so important to conceal his radicalism behind his barbershop American facade—eating hot dogs, attending baseball games, patting the *derrières* of presidents of daffodil societies.

Prentice had tried and failed to get a major league baseball club back into Washington. Failing that, he had succeeded in promoting a spring exhibition game every year between the pennant winners of the previous year. He was always there cheering lustily, eating popcorn—and how could anyone suspect deviousness in a President with such old-fashioned tastes?

''What did you want to see me about?'' asked the President.

Tupper looked sourly at the Secret Service men on the running boards. He didn't trust anyone anymore. He slipped the envelope along his knees to the President's knees. Prentice opened the envelope, still bowing and smiling to the few people looking his way and slipped out the photograph. He glanced at it briefly. Then did a startled double take. One man was passionately kissing another man on a bed. Both stark naked.

The man on top was George Blaser, the Secret

Service deputy who had committed suicide five days earlier.

"Where did you find this?" asked Prentice.

"Tasio's safe," said Tupper.

The President threw out the first ball himself, smiling jovially. He threw much better than any of his predecessors because he'd played the game once. He still loved watching good baseball, an old-fashioned taste. The populace had gone over altogether to professional football, which Prentice thought was just organized violence. Appropriate to the epoch, but not for Prentice. He got enough violence on the job.

It was a very good game—between the Baltimore Orioles and the St. Louis Cardinals—and Prentice cheered at the long balls, shuddered at the close ones, stood up and sat down, ate popcorn, and forgot all about the job, and about Central America and his private civil war for a full two and a half hours.

It was only on the long ride back to the White House that his mind sprang back to the unpleasant picture in his pocket. Blaser. He knew him only slightly. He'd had much to do with assignment of Secret Service personnel—and recruitment, too. A prime object of blackmail for one of the top mobsters. The possibilities for mischief were infinite.

Silence reigned in the Presidential limousine. Both Prentice and Tupper were sizing up the two Secret Service outriders on the running boards, wondering whether they had been assigned there by George Blaser, now defunct.

As they passed through the East Executive Drive gate, Prentice said wanly: "Sex is a terrible thing. Avoid it."

"Never touch the filthy stuff myself," said Tupper.

Joplin was waiting for him in the little upstairs study just outside his bedroom. He was dressed in a business suit, as inappropriate on his tough rangy frame as a chemise on a monkey. He overflowed the little red leather chair in all directions, arms hanging almost to the floor. Prentice half-sat, half-leaned against the windowsill and studied his man silently. That long, seamed face weathered in a dozen guerrilla actions from Riga to Detroit with stopovers in Rumania and Hungary. He exuded power. Physical power. Once set on a course he looked hard to deflect. The little room seemed much too small to contain him.

The long Presidential silence would have unsettled lesser men. Not Joplin.

Prentice used his old technique for openers. Don't defend, attack. Make the other fellow defend. "What's bugging you, Joplin?" he said. No friendly diminutive. Not yet.

"I've been reading the newspapers," said Joplin flatly. No strain in his voice at all.

"A bad habit."

"Killing lawyers. I don't like it. That's how it started in Rumania. Killing lawyers. When the lawyers are dead, they can kill anyone."

"A bad business," agreed Prentice. Let Joplin talk himself out. Get it out where he could examine it and tear it apart.

Joplin was not one to run off at the mouth. The silence grew oppressive.

Joplin picked at a calloused thumb. The President looked at him. Time passed.

"I didn't mind hitting the Tasios, the Schotzes. They hit a lot of people in their day. Why lawyers?

Civilians." Joplin was respectful and contemptuous of
civilians at the same time, as were a good many people
in his business. One didn't kick civilians around any
more than one kicked a dog around. It wasn't done.
Still, they were only civilians. One measured out one's
respect in teaspoons. Killers were in a club of their
own, and they no more knew what made the civilians
go round than the civilians knew what made them go
round.

"Because they get in the way," said Prentice.

"It'll be women and children next," said Joplin.

"If they get in the way," said Prentice.

The simple brutality got through to Joplin. The
seamed face showed a glow of passion. Joplin stood up,
much too tall for the room. "That's what I figured. I
want out."

"Sit down," said Prentice, every inch a Presidential command.

Joplin glared. Then he sat. What choice had he?

"I didn't know you were so sentimental about
women and children, Joplin," said the President, pushing him to the outer extremities by sheer brutality.
Making him expose himself.

"Why women and children?" spat out Joplin.
"What is this?"

"Civil war," said the President. "No more and no
less. In war people get killed. Women and children
along with the others. In Dresden 135,000 were killed
in one raid, mostly civilians. Many women and children."

Joplin grunted. "That was World War Two."

"This is Civil War Two."

He let it lie there a long while. Joplin was listening
now. Listening hard, eyes on the floor. He let him wait.

"Jop," said the President using the diminutive

now that he had him where he wanted him—using it almost tenderly, caressingly, with one syllable changing the temper and mood of the colloquy altogether—making it at one bound a conspiracy rather than an argument, "crime is the biggest business in this country. Bigger than steel, automobiles, and oil added together. We as a nation have endured this for almost half a century with a sort of easy-going cynicism, using mobsters as laugh lines, while they ate away at our vitals. Poison. We thought the money didn't matter. There was enough to go around, let the crooks have a few billion. But with the money went the power. They've corrupted the police, then the judges, and now, Jop, it's creeping very close to the White House itself. They've infiltrated Treasury, I don't trust the Secret Service. I don't trust the FBI. They're deep into the Interior Department and I strongly suspect the next objects of their attention are the Army and Navy."

He stopped and let it sink in. Joplin was staring at the floor, stubbornly. He didn't believe it. He didn't want to believe it.

"What evidence have you of any of this?" asked Joplin, frank hostility in every syllable.

"Not much," said Prentice casually. "One reason we haven't got the evidence is that most evidence—through a long series of Supreme Court decisions—has been held to be illegal. You can't tap phones. You can't seize evidence in a man's house without first warning him you're going to enter it and search it, so naturally the evidence isn't there when you search. The web of protection around the guilty—especially the rich and powerful guilty—is far too strong now even for the federal government to break through." He smiled. "And who has woven this web of protection around the organized crime? The lawyers. If the modern lawyer had been around in the nineteenth century, fingerprints would have been against the law as an invasion of privacy. That's why we're killing lawyers, Jop. You've heard of the Gordian knot, I think. It was much too complicated to undo. Alexander the Great cut it with a single blow of his sword—which is the only way to handle Gordian knots.''

Joplin's face still looked undeviatingly, stubbornly, at the floor. Prentice let him stare for a while.

"Last year the profit from illegal mob activities— gambling, loan sharking, extortion, prostitution, heroin, cocaine—was in the neighborhood of fifty *billion* dollars. You can subvert a lot of people with fifty billion dollars. Ultimately you can subvert a whole nation— and that's what's being done.''

He picked up a photograph he had carefully left on the top of the desk and tossed it to Joplin. It was a photograph of an addict, the bony face, the starved eyes, the anguished mouth...

"In Detroit alone the rate of addiction has gone from one in ten thousand citizens in one area to one in a hundred in five years. In another five years, it'll be everyone—including the children who come into the world hooked. In spite of any nonsense you may have read to the contrary, drugs are the Mob's top income-producer. It is destroying the moral fiber of the city. Those not hooked are being robbed, assaulted, or killed to get money for junk. The city is becoming a city of victims, and what has happened in one city *will* happen in the others, one by one—New York, Chicago, Milwaukee, San Francisco—all of them.''

Silence filled the room. Prentice examined the

rocklike visage for signs of softening; there were none at all.

Very tough fellow, Joplin.

"No country has ever survived this sort of assault on its moral underpinnings. Rome collapsed in four hundred years, but of course the rate of change then was much slower. In our century change moves at twenty times the speed of ancient Rome. At best we have twenty years before the nation collapses."

The President studied the bony face. Nothing. He played his trump card.

"You must also consider our dear enemy, the Soviet Union. They are great students of history, the Soviets, much taken by Marcus Cato's famous statement: 'Carthage must be destroyed.' And Carthage *was* destroyed, which left Rome the only great power in the world. From the very beginning the wise old owls in the Kremlin have concentrated on destroying their great rival from the *inside,* so much easier than conquering them from the outside. Every little Marxist in South America is helping the cocaine trail to the U.S., partly to make money to finance revolution but most to corrupt us, demoralize us, victimize us."

Joplin was listening now. Sullenly. But listening, Joplin needed a villain. Prentice did his best to provide one.

"Drugs are part of Soviet foreign policy and possibly even China foreign policy. Drugs have been adopted as foreign policy by the highest levels in the Kremlin. First, they depended on heroin but that seemed to reach only the lower classes. Cocaine is a far more deadly weapon, reaching the educated classes, the leaders, destroying the best of our people, the most valuable of our thinkers and doers."

Prentice read from the document on his knee in his very dry, unemphatic, silver-tongued voice: "The rate of addiction among officers and enlisted men in Vietnam doubled from thirty to sixty percent in one year, 1970. The success of this policy in Vietnam was so great that the Kremlin decided to direct its efforts toward U.S. civilians in U.S. cities. Its success in this field can only be judged by the doubling in two years of the addiction rate in three cities—Chicago, New York, and Detroit...."

Joplin made an eloquent move. He reached out one great apelike arm. Prentice put the document into his hand. Joplin scowled at it—FOR THE PRESIDENT'S EYES ONLY glaring at him in red from the cover. Prentice let him take his time. When he was through Joplin looked straight into the President's eyes—the first time his eyes had come off the floor.

"This is civil war, Jop," said the President wearily. "And in war you don't worry about a few dead lawyers. The lawyers are weaving a web of conspiracy in which the country is foundering in its own civil rights. We have very little time to stop them. Because if I don't stop them fast, they're going to stop me. They're on to me, Jop. I have kept my civil war secret not only from the public but from *them*—but I'm blown, Jop, blown. They're going to move in fast because they have to. Two ways. First, if they can do it—exposure. I'm very vulnerable to exposure, Jop. And they won't stop at that either. There is the other time-honored way of getting rid of Presidents—killing them." Prentice smiled, a little crookedly. "I think, Jop, knowing my adversary, that they will try both— murder *and* defamation—but which comes first, that I don't know."

Joplin's eyes glittered with the joy of combat. He

had his villain now and he had his hero. Life was very simple for him, a matter of certainties. He needed certainties.

"You sneaky bastard," he said. "I might have known you'd talk me around. Okay. What's the action?"

The President smiled. "I'm glad you're on my side. I . . . don't trust many people anymore. Not more than three or four." He stared out of the bulletproof glass. "It was the Praetorian Guard who usually assassinated the Roman Emperors, you know."

He sat down at the desk, facing Joplin. "Here's my plan," he said.

An hour later Joplin was on his way back to Utah and the President was in bed, first locking all the doors, including the one to his bedroom, which he had never done before.

Ferrier arrived at the bedroom office the next morning at 8:00 A.M. Washington was an early town. The President was dressing; Rosemary had already fled. Ferrier carried a package wrapped in white tissue paper, which he unwrapped slowly and without comment before Prentice's inquiring gaze.

It was a rose bush in full flower. Prentice examined it with his expert eye, and recognized it instantly.

He looked out the bulletproof glass at the spot where it had been. Another bush was in its place.

"The CIA is very thorough," said Ferrier wryly. "We never uproot a rose bush without planting another in its place."

Ferrier pulled the bush out of its pot, and at the roots was a cube of stainless steel, matchbox-size. Wires ran from a hole in its side right into the root of the bush. Prentice inspected it. The wires seemed to become the roots.

"Oh, they don't stop there," said Ferrier. "The wiring runs through the plant, and it's a real rose plant. The branches have been trained to grow right around the wires, swallowing them. Must have taken years."

"What does it do?" asked Prentice.

"Communications," said Ferrier. "The very best. That's what bothers us. We didn't think anyone but us could miniaturize like that." He pointed to the tiny cube. "Even with us that's highly restricted. Only the CIA and the Air Force have it—and only certain highly selected bits of the Air Force. Worrisome that that kind of gadgetry gets around."

Ferrier took the President's paper scissors from the desk and snipped off a rose and showed the stem to the President. A tiny wire was at the base of the root, the thorns growing right around it.

"Outrageous," said the President, a rose lover, "doing that sort of thing to a rose. But why? What is it for?"

Ferrier shook his head. "We don't know. It could be used for a lot of things. To home in a missile, perhaps. Or an airplane. Or for telemetry of many sophisticated sorts—like detonating a bomb placed under some other rose bush. Or anywhere."

The President put the wired rose into his buttonhole, casually. "I need men, Paul. A lot of men. And I need them fast."

He told him how many men he needed. Ferrier blinked.

"I haven't got that many. Not operational. Not here."

"Bring them back from abroad. The priority is here."

"Mr. President—" Ferrier didn't know how to put it. "You don't know what you're asking. A lot of those men were picked for one reason only—their ruthlessness—and I wouldn't trust them in this country much less with a sensitive assignment such as the one I *think* you have in mind."

Blowing people's heads off, thought Prentice, was not all that sensitive.

"Many of them can't even speak English."

You don't need English to pull a trigger, thought Prentice.

"They're all nationalities—Poles, Czechs, Arab terrorists, Uraguayan urban guerrillas, Algerian hoodlums—you can't let that kind of flotsam run loose here."

"I don't intend to let them run loose," said the President. "They'll be on a very tight rein, and they'll be out of the country within two days."

Ferrier curbed his crazy desire to ask questions. "How many do you need again?"

Prentice told him.

Ferrier rubbed his chin. Speaking out ran against his deepest grain: "Mr. President, sooner or later questions are going to be raised. Senator Blair has already asked me—"

"What?" said the President sharply.

"Whether the CIA had any knowledge of these gang killings."

"Senator Blair asked *that*?" said the President. "Right out of the blue? Just like that?"

"Right out of the blue. Just like that."

"When?"

"Yesterday. On the telephone."

"You sure it was Blair?"

"Should I suppose it was anyone else?"

"I don't know," said the President. He especially didn't know why Blair should be guessing so accurately, so brilliantly. Someone must have tipped him.

"What did you tell him?"

Ferrier let a ghost of a smile cross his face. "I asked him *what* gang killings?"

The President grinned. "What did he say to that?"

"He used a very dirty word. Before he got any further, I told him the CIA's sole function was abroad. It had no, repeat *no* operatives in this country at all. Not one."

The President nodded appreciatively. Ferrier was as good a liar as he was.

"Besides men," said the President, "I need a few other things."

He told him what he needed.

CHAPTER
TEN

The camp stood on a heavily wooded plateau high in the Rockies. Tall firs masked the wooden huts, most of them anyway, and all the top secret stuff was kept under wraps deep in the Utah woods. But they couldn't very well keep the exercises altogether under cover. Out on a field sat a replica of a Manhattan town house, one of the grandest still standing, granite walls fronting the house with a small sign lettered Fifth Avenue. It had to be a real granite wall, because they were testing the armor-piercing rocket.

Joplin, in blue jeans, watched from the shelter of an earth bank, forty yards away, eyes on his watch. They were running slow, but he'd told them to take their time and for godsake to get it right. It was always slow the first time. He looked up at the sky. No airplanes passed this way except now and again, those of a few rich ranchers on their way to their hunting lodges. Of course, the satellites were up in the sky and Joplin wondered what the Russians thought of this exercise. He had a few dummy cinema cameras around—just to puzzle them a little further. Was it a film or wasn't it? He didn't really give a damn what the Russians saw and he doubted whether the Mafia had any satellites. Not yet.

"All right, get on with it," he shouted. It was a mixed crew he was shouting at—two Arabs, four Czechs, and three Chinese. Prentice had personally selected this mixed bag because, if caught, they would thoroughly befuddle any FBI men who picked them up. (God forbid that any such disaster should occur.) None of them spoke English. None had the faintest idea what he was doing or why. Beyond the barest outlines, that is. Get into the house and kill everyone. Then ransack the place and bring every scrap of paper in it. All within twelve minutes—a tall order. That's why they were practicing.

There was a muffled crump. It wouldn't wake a light sleeper at two hundred yards, Joplin figured, even in the 4:00 A.M. silence of Manhattan (virtually the only time the place was reasonably quiet). Joplin watched the neat rectangle it blew into the black stretch of the front wall of the fourth story—behind which lay eight inches of steel plate. God help them if the steel plate was thicker than that. Behind the steel plate lay the safe, and the only way to do the job fast was with Harrian rockets designed for use against Russian tanks.

The grappling hooks were already in place and two Chinese slithered down the ropes from the roof and into the hole. Thirty seconds. Not bad—not good. He listened for the sound from their silenced machine pistols. Nothing. Good. There'd be the flashes, of course, but who would be looking at a four-foot hole, four stories high at 4:00 A.M.?

Inside, the Chinese were sending bullets into a dummy on a double bed, into two other dummies who might be guarding the door. (They were just guessing about that. There might very well be nobody. Always be overprepared.) One was downstairs now, wiping out the dummy of a very real butler who had been with the man for years. Too bad, one of the innocents in this operation.

Outside, four Czechs were going down the ropes into the hole; veteran safeblowers all of them, they went right to work at what were very real safes. Nothing subtle about this job. Get it done, noise or no noise, but all in one big bang—the granite walls would muffle the racket from outside. The advantage of four Czechs was they could talk to each other in their bewildering language. The last Chinese stood guard on the roof while the two Arabs slid down the rope into the house. Arsonists and general all-around thugs they were. Their jobs were to kill any cops who had the misfortune to blunder onto the scene, and to burn the place to a crisp after the others had left.

Inside, the Czechs blew the very real, very tough inside safe wide open, seized very real papers, and put them in the precise canvas bags they'd use on the real job. One Arab and the rooftop Chinese sprayed rubber bullets on a couple of simulated cops Joplin had sprung on them as a surprise. The rubber bullets hurt like hell, but Joplin wanted accuracy.

The team came pouring out of the hole in the wall, scrambled to the roof and away over the rooftops—or what would be the rooftops. They had only one in Utah. Joplin looked at his watch. "Sloppy!" he shouted. None of his hoods understood English—except for a few phrases Joplin had taught them like "Get on with it" and "Sloppy." He hadn't bothered to teach them "Well done" yet. He could do that later, if the occasion arose.

"Take a break," he shouted.

Mitch sauntered out from the cover of the nearest tree where he'd taken shelter from the rubber bullets.

"Are you the director of this B movie?" he inquired. He was a fun-loving Welshman. Loved killing people, also jokes. "It won't get second billing in Buffalo."

Joplin contemplated him sourly. "You got anything but jokes on your mind?"

"Two consignments of extras, Belasco," said Mitch flippantly. "You could make a hell of a crowd scene."

Joplin ran his hand over his face. "Christ! How many does that make?"

"Just this side of four hundred." Mitch grinned cheerfully. "Come have a look. Blackbeard himself would faint dead away with fright at the sight of this bunch."

The two men walked briskly through the camp, past scenes of carefully calculated carnage. On one side of them there was a wooden front, like a movie set, of a very real country house in Beverly Hills. A man leaped from a moving car with a blazing submachine gun cradled under his arm, right through a window. The two men paid no attention. Farther along, on a bit of highway, three cars passed them at 100 miles an hour. The second one edged in front of the leading car while the third car drew alongside and then both slowed the runaway down—finally jamming him to a halt, far down the road.

"Where are we going to house them?" Joplin asked Mitch.

"I've set them to felling trees and I've told them if they expect to be out of the rain tonight, they've got to put a roof over their heads. You'd be surprised how that hurried them along."

Joplin grunted.

The two men stopped to watch another display. A man dressed as a lineman was on the top of a telephone pole, with a line of rope hanging down. A motorcycle with a robot aboard chugged down a road. The man on the telephone pole came zooming down the rope on a little pulley and seat arrangement, spilling the robot in the ditch. The fake telephone lineman stepped out of the rope and pulley arrangement, righted the motorcycle, and drove off.

Joplin scowled. "What makes you think the motor-cycle will still run?" he asked the man in charge.

"We have three other possible getaways. His feet, hitchhike, or as a last resort, the car he came in—which we'd rather not use because we think the FBI will figure that's the dead man's car and get themselves hopelessly confused when they trace the number."

Joplin didn't like it much. "Are we sure it'll *be* a motorcycle?"

"He's a motorcycle nut. Always travels that way, and *always* that road."

Joplin nodded and went on.

At the edge of the forest he found his newest batch of hoodlums. Some were cutting down trees that others were feeding into a screeching power saw. Out came instant lumber. Thugs of various nationalities hauled the green timber away and were erecting huts with it. Two had already erected under the direction of one of Joplin's regular hoodlums, who was now shouting instructions about the roof.

Joplin inspected his newest recruits and beamed with delight. There were Turks in fezzes with great mustaches flaunting their virility—which seemed obvious enough without them. A tremendous black man, bald as a knife, his torso a massive twist of muscle, looked like a Michelangelo figure on the Sistine ceiling. There were a couple of massive Kurds—where in hell did Ferrier find these people?—tall as telephone poles, using their great height to lift the new boards into place on the new huts. There were quite a few Chinese—a lot of discontent in Formosa—which Ferrier had used for recruitment; there were grinning, graceful Italians from the poverty-stricken south of Italy, and of course, a smattering of Corsicans (Ferrier loved the Corsicans for their agility in tall building jobs and their lighthearted absence of conscience on closeup jobs, to say nothing of their intimate knowledge of Mafiosi methods of protection); there were true Rumanian gypsies with black hair and supple bodies singing their wild songs in defiance of the screeching power saw; there were Hungarians, Germans, Poles, and one lone Japanese, a tree trunk of a man who looked like a refugee from professional wrestling.

"Is there an American in this lot?" asked Joplin.

Mitch shook his head. "Nor an Englishman, Irishman, or Frenchman," he shouted over the buzz saw. "Too civilized, those people."

The Welshman gazed at the scene appreciatively. Wouldn't Goya like to paint that scene! Or Holbein. Or, for that matter, George Grosz. Any painter who had real guts and a powerful line. Were there any more painters like that? Now they painted soup cans, not people. "We should have a resident Goya," he shouted to Joplin.

"Who?" asked Joplin.

"Let it pass! Let it pass!" said the Welshman. Joplin was not one who would know about Goya. He was the kind of man who should have been *in* a Goya painting, not one standing in an art gallery looking at one.

Jerry Patch (a shortening of his real Polish name, which was unpronounceable) picked his way through the tumult and touched Joplin on the sleeve.

"The Boss," he said, and held his hand to his ear, simulating a telephone.

Joplin nodded and departed instantly, walking back through the camp where practice was intensive. One man held a little short rifle with a grappling hook stuck in its muzzle. He fired it and the grappling hook sailed gracefully through the blue sky pulling a nylon line behind it and lodged on the roof of a building. The other end of the line was fastened tautly into a hook in the ground and three men were running up the taut rope on a powered set of pulleys, the little engines spitting black exhaust puffs behind them. Farther on, a murderous little tank—it barely came up to Joplin's waist—shot past him and piled right through an oak door spitting rubber bullets to each side of it.

Joplin's office was a little log cabin he'd lovingly built himself in memory of his Baltic boyhood. The white telephone was kept locked in a stout wooden case that he allowed no one else to touch. Above the case a light blinked on and off. Joplin pulled out a set of keys and unlocked two great padlocks.

Joplin picked up the receiver and sat down. Silence. This could last a long time. Sometimes the

President was busy or had visitors. He knew a light was blinking on the White House desk. No one would pick up that phone except Miss Doll or the President, and they were not always there. Minutes passed.

Prentice began without preamble.

"Fiesta is Saturday night," said the President.

Joplin deducted two days because it was Tuesday and implanted Thursday in his mind. If the call had come on a Wednesday, he'd have deducted three, if Thursday, four, and so on; nothing was ever said straight in these calls. Thursday would be the night of the long knives, the like of which the U.S. had not seen in its history.

"I hope all your girls are in a party mood," said the President.

Joplin's seamed face creased into his wryest smile: "Breathless with anticipation," he said. "Positively agog with girlish enthusiasm."

Two thousand miles away, the President smiled. "You've looked over their evening clothes, I hope? We want only the last word in fashion at this party. The girls would be seriously embarrassed if any of them were caught in last year's duds."

Joplin grinned. "I think we can safely say we'll knock their eyes out."

The President permitted himself a little smile of appreciation. He was going to miss these conversations with Joplin when it was all over. "Be sure you get the girls home before midnight." (Translation: 4:00 A.M.) "You wouldn't want them to turn into pumpkins, now would you?" said Prentice and hung up.

Joplin was left with a dead phone in his hand. He looked at it tenderly, as if it were a person, before cradling it in its wooden case—which he locked again with its huge padlocks.

The moment he hung up, the President stood up in the redecorated Oval Office with its Vermont barn red walls. He got a deep pleasure out of his newly painted office, partly because he loved the muted red, a very American color, but mostly because traditionalists were shocked to the marrow by it. He enjoyed shocking them.

He looked out the window at the electronic rose bush which had been tenderly replaced just where it was before. Ferrier's men had put it back exactly as it was—still not knowing its secrets—on the theory that they could at least keep an eye on it. If it were replaced they might never find the replacement.

The President looked at his watch, adjusted his tie in the oval mirror—a treasure of early Americana—patted his pocket to see that the little revolver was in it (he must remember never to do that in public, he thought), and strode out of the Oval Office. The Naval Officer with the black box sprang to his feet and scurried after him. Two Secret Servicemen—why did they all look as if they'd been to Princeton? We must get some Yale men in the crowd, thought the President—added themselves to the cortege, one in front and one behind. The unwieldly procession picked up Tupper in the Appointments Office—he had been waiting for twenty minutes—and marched into the elevator in the West Wing. The elevator rose at its dignified White House pace.

There was a vast silence in the elevator. There always was when he was in it, thought Prentice. All eyes front, everyone very solemn. "How are you feeling, Tup?" inquired the President with solicitude.

"Hemmed in," said Tupper sourly.

The President inspected this remark. He and Tup had a private language too, which they made up as they went along. One had to guess at the meanings.

Something was crowding him, and not on that elevator either. He hazarded a guess: "Is Big Daddy making trouble?"

"Keeping me awake nights."

"We'll have to get you a sleeping pill."

"In a very big hurry," said Tupper savagely.

That didn't sound good at all. Tupper was the most easy-going man he knew. He rode out crises of hurricane proportions without moving a muscle. He'd never heard Tupper sound like this.

The elevator door opened and the cortege marched down the West Wing and into the main conference room where the rest of the National Security Council was assembled—Osgood Carruthers, Secretary of Defense; Major General Dyke (what was he doing here? wondered Prentice; Ordnance wasn't usually in on this show); Roger Jackson, Secretary of State; the FBI head Jeremy Fisher, looking even more ferocious than usual; Paul Ferrier, of course, whose remote eyes always set him apart from everyone else in the room. (That's what intelligence did to people—set them apart from their fellows to the point they thought themselves a separate species, with different rules.) Paul Wright, Secretary of the Air Force; Tom Bakke, Secretary of the Army; Peter Dewey, Secretary of the Navy; and, of course, the white-thatched adviser of Presidents, Everett Quincey. Too damn many people, thought Prentice for the hundredth time. He was a loner by nature. Two people were too many. How the hell could you make a decision with a mob like this? That's why they'd made that blunder at the Bay of Pigs; nobody had dared to open his mouth and state the obvious.

Prentice took his place at the head of the long conference table and gave a smile, a nod, and a first name to every last man there—Osgood, Roger, Jeremy— all of them. They murmured "Mr. President" back. Prentice sat down and launched an attack, as was his wont, before someone else did.

"I am getting a great confusion of information about the situation in northwest Africa. Your information, Paul, which says things could hardly be worse, conflicts directly with that of Army intelligence, which says that while things are not ideal, no real threat is coming from that area."

"Not a difference in information," said Ferrier, easily, "just interpretation. The CIA is by nature pessimistic; the Army by inclination . . ." (with a shade of overt contempt) "lazy. It's easier to be optimistic than pessimistic."

That set off an uproar. Ferrier was protecting his chief from the gang war issue.

It didn't last. It couldn't. Jeremy Fisher was not to be gainsaid for long; although Prentice was studiously avoiding his eye, he could not avoid his voice. He cut through the spitting intelligence quarrel with three words that brought a shocked silence to the room.

"Civil war, gentlemen," said Jeremy Fisher.

This silenced everyone, including Prentice. Civil war? His own idea exactly. But not one he voiced publicly. Not Prentice. What was Jeremy Fisher doing running around with his ideas? Fisher wasn't bright enough. Prentice had personally picked him to be not very bright because too bright an FBI chief would be a very great menace to his operations. Here he was sprouting bright ideas. Whose?

Fisher was saying that the non-Communist world was being shaken from San Francisco to Tuscany by internal riot. "Our mistake," said Fisher, "is that word riot. It's really civil war, fought with underground armies, out of uniform, but united in aim and objective. Urban guerrilla violence is the new kind of civil war." And he went on to list them, from Ulster to Poland—the communist, the non-communist—and pull them together brilliantly into one pattern of civil disobedience to central authority avoided only, he said wittily (and wit had never previously been known to be his strong point) by Luxembourg and Sikkim, both well out of the main stream of history. (Who is writing his jokes? wondered Prentice.)

"Looked at in this light," said Fisher smoothly, "the gang wars assume a whole new menacing pattern. They are not simply a struggle for gang power which, though regrettable, the civil authorities can safely dismiss as irrelevant to their real concern. These gangs now control police, judges, mayors, maybe some governors, and some say even higher authorities."

How about the FBI itself? Prentice was thinking.

"And now we have very strong evidence that a foreign power—the Soviet Union—is assuming a major role in gang affairs, with a deliberate aim of subverting this nation by crime, corruption, and above all—drugs. The FBI has no other explanation for gang killing on this scale. It has gone beyond one gang wiping out another; it has become almost gang suicide—and that is ridiculous. Why should they do that? Only a national government, we feel most strongly, could mount such *offensives*—and there is no other word for violence on this scale.''

What was he leading up to? wondered Prentice, his mind going at lightning speed. He had to head it off and how could he head it off unless he had some clue as to where Fisher was headed, what he was after.

''. . . wiping out Tasio who was a very tough customer,'' Fisher was saying. ''A very tough customer. He once hung one of his gorillas on a meat hook and beat his brains out with a baseball bat with his own hands . . .''

There it was—Prentice's fictitious anecdote he'd fabricated for Hasbrouck—just to see how far it went and by whom it came back to him.

Hasbrouck.

Hasbrouck was writing the jokes. But why? Prentice didn't know that Hasbrouck even knew the FBI head. His witty chum knew a lot of people around Washington, most of the important ones, but the FBI chief was not only outside his regular orbit, but normally his bitter enemy—he and his whole department.

''. . . this not only puts the whole gang war scene into a new and menacing light, but it also means we must take new and more drastic steps to combat it. We need fresh weapons.''

Uh-oh! thought Prentice.

''Major General Dyke,'' said Fisher, ''would you take over on the question of weaponry?''

That's what Dyke was doing here, thought Prentice grimly. Fisher had brought him. Very interesting. Someone was certainly doing a lot of thinking for Fisher. Hasbrouck? Why? Tasio had been his client but Tasio was dead. And what long-range objective did Hasbrouck have in mind?

Major General Dyke, the very model of a stuffed-shirt Army general, was pontificating at some length about weapons used in the gang killings which ordinarily should have not been in their hands. "The high explosive in the Tasio murder was of a very light-weight concentrated sort—highly restricted even in our own armed forces. Even so well-equipped a gang as the Mafia could not lay hands on it. Only a foreign power— and we had hoped not even them. Then there was the means of ingress. We have some evidence that it was by helicopter—and it must have been a new silent helicopter like our Army Bell X-20, which is very top secret indeed."

Prentice cut in to get the thing back into his hands. "What makes you think that?"

"Simply," said Fisher, taking the play away from Dyke, "by eliminating all other means of ingress as impossible."

"Pretty tenuous," said Prentice. "Jeremy, all of this *police* work," bearing down hard on the word police, as an activity well beneath the contempt of the National Security Council, "just what relevance has this to our larger concerns?"

"It *is* our larger concern," said Fisher. "That's what I'm saying. I need—"

"What now?" asked Prentice wryly. "Tanks? Planes? The FBI is already the world's best-equipped police force."

"We need," said Fisher, "direct access to the Army—*when* we need them. I'm just asking for a co-ordinating unit so that we could, if necessary—and, believe me, it is—call on the big stuff—yes, tanks and planes. Because that may very soon become necessary."

Over my dead body, thought Prentice. But not

aloud. Not, for God's sweet sake, aloud. He must head it off but not seem to.

"What would the Army think about *that*, Tom?" asked Prentice of the Army Secretary. Trust the Army to fend off any borrowing of its toys.

"Well," said Bakke unexpectedly, "Jeremy and I have talked this over and come up with a plan which should be fairly easy. It just needs a communication center so we could maintain instant twenty-four hour access to each other. It would be a very good exercise for us—since this kind of guerrilla warfare seems to be the going thing."

Somebody has been brainwashing him, too, thought Prentice.

"So the FBI would wind up commanding Army tanks in street battles," said Prentice. "As Commander in Chief of the Armed Forces I don't think I'd like that even if you would, Tom."

There was an immediate horrified protest from both men that there was no question of Prentice yielding one bit of his command responsibility. The White House would be kept fully informed, at every step, but of course the White House was pretty busy and in case of immediate emergencies, well, after all, the FBI didn't call the President every time it let fly a bullet at a felon, did it? This was the same thing except with different, more deadly weapons demanded by a different, more deadly situation; didn't Prentice understand that?

Prentice understood it only too well. The FBI would have access to Army material of the most awesome sort; Army and FBI would be putting heads together on all sorts of preventive measures and retaliatory steps, which could overwhelm his little task force in the Utah woods. An Army and FBI intelligence combine would be operating, not so much behind his back as around his flank, finding out things and taking steps, before he knew of them himself.

And yet he could not block this dreaded thing without making himself conspicuously obstructive. It was too sensible. It was also the worst news since he'd undertaken, all by himself, this vast enterprise. Thank God the fiesta was only two nights away. They couldn't get the combined operation working by then.

He hoped.

Back in the Oval Office, Prentice and Tupper faced one another silently. Finally, Tupper looked around him: "Is this place bugproof?"

"Is any place?" asked Prentice wearily. "Go ahead."

Tupper lay the piece of paper before him. He pointed to a name. The same name.

"Big Daddy keeps coming up with him."

"We already knew that."

"I wasn't playing around with hot money accounts this time," said Tupper. "I was asking Big Daddy all sorts of questions about lines of economic force. Very sophisticated stuff I learned from the Banking and Commerce Committee and the World Bank and the United Nations narcotics team. Whatever tune you play on Big Daddy you come up with *that* name. He's the big cheese himself. He *must* be. There's no other explanation."

Prentice had already reached that conclusion. But of course it would be upsetting to Tupper. He hadn't confided in anyone.

"Well?" said Prentice.

Tupper let it lie there a long while. He glanced around the room, still worrying about bugs.

Finally he blurted it out: "Chief, I don't know what you are up to, but . . . I can't avoid certain . . . speculations."

"I'd rather not hear them," said Prentice dryly.

With his inside information and his intelligence Tupper could hardly avoid having some pretty shrewd guesses, but it was always best to leave these things unspoken. Things suspected were one thing, things known were altogether different. If there were (heaven forbid) a Congressional investigation later, Tupper could take the stand and say with absolute honesty that he knew absolutely nothing. (What anyone suspected was nobody's business and was inadmissible anyway.)

"He's very dangerous underneath that smiling exterior, Chief," said Tupper. "I've known him for twenty years."

Prentice was surprised. "You learn something new every day. I shouldn't have thought you'd mix in those circles."

"He's an old friend of the family. Very old. My mother still sees him now and then when he goes to his Connecticut place. He was up there last weekend. There was a very great gathering of his big-shot pals. Publishers, mostly. A few bankers. Mother went to dinner and she said there seemed to be one topic of conversation—you."

Prentice blinked. He didn't like it much. "Well, it's nice to be the center of attention."

"I don't know who put forth the idea first. One can rely on Mother only so far. But the idea they were all kicking around was whether you had a hand in these gang killings."

Prentice felt a chill clear to his toes. He'd already known the organization had spotted him. But if this idea was to percolate down to the public, he'd be so busy covering his tracks he couldn't operate at all. Perhaps that was the idea of bringing in the publishers. A few trial balloons, no matter how carefully released, would bring the whole pack of journalists down on his skull.

"Mother is pretty scatter-brained and she would not even have remembered any of this except they were all using a very dirty word."

"What word was that?" asked the President.

"Impeachment," said Tupper.

CHAPTER
ELEVEN

The familiar voice on the tape recorder was saying: "Anti-matter exists. Repeat anti-matter. Anti-matter nuclei in the primary cosmic rays. Repeat primary cosmic rays. Encoding the accelerator with gamma rays."

The President pushed the stop button and the tape recorder stopped. He rubbed his chin, his eyes sad. Whitney, the young Yale lawyer, was looking at him accusingly.

"Who was he talking to?" asked Prentice.

"We don't know," said Whitney. "We picked it up from a rooftop on a directional antenna. I thought you might know, Mr. President. After all, he *is* your best friend." The rebuke was blatant and, in a Presidential aide, unforgivable. Prentice forgave it anyway. These were trying times. Spying on one's best friend was simply not done, at least not among young liberal Yale lawyers. It was a little like Henry Stimson's engaging remark about employing spies: one doesn't read someone else's mail. Dear old gentleman—such a quaint sentiment.

"Whitney," said the President, "you must not think about these proprieties too much. Just carry out the orders. You know very little about the whole picture." Don't pass moral judgment on what little you know. He didn't say the last bit. Whitney already looked properly abashed and he didn't want to push him into overt hostility. The education of a Yale lawyer into the new realities.

The fact that he had to call Whitney to order at all bothered Prentice. He hadn't had to do that with any subordinates for a very long time, and it showed glaringly how far over the line he had strayed. But then all recent Presidents had strayed—each farther than his predecessor. Kennedy (and before him, Eisenhower) with the planning and execution of the Bay of Pigs idiocy, which would not even have been contemplated by earlier Presidents. Johnson with his Gulf of Tonkin assault on the U.S. Navy, which he had used to justify the whole Vietnam escalation—a fabrication from start to finish. Now here was he, Prentice, fighting a civil war only he knew about. Oh, for the old Stimson simplicities!

He pushed the start button and listened to the familiar voice again. "Repeat primary cosmic rays" (a bit of emphasis on *primary* he hadn't noticed before). "Encoding the accelerator with gamma rays . . ." He switched it off. He didn't like that word accelerator a bit.

"It doesn't seem to be in any code book," said Whitney.

Prentice smiled. It wouldn't be in any code book. It was schoolboy code. He and Hasbrouck used to do it at Groton all the time to get around proctors and teachers and they had been particularly attracted to physics and space talk because that was hot new science fiction then, not fact as it is now. Anti-matter was only a hilarious schoolboy joke then. Anti-matter was the enemy—the other side—whoever he might be. He and Hasbrouck had always been on the same side. Most of it was fairly simple to Prentice. Anti-matter (enemy) exists (look out!); anti-matter nuclei (enemy agent) in the primary cosmic rays (well, primary meant the head man, in short himself; cosmic rays might mean anything of high import, the White House probably. But then, they didn't appear to suspect him as the nuclei itself, but as an agent close to him. Who? Ferrier?)

Then that bit about accelerator, which was downright alarming. When he and Hasbrouck had been in school there had been no such thing as an atomic accelerator. It had been invented since then. But it was easy to slip such a thing into the old schoolboy code—and it could only mean one thing. Accelerate! Pick up the pace—move up the operation. What operation?

Prentice looked at Whitney piercingly, eyes somber. "I want a twenty-four hour surveillance—every word he says—in his office and his home, and not simply from the roof tops. I want his telephones tapped. All of them."

"We'll need a court order," said Whitney.

"Forget it," barked Prentice. Whitney looked alarmed at first, then mutinous. "In the case of a clear and present danger to the national security, the President may take such measures as he sees fit to preserve the nation. This is such a clear and present danger." The awesome power of the Presidency was behind every syllable, straightening out Whitney almost visibly. Oh

God, thought Prentice, the damned job was getting in every way more and more like that of the Roman Emperors—part Jehovah, part clown—equal quantities of each. For the first time since he held the job, he felt if only for the tiniest second that he might prefer some other line of work. He banished it.

"Anything else?" asked Prentice dismissively.

Whitney almost snapped to attention. He had not even sat down. Prentice could see a visibly growing deference that had not been there before. He could make a valuable ally and aide of Whitney one day—given time, of which there seemed precious little.

"There's lots more on that spool," said Whitney, "all nuclear reaction sort of stuff."

"Better leave it with me," said the President. "Get on with it."

When Whitney left he picked up the purple phone and told Miss Doll to head off everybody. *Everybody.* He had work to do. The only exempt ones were Ferrier and Joplin and they both had direct phones. Then he locked the door to the Oval Office, a most recent precaution.

Alone, Prentice prowled the Oval Office a caged lion. Well and truly caged, and the cage was getting smaller. The weapons were slipping out of his hands. He reviewed the bidding. The National Security Council meeting had revealed the unexpected and thoroughly alarming alliance between the FBI head and Hasbrouck. Or was alliance too strong a word? Clearly, they had been talking together—and there was only one topic of conversation they could share. The gang war (or what they thought was a gang war). Prentice preferred to think of it as the forces of light overcoming the powers of darkness, but then they probably thought of it as the other way round. Up to now the FBI had been truly neutral, a law enforcement agency, nothing more. Now he wasn't sure.

The National Security Council had forged a link between FBI and the Army with his reluctant compliance. The thought of Army muscle attached to FBI civil intelligence chilled his soul. Then there was the dead Secret Service deputy, George Blaser, a prime target for blackmailing by the syndicate, which made the whole Secret Service suspect. His Praetorian Guard. He smiled wryly, remembering his ancient history. Ten Roman Emperors with their families and their friends—assassinated within a single decade—oh, they made a clean sweep of it in the old days.

Prentice looked over the lovely curving bookshelves where he had put—as a constant reminder of the mockery of power—Gibbon's *Decline and Fall of the Roman Empire*. He pulled out volume three, opened the book at random and read: "... Maximus, who found himself encompassed on all sides, had scarcely the time to shut the gates of the city. But the gates could not long resist the effort of a victorious enemy; and the despair, the disaffection, the indifference of his soldiers and people, hastened the downfall of the wretched Maximus. He was dragged from his throne, rudely stripped of the Imperial ornaments, the robe, the diadem, and the purple slippers; and conducted like a malefactor to the camp and presence of Theodosius, at a place about three miles from Aquileia; Theodosius abandoned him to the pious zeal of the soldiers, who drew him out of the Imperial presence and instantly separated his head from his body."

Just one of many Emperors, dragged, stripped, and killed, rather more pleasantly and swiftly than many, by his own troops if not by his own bodyguard. Prentice's bodyguard was the Secret Service. He put the book back into place and resumed his prowl, thinking about poor Maximus. They always dragged them from the throne, poor fellows. He looked at the black leather revolving chair that was his own throne. Would they drag him from that? He sat down, revolving slowly from side to side. I'm beginning to feel sorry for myself, he thought, and that will never do. With an impish grin, switching his mood to one of playfulness— the only way to maintain his sanity—he played shamelessly with the newest toys that Ferrier's men had built for him. Underneath the desk was a button. He pushed it. This plastic bulletproof screen sprang out of the floor at bewildering speed, noiselessly. He had no idea when he might need such a thing, but one never knew. It had been his own idea—knowing how many odd delegations wandered in and out of his office. The sight of a gun in a hand and he'd have this instant plastic protection. One never knew.

The idea of the chair had been Ferrier's. The chair button lay next to the plastic screen button. Both needed a good hard push so that they couldn't be triggered accidentally, both looked like parts of the desk. Even Miss Doll had noticed nothing and she dusted his desk every day. Prentice pushed the other button; the chair and the President of the United States disappeared into the floor. It almost took his breath away. In the darkness, he felt for the other button right under the chair. Within a second and a half, he was back in the Oval Room. Marvelous gadget. It restored his humor altogether.

He was thinking furiously now, pulling all the pieces together. Hasbrouck—his oldest friend—was it betrayal? Was it treason? Or was it simply Hasbrouck's habit of taking on the toughest opponent, trying to solve the toughest puzzle, trying to outwit the brightest men in the room with his own gleaming intelligence? Was it just Hasbrouck being his own sparkling competitive game-playing self. That's why he represented Tasio—to say nothing of two other notorious gang leaders—because he'd been attracted by the sheer difficulty of the thing. This had led him first into defending them in court (which was not so difficult, given the huge array of civil rights rulings), but later into defending them philosophically and ethically—finding in society, or in the remorseless logic of history some ethic for siding with the atrocious Mob chiefs. Wasn't that just like his brilliant friend? Then, of course, came the supreme challenge. Having discovered (*if* indeed he had discovered) Prentice's private civil war, had he undertaken—single-handed against the power of the President—to head it off? It was the kind of challenge that would fatally attract Hasbrouck. To outwit and outgun a man who had all the weapons of the Presidency in his hands.

Prentice pushed the button again and listened for the third time to the prattle of the tape recorder. "Antimatter exists." He shut it down again. Why would Hasbrouck be using that old schoolboy code? The only people who knew it were his old classmates at Groton. He ran through the class, one of the most brilliant in Groton's history—himself, Hasbrouck, Soames, Stern—

Stern!

Prentice picked up the purple phone and asked Miss Doll to put him through to Tupper. When he got him, Prentice asked abruptly, "Tup, that party your mother went to last weekend—was Stern there?"

Tupper was surprised: "Yes, he was. I meant to tell you and it slipped my mind. How did you guess?"

"I wish I hadn't," said Prentice, and hung up. Stern!

The President put his fingertips together, one by one, an old habit when he was lost in thought and contemplated Stern, the malevolent Stern. There'd been sparks between them for forty years. The brilliant, malevolent Stern. He and Stern had been political partners, frequently reluctant ones, for thirty years. Prentice was always well ahead—miles ahead—in the race because he was by nature a winner of elections. Stern, with his dark satanic brilliance, had run for office only once—for State Assembly—and had been massacred at the polls. His career had been one long succession of appointive offices—aides to Lieutenant Governors, political manager of Senator Chase of Wisconsin (and a bloody good one), party fund raiser—until he'd come to roost in the White House as Press Chief of a President who'd never let his personal likes and dislikes interfere with appointments. Stern was more than able; he filled a crevice in Prentice's armor, always pointing out the weaknesses he himself had failed to notice, shoals and pitfalls in popular opinion he'd not taken seriously enough. For a man who'd spent most of his life being disliked both by those who knew him and those who didn't, Stern was astonishingly expert at public relations—which was nothing more nor less than the art of being liked. It was a paradox but politics was full of paradoxical situations.

Prentice then considered the alliance of his oldest friend with his oldest—well, rival. Stern and Hasbrouck, both brilliant in different ways, one a master of the underground maneuver, manipulating popular will when it didn't know it was being manipulated, the other a master of the above-ground, courtroom, fully legal ploy.

A formidable combination. But what on earth brought the two together? They didn't like each other.

A grimace of pain twisted his face. It was just possible their mutual hatred had been overmastered by raging envy. He had the job they both wanted and neither would ever have. He swung around in his chair and looked across the lawn, tasting bitterness. He had never felt so alone. No matter how many friends one had when one entered the office of the Presidency—and he'd had scores—one wound up totally alone, friendless. The job dissolved friendship like acid on paint.

He thought again of poor Maximus. "...the despair, the disaffection, the indifference of his soldiers and people." Disaffection, what a Gibbonesque word! That's what he was suffering, the disaffection of his best friend.

Prentice rubbed his hand over his face, a gesture he sometimes used to wipe out unprofitable thoughts, and get on with more profitable ones, and forced himself to think about that dread word impeachment. He had bet his last political dollar against any such thing happening because of that wonderful and awful word *omerta*. It had been silence that had built up the Mafia to its awesome invulnerability, and it was Prentice who had thought all by himself what a vulnerability it also was. They couldn't fight in the open. They couldn't enlist popular opinion. They had no weapons to fight in the open. He was slaughtering them in silence because they couldn't come out of the shadows to admit their very existence. That was what he had always bet on. But if they'd enlisted Stern, an expert at popular opinion, a man in his White House family.

Prentice picked up the white phone, activating the light over the wooden box in the Utah woods. Then he put the phone down again. It might take a while to find Joplin. He picked up *The New York Times* and read Lamport's story for the second time. He'd glanced through it before. Now he read it in a new light:

"The FBI higher command is now speculating on the possibility that the gang killings might not be gang killings but something else. Just where this line of speculation could lead is anyone's guess. This kind of massacre had been a Mafia specialty only in the lower echelons of gangdom. The big boys do not kill each other, if indeed they could. To the student of gang warfare the slayings have crossed lines of hostility in ways that defy all reason. Therefore the idea is being explored that some other force, hitherto unknown in underworld circles might be at work."

Why had he not noticed that paragraph before? Partly, thought Prentice, because it was far down in the story, deep in the second column on page two, which meant Lamport himself didn't take it very seriously yet, but was just trying it on. What gave Prentice pause was that phrase, "the FBI higher command." The FBI higher command never, never told the press its speculations, its interior thinking, only the hard facts—a crime had been committed, a crime had been cleared up. Little in between and never speculation. What was causing that change of attitude?

He grinned wryly. Here he was, President of the United States, wondering haplessly why one of his own executive bureaus was acting in such a way. In any other conceivable set of circumstances he, the President, would simply have lifted the phone and asked the agency to explain what in hell it was about. About this, he could not. He was acting like a common malefactor— just as Maximus had been treated.

The light over the white phone was blinking. Prentice picked it up: "Jop, can we move the fiesta forward by twenty-four hours?"

"Christ, no!" It was an explosion of negation. Joplin didn't volunteer any explanations and Prentice didn't ask for any. Jop would know he wouldn't ask such a thing unless it were crucial and Prentice didn't need reminding of the split-second logistic problems which already strained his little task force's facilities to the utmost. If they could have changed, Joplin would have done it—however awkward were the problems it would pose. When Joplin said No, it meant it couldn't be done.

"Just asking," said the President with a cheeriness he didn't feel. "So be it." He'd have to try to stay alive for thirty-six hours. "Jop, stay in touch. Call in every four hours. I may need you. If Highway 1 is out, use Route 66." There had always been an alternative communication system, used only late at night, and rarely then.

He hung up, and resumed his prowl around the office.

Assassination. A rich subject of folklore. Circling the Oval Office like a caged cat, he thought of all the Presidents who had been extinguished in office. Abraham Lincoln in a theater—a well-scheduled, well-advertised night out. Garfield on the way to the train for a holiday, also well-advertised. McKinley at a public appearance, well-advertised, thoroughly scheduled, at the Pan American Exposition. Andrew Jackson had almost been killed at another scheduled affair, a state funeral. Kennedy met his end in a cortege whose route and exact times had been in all the papers.

Adolf Hitler, a man around whom more assassination plots had been concocted than any man in history, had avoided it largely because he was always late to appointments, sometimes by hours, sometimes canceling them abruptly at the last moment. Hitler was hell on an assassin's plans. But he was never assassinated.

Prentice picked up the appointment pad. It was rich in well-scheduled assassination possibilities. Starting with a White House luncheon one hour from that very moment. State party chieftains discussing strategy for the next election. A great place to pick him off. At the risk of incurring party displeasure at the grass-roots level where it could do serious damage, he would not be there. After all, one's candidacy for re-election depended entirely on one's staying alive. They wouldn't find out about his illness either until the very last moment when he would be stricken by . . . what? Never mind. His doctors would order him to bed. Let them think up what for. They'd done it before. Now about tonight—if he couldn't make luncheon, he certainly couldn't make a State Dinner—or could he? Maybe he could at that.

He picked up the green phone. "Ferrier," he said, a great grin spreading over his face, "do you remember that scheme of yours which I denounced as illogical, paranoid, ill-begotten, fantasy-ridden and I believe, insane?"

"Yes, I do, indeed," said Ferrier, bleakly.

"I've changed my mind," said the President. "We'll put it into action immediately."

CHAPTER
TWELVE

The State Dinner—these affairs had always been the bane of Prentice's life in the White House—was at the Kennedy Memorial Center. An exclusive affair for two thousand diners, including embassy staffs from more than one hundred nations. Oh, it was a colorful throng, all right, fezzes and turbans from the East mingled with white tie and tails, which was becoming almost a court costume in the U.S.A., seen nowhere else except Presidential dinners. But this dinner wasn't Prentice's baby; it was the State Department's welcome to Sheikh Mahout of Kuwali. The President of the United States was there because Middle eastern oil was still an important bargaining counter in world power plays and was certainly worth a good dinner.

The arrival of all those white ties and turbans was a great show under the stars on the warm spring night by the Potomac. The Secret Service, like Secret Services everywhere, would have liked to sweep the onlookers back two hundred yards from the entrance. But there was politics to be considered. The visitors from abroad, to say nothing of the ambassadors, wanted to be seen. It would seem rude to push the people back to where they could not ooh and aah a little bit. There were too few opportunities for that kind of buzz in Washington anyway. Consequently the crowd pushed forth quite close to the canopy—although that part of it was a very selective crowd with special tickets issued by State, many to its own huge staff of employees and their families. Searchlights played on the red-carpeted entrance, drenching the limousines with brilliant light. The cameramen obscured the distinguished visitors as always, and TV technicians were perched precariously on their trucks. The place swarmed with Secret Servicemen trying to be unobtrusive and not succeeding, as the distinguished visitors poured out of rented Cadillacs in stately procession.

The Suleiman of Swat, in gold burnoose, arrived with his six wives, who were wrapped in solid silver cloth. In contrast to all this opulence, the communist ambassadors arrived in their drab sack suits that looked like bargain basement stuff from a fifth-rate department store; this was the new form of ostentation—vying with one another for the good will of the world's proletariat. Our suits cost less that yours—that was the message. The capitalist democracies were in gleaming white tie and tails, their wives dressed to the nines. The trouble was that the wives weren't very attractive, aged and bulging in the wrong places with capitalist prosperity that no amount of tulle would disguise. The tiny eastern communist wives with their twelve-inch waists were knockouts. There is no doubt about it, a certain amount of malnutrition does something for a woman's body and chinline.

The twelve-ton Presidential Lincoln arrived last, and a great roar went up as the great U.S. father-figure—the President serving both kingly and prime ministerial functions at one go—stepped out. During Prentice's Administration, there were fewer of these state appearances of the Great White Father before the screaming unwashed multitude because he simply did not believe these visitations had the slightest effect on the way the electorate voted. But a few of these events couldn't be avoided, not for vote-getting, but for diplomatic reasons. This was one.

To the security forces on the surrounding rooftops, where the Presidential arrival looked like a No play from the second balcony—remote, theatrical, unreal—the President took God's own time to get out of gun range. He smiled, waved, doffed the silk top hat that Kennedy had banished and Prentice brought back. He was alone. The First Lady had had an unfortunate chill, a diplomatic chill. Then, with great and to the rooftop watchers, maddening deliberation, he swept up the red-carpeted stairs, the black opera cape (Prentice had borrowed that theatrical bit from President Roosevelt, and used it with stunning effect) billowing around him, and disappeared into the great edifice.

The TV cameras picked out the Presidential figure the moment he swept into the Great Hall, where the reception before the dinner took place. The cameras were in the balustrades far above the action and the wide lens took in the whole splendid scene in color. Every last one of the two thousand guests were in the hall, most of them trying to get close to the President. It was a security nightmare, since the Secret Service simply couldn't sweep away the ambassadors and the distinguished guests as they could the ordinary voters.

The scene was a swirl of color, a maelstrom of costume, very much more difficult to keep under proper observation for the sheer variety and razzle-dazzle of the dress. Also, the President was darting from hand to hand—pausing nowhere—in an effort, it seemed, to greet everyone (where usually he paused to exchange a few words with the diplomats he knew best).

The Secret Servicemen simply could not keep up, and when the shots came—*three* said some, *four* said others, still others thought only one—it was impossible to tell where they were fired from, so great was the confusion.

Only one shot counted. It went straight into the forehead of the President, and by a miraculous accident of timing, a TV camera with a zoom lens had the Presidential face in close-up and registered the impact— the microsecond of disbelief in the features—before all expression was blotted out. Then a mass of figures swept over the figure and chaos ensued.

Prentice watched the terrible and terrifying scene from start to finish on television in a hut in the Utah woods. When the shot struck his double he went white with horror, although he had anticipated the very thing. He stood up, swaying, and Joplin put a protective arm around him for fear he'd fall. Joplin never took his eyes from the screen. He wanted to see what happened next because it was very important.

Pandemonium happened next. The commentator was so overcome with the history he was witnessing that he could do little more than gasp: "The President is shot! The President is shot! He is down!"

Prentice was saying: "The poor bastard! The poor bastard!" It had never occurred to him that another man would be killed for him.

Joplin's craggy face looked Jehovah-like; there was even a glitter of triumph in his eyes. For the fact was he'd still had a few doubts about the authenticity of Prentice's self-proclaimed national emergency. The assassination had swept them away.

Ferrier, finger on his lip, looked as if he were watching a chess game—an intensely cerebral chess game—in which the right move had been made in the nick of time. At times like this he went ice cold with self-satisfaction. Not a spark of emotion in him.

"Where did you get that man?" demanded Prentice.

"Model agency," said Ferrier, thin-lipped. "He made his living impersonating you in whiskey ads."

"Do they know he's—"

"Nobody knows. Nobody at all. He lived in a three-room apartment in Queens. No wife. No family at all to speak of, he told me. I told him there was a very large risk in what he was doing."

The three men were alone in the hut Joplin had built himself in the Utah pines. The voice of the TV commentator babbled on, saying nothing at great length, because the event eclipsed talk in a tidal wave of horror. Joplin turned down the sound, leaving only the dancing images, Secret Servicemen trying to claw through the gaily dressed weeping women, the white-tied, thunderstruck diplomats.

"They're a little late," said Ferrier, "as always." He had a low opinion of the Secret Service and since the Blaser suicide his opinion had dropped ever lower.

"What do we do now?"

Prentice was thinking furiously. "No one, you say, no one at all knew?"

"No one."

"No family, no friends, to miss him?"

"Well, ultimately someone is going to come looking—if only his model agency."

"I only need three days."

"For three days, no one at all will ask any questions, I guarantee that."

"Bury him!" said Prentice in a fierce exultant whisper. "Bury him! We'll have a big state funeral." It cleared up a lot of pressing problems. They couldn't assassinate an already assassinated President and they couldn't impeach one either. It was hard on the poor fellow; it was also providential.

"We'll have a big state funeral and see who crawls out of the woodwork. The President is dead, long live..." said Prentice—and stopped. The Vice-President! "Where the hell *is* McMillan? Has anyone heard from him?"

"He's in northwest Africa, where you sent him," said Ferrier, dryly.

"Where, in northwest Africa?"

"Ruanda—at the last report—which was yesterday."

Prentice couldn't suppress a bleat of grim laughter. "Well, the stupid bastard is President—for a few days. That's about as much of him as the country could stand."

"Are you quite sure you want to do this, Chief?" said Ferrier quietly. "McMillan will be President, with all the powers and prerogatives. You can't be ordering B-52's around at will any longer—or setting up secret operations in the woods in Utah."

That gave Prentice pause. He thought about it. The

operation existed because of the President's great powers and even greater resources of men and machinery. Cut off from those . . .

"Three days," whispered the President. "That's all I need. How long will it take McMillan to get back from northwest Africa?"

"Five hours and twenty-five minutes," said Ferrier, a precisionist. "He'll not dawdle. And he'll take the oath of office in the airplane—like Johnson. Only he won't have your widow there as Johnson did Kennedy's."

Prentice scowled. He didn't like that. He considered it. "Truman said it was like a ton of bricks hitting him, or something like that. He didn't settle down to real command responsibilities for weeks. Even Johnson, a much more assertive person, didn't grab the reins in three days. He couldn't. That dumb bastard McMillan couldn't take hold of a fruit stand in three days. The rest of Washington will be so occupied with the funeral and so stunned by the disaster that no one will do any serious thinking until next Monday at least. By that time, I'll be back in the Oval Office—after I've done what has to be done."

The CIA chief looked at Joplin, who looked back stonily. Joplin knew where his loyalties lay. He was a man of action and to him the whole thing was the ultimate simplicity. The plan had been rehearsed. Carry it out. Even Ferrier's infinitely more complicated brain couldn't help but agree that the simulated death of a President contained dazzling possibilities. He shrugged, a gesture which on him meant okay, let's get on with it.

"What do you want me to do?"

"Get back to Washington and go straight to Rosemary."

"If I can get in."

"You can get in," said the President. "She has great trust in you."

"Am I to tell her . . ."

"Nothing," said the President. "She couldn't carry it off. She'd be overjoyed and it would show for twenty miles. No, she'll have to stick it out for three days like everyone else."

"If she gets near that body, she'll know. He doesn't look all that much like you."

Prentice had already thought of that: "I don't think she will want to. She has a hatred of open coffins that dates back to being forced to look at her dead mother. Believe me, she won't look at the face even if she's brought to it. But you must use her to see that no one else looks too closely. Tell her to issue orders it's to be a sealed coffin; the President is too badly damaged to be looked at. She's the widow; she'll have absolute authority over all funeral arrangements. One thing we must avoid is that barbaric public viewing bit. None of that."

Ferrier sighed. "I'd better get off," he said. At the door he thought of something: "Keep in touch by the red route. Only the red. It's by satellite—and there's no way to cut it."

He left.

The TV screen still swirled with its gay figures, its wild colors. It looked, Prentice thought, like a costume ball, very festive, full of merriment and laughter.

He turned up the sound.

"The President is dead," said the commentator with enormous finality.

CHAPTER
THIRTEEN

The Bell X-20 whirred silently through the velvety night, the lights of Manhattan dead ahead. It was coming in from the sea below radar cover, hurtling along at 120 miles an hour. Prentice was in the pilot's cockpit along with Joplin and the pilot. He'd had to exert every last ounce of command authority to come along; the argument that prevailed finally was that he had to make fresh decisions on the spot. Things were not going as planned. Not a bit of it. He'd had to make some last-minute changes of plan.

In his lap, Prentice had a tiny TV set whose screen glowed up at him. McMillan was making his first address to the nation as President: "In this grief-stricken hour..." he was saying, his plump visage a mask of pious worry.

"Oh, my God," muttered Prentice angrily.

"...I appeal to each and every last American..."

The bastard was using his own speechwriters, thought Prentice savagely. Merriwether wrote that. That each-and-every-one-American was a Merriwether favorite and Prentice was incessantly cutting them out of his own speeches.

"...to unite in prayer for the safety and well-being of our country. I pledge in this most solemn hour the entire resources of our mighty nation to track down and bring to justice the foul malefactors who had perpetrated this evil deed." God in heaven, what malarky, thought Prentice.

Aloud, he said, "Well, you're not doing very damned well at it."

For the first time in the history of Presidential assassinations, the murderer or murderers had got clean away. It had been a brilliantly executed coup in the Great Hall, and in the confusion of sheer numbers, the Secret Service had been unable to collar a single suspect. Reviewing the tapes of the murder scenes—played over and over on TV—Prentice was struck by how little protection the Secret Service had afforded his double. There seemed to be no Secret Service men near him and the air waves were clamorous with explanation as to why this had happened. A mix-up in orders; the thickness of the crowd; the very importance of the visitors, which prevented Secret Service men from pushing them aside as they pressed close. Balls, thought the President. The Secret Service had no such compunctions usually.

The X-20 was over lower Manhattan now at three hundred feet in the 2:00 A.M. stillness, visible now to naked eyes—if there were any open at that hour—and to police surveillance. But a silent black helicopter traveling at 120 miles an hour was a hard thing to detect much less stop, even by the most sophisticated electronic sensors. In one minute and ten seconds, it had sped from the Battery to Ninety-second Street and Fifth Avenue, where it settled silently on the roof of one of the last really elegant town houses in the city—so swiftly that the tough Sicilian on guard had no chance to focus his muddy wits on an emergency he had not been trained to deal with. The Bell X-20 came down vertically right over him, and the man had just raised his head in startled realization when Joplin leaped from the helicopter and silenced him. A burble of blood from the throat and that was that. Prentice stepped out over the corpse from the copter's front seat; from the back poured two Arabs, four Czechs, and three Chinese, faces blacked, costume black as night, carrying ropes, block and tackle, submachine guns. Prentice personally lifted out the delicate electronic equipment he'd insisted on bringing to this fiesta. He'd made a few last-minute changes in the plan.

Things on the outside world were moving with far greater speed than he had expected. He hadn't expected McMillan back in the States that fast; or to take over so completely. Something was very wrong somewhere— and he wanted to find out why. That's why the electronic equipment. That's why the new plan. Joplin hadn't like it.

He and Joplin sorted out the cable and Prentice, squatting under cover of the parapet, screwed the tiny Japanese TV camera on the end of the cable. Joplin was setting up the little Sony TV set and plugged it in to the cable. Prentice lowered the little TV camera from the rooftop to the second set of windows from the top, keeping it close to the side of the building. It stopped at the lone window that was still lit. One of the Chinese lowered the tiny directional mike to within an inch of the camera. Joplin adjusted the little Sony, and the scene on the TV screen gradually cleared. Prentice handed the cable to another of the Chinese and crouched beside Joplin, still sharpening the image.

Everett Quincey, the white-thatched adviser of Presidents who never took his advice, was leaning back in a big black leather armchair, remarkably like the one in the Oval Room, thought Prentice in a flash of divination. He was speaking, but no sound came. Prentice leaned across to the Chinese and turned up the sound dial on the microphone.

"... not doing badly at all, considering everything," Quincey was saying, radiating geniality all over the little TV screen. That was his greatest asset, thought Prentice, that goddamned benevolence. Under the cloak of benevolence he could swindle a widow out of her own orphan. The most beloved man in the U.S.—and the biggest son of a bitch, thought Prentice.

"After all," said Quincey, "we must consider McMillan's limitations. He is not the brightest man in the world and he has been staggered by the magnitude of the burden. He has the world's sympathy; he will grow in the job." Positively oozing good will to mankind from every pore, thought Prentice coldly.

"Let's hope he doesn't grow too big for it," said another familiar voice.

"Stern," whispered Prentice.

He made a twisting motion to the Chinese. "Slowly," he whispered. The little camera panned the room flashing past one figure, settling on another—Stern, smoldering with his usual slow fire of malevolence. "Are you sure you can handle him, Everett? The job blows them up like balloons."

Prentice grinned in the darkness at this direct hit. Joplin scowled and drew his finger across his throat. Prentice smiled and held up his hand, as if to say "Cool it."

"I despise the bastard," flashed Stern. "You can buy McMillan and sell McMillan. He's got a heart of solid blubber. Be careful, Everett, because the first man who gets his ear is going to buy him just as completely as you have."

From off-screen came another very well-known voice. The moment he heard it Prentice's face froze. "Who killed him?" said Hasbrouck. "*Who killed him?* Haven't they *any* idea?"

Prentice motioned to the Chinese holding the camera cable to turn it slowly to the right. The Chinese panned the room and came to rest on Hasbrouck standing by the fireplace. He looked, thought Prentice, more terrible than he'd ever seen his gay Gallic friend, his eyes black holes of fury.

"For Christ's sake, who killed Prentice?" he was saying. "Eight hundred Secret Service men assigned solely to protect the man! Not one of them was near him when he was needed, and not one has come up with a single idea. What the hell is this?"

On the rooftop Prentice felt a sudden immeasurable relief, a lifting of spirits he desperately needed. He looked at Joplin. "I think I've made a terrible mistake," he whispered.

Joplin's eyes were glued to the glowing little Sony screen.

On the screen Hasbrouck seemed a man possessed, torn with rage. Out of control. Prentice had never seen him out of control since they were boys together.

"The Secret Service was terribly hampered by the

crowd.'' Everett Quincey's benevolent voice spread oil on the waters.

"Bullshit!'' spat Hasbrouck. "This is the very job they're supposed to do, and incompetent as those goddamned idiots are and always have been, they are not *that* incompetent because *nobody* could be that incompetent. They were looking the other way. Goddamn it, Quincey, the whole thing stinks to high heaven of conspiracy, and you're much too smart not to know it.''

Prentice quickly took the cable out of the hands of the Chinese and spun it around personally. He wanted very much to see Quincey's reaction to that. The camera was a kaleidoscope of blurred image and then rested on Everett Quincey, his eyes fixed across the room. He was not smiling now; he was just glowing with sympathy for the whole of grief-stricken humanity. "We know you loved him,'' murmured Quincey. "You mustn't let it affect your judgment, Jacques. Prentice is dead. Nothing can be done about that. The time has come to bind up the nation's wounds.''

"My ass!'' roared Hasbrouck. "Bind up the nation's wounds, my fucking ass! Who do you think you are, Abraham Lincoln? The time has come to solve a murder story that stinks to the heavens. I'm not to be put off by your pillaging the Gettysburg Address for suitable phrases, Quincey, and I'm not going to pledge allegiance to that unholy shit McMillan. I am going to find out who did this thing and tear his head off...''

Prentice put his mouth next to Joplin's ear. "We've got to get him out of there. He has no idea what he's got himself into.''

Joplin grimaced in pain: "This thing's been rehearsed to a split second. The rockets are going to hit that window in—'' he looked at his watch, "just three minutes and twenty-seven seconds. *How* are we going to get him out of there?''

Prentice considered, very hard, and very fast. "Where are the rockets coming from?"

"Central Park." Joplin pointed to the precise patch of bush where the Albanians already lurked.

"Red network," murmured Prentice.

"Oh, my God!" Joplin's lips framed the words but didn't quite utter them.

"There is no point in having all these facilities if one doesn't use them," murmured Prentice, feeling an immense elation. The defection of Hasbrouck had torn him more deeply than he'd been aware. Already Joplin was unstrapping the telephone swinging from his leg. He fished in the leg pocket, pulled out a small square of coded cardboard, and pushed it into the base of the telephone. An electronic modulation of 1276 cycles sprang twenty-six miles in the air and there it nestled into a satellite of gleaming titanium, where it was modified to 1346 cycles and then sent earthward again to a switchboard in the Virginia hills. "Podium," said the man at the switchboard.

"Lodestar," said Joplin, the code name of the exercise.

He looked across at Prentice questioningly.

"Tell him you want the private home number of Everett Quincey at 1289 Fifth Avenue. It's in his black book—and tell him to be sure to get 1289 Fifth Avenue, because Quincey's got twelve other homes."

Joplin's face registered his black disapproval of a man with thirteen homes. Into the phone he said, "Everett Quincey's private number 1289 Fifth Avenue, New York." There was a pause. On the TV screen the argument was raging in the living room between Stern and Hasbrouck.

"What do you plan to do?" Stern was saying.

"I'm going to Lamport of *The New York Times* and tell him who has really been feeding him this horseshit he's been printing."

"You are as deeply implicated as we are," said Stern, glowering.

"Gentlemen, gentlemen!" murmured Everett Quincey. Always the peacemaker, thought Prentice. Any moment he'll be recommending wage and price controls as a solution to his assassination. That was Quincey's solution to every problem—a device he'd swiped from Baruch.

"Okay, ring it," said Joplin to the Podium operator. He handed the phone to Prentice. "Your baby from here."

Prentice, his eyes on the little Sony screen, could hear the blips that meant the phone was ringing in the apartment underneath him. Sargent, the Quincey butler—Prentice knew him well and could see the florid face in his mind's eye—answered with a simple "Hello." None of your "Mr. Quincey's residence." Just "Hello." Rather a distant "Hello."

"Mr. Hasbrouck, please," said Prentice, assuming an English accent he greatly enjoyed. "Hart, here, Mr. Sargent." Hart was Hasbrouck's butler and the two men, Hart and Sargent, knew each other well. "Tell Mr. Hasbrouck it's extremely urgent."

"Just a moment, Hart."

Silence on the telephone. "Get Jacques on the box," muttered Prentice. Joplin took the cable and twisted it until Jacques was in close-up, his lips still twisted with fury. Joplin held his watch up to Prentice's eyes. "Two minutes," he said in Prentice's ear.

On the TV screen they saw Sargent arrive and whisper in Hasbrouck's ear. A look of annoyance. Then he nodded. To Prentice's horror the butler handed him a telephone, picking it up from the nearest sidetable. Damn, thought Prentice, the place was rife with telephones. He had hoped Sargent would lead Hasbrouck out of the accursed room which the rockets were due to hit in just under two minutes.

"Hello, Hart," said Hasbrouck.

Prentice could hear him on the phone and see him on the screen. For a moment he stood paralyzed.

"Hart, are you there?"

Prentice closed his eyes briefly and then spoke low and urgently, "Hasbrouck, it's Prentice. For gods sake, don't move a muscle of your face." He could see on the TV screen the words hitting Hasbrouck like bullets. "Steady boy, steady," said Prentice, "calm those face muscles. I want to see the best courtroom performance of your life."

Already Hasbrouck's handsome Gallic face had become a mask, though the muscles of the jaw were pulled tight, very tight.

"Now, just listen very hard, my friend," said Prentice. "You have fallen among thieves and we want you out of that room. Don't argue. Just say yeah from time to time to throw the others off."

Instantly Hasbrouck said casually, almost flippantly, "Yeah, yeah..." Listening hard.

Thank God for boyhood friendships, thought Prentice. He'd got through to Hasbrouck in seconds. It took thirty years of intimate acquaintance to bring such instant understanding.

"Rockets are going to hit that room in just—" he looked again at Joplin's watch, "one minute and thirty-two seconds—and no power on earth can stop them. Don't say anything—just *listen*. I want you to hang up that phone twenty seconds from now. Just say 'Yeah, yeah, well I'll tend to it in the morning,' something like that. Then I want you to say 'Christ it's hot in here,' walk to the big window—the one you're looking at right now. Throw open the window and you will find a rope waiting for you."

The Chinese were already lowering it from the roof.

"Grab that rope and hang on for dear life. There are knots every three feet so don't worry too much. Don't look down. Just hang on."

The second hand on Joplin's watch had crept around another twenty seconds.

"Okay, boy—*now*," said Prentice, his eyes on the TV screen.

Hasbrouck's face was a mask of impassivity. The eyes glittered with something like madness, but then one couldn't do much about eyes.

"Yeah, okay, I'll take care of it in the morning," said Hasbrouck, a miracle of mildness. "Go to bed, Hart. I won't be back until very late."

Hasbrouck hung up the phone and turned his glittering gaze first on Stern, then on Quincey. "Christ, it's hot in here."

On the rooftop, they watched him walk straight to the window where the little TV camera was taking the pictures and open it. The rope dangled right in front of him.

"Good-by now," said Hasbrouck politely, and grasped the rope. The three Chinese and four Czechs, the rope across their shoulders, sped across the roof. Hasbrouck shot skywards.

Prentice and Joplin lifted him to the roof.

"Welcome to Sherwood Forest, Friar Tuck," said Prentice. "Now get your stupid head down before it gets blown off."

He pulled him down under the protection of the parapet.

Twenty seconds later, right on schedule, the rockets hit.

CHAPTER
FOURTEEN

Even on the rooftop directly overhead, the crump of the two rockets was not very loud. The two Chinese—just as they'd rehearsed again and again in the Utah woods—were over the side and down the grappling ropes. After them farther along the rooftop went the four Czech safeblowers with their canvas bags. The two Arab arsonists stood by instead of following down the ropes. Prentice had changed the plans.

Hasbrouck watched all this with the superb detachment of a man too dumbfounded to be surprised. His brain was ice cold.

"Why blow holes in buildings?" he asked, quietly. "They could have gone in the window."

Prentice was staring down Fifth Avenue, first right, then left, looking for patrol cars and hoping there weren't any. "Stun the occupants. We didn't know who'd be there. We didn't expect *you*, Jacques, for instance. The other reason . . ." He faced his old friend with a little smile. "There's a safe down there with eight-inch steel front and sides. We want to examine a few things inside it. There are, we hope, a lot of explanations inside that safe."

He swung his lanky frame over the parapet and grasped the rope.

"Safeblowing?" said Hasbrouck in tones of only mild surprise. "You?"

"Yes, and a damned good one," said the President. He started down the rope, firmly avoiding looking down. Far far uptown, was that a siren in the wind? He hoped not. Hasbrouck leaned over the parapet, his eyes wild.

He asked the most fundamental question of all creation.

"Why, Harry? Why?"

Prentice, clinging to the rope four-stories high, couldn't repress a bark of laughter. "This is not the time to explain the facts of late twentieth-century life to you, my friend," he shouted, and swung into the neat oblong hole made by the rocket.

The room had disintegrated into a morass of overturned chairs, dust, smoke, and haze. One naked light bulb had somehow survived. Joplin was crouched over a still figure that lay face down. Joplin turned it over. Stern. Eyes open. A jagged tear in his chest. "He's gone," said Joplin, harshly. "Your dear old school chum."

Prentice sighed. That was the end of *that* rivalry. Funny about school rivalries; they never ended. Stern had not really wanted to be President or Governor of Wisconsin; he had only wanted those jobs because Prentice had had them, and he wanted what Prentice had achieved, all of it, and he never got any of it. If he'd gone to a different school or even the same school at a different time, he'd never have harbored any of those ambitions.

"I ruined his life, Jop, and now I've killed him," said the President sadly. "Too bad. I'd like to have had a few words with him. I owe him an apology."

"Balls!" said Joplin explosively.

The other figure lay where they'd last seen it, in the corner. The two Chinese had removed the wing chair overturned on him and were wrapping him in a canvas bag. Quincey had had his distinguished thatch of white hair badly mussed. Otherwise he was okay. As Prentice watched, Quincey's eyes flicked open and stared straight back into his. The Chinese impassively wrapped the folds of black canvas around him as if he were a mummy. Gently, as Prentice had instructed. This was the change of plan. Quincey was not to be extinguished just yet.

Prentice stepped around the Chinese and down the hall past the dead Sargent. Poor fellow, there weren't all that many good butlers left. Prentice knew the town house well. He'd been there many times, raising money for his candidacy. At the back of the corridor was Quincey's study. A big much lived-in room where Quincey had spent most of his time when he was in this one of his thirteen homes.

The desk was open and Prentice went through it. Drawers, cubbyholes. It was doubtful that Quincey would keep anything in there of great delicacy, but one never knew. There were letters in the cubbyholes, bills for his country house in the main desk drawers—all spectacularly large—and photographs of his grandchildren. He found more photographs in another drawer. Photographs of his house in Virginia. Beautiful place. Vine-covered. Prentice gazed at it appreciatively. Underneath more photographs of people and parties at Wistaria, which was the name of the place, merrymakers, in those party poses at tables under the stars. He was a great party-thrower, Quincey. Prentice glanced idly at these photos and cast them aside, delving further into the desk. Suddenly he stopped dead, and picked up a party photograph he'd discarded. His gaze zeroed in on one very pretty girl—laughing, festive. Fenella Jones. Well. Well. His pretty sub-sub-assistant. Thank God he'd never told *her* anything.

Joplin strode into the study.

"Cops," he said, not at all worried. "Squirreling down Fifth Avenue from up Harlem way." He went straight to the far wall as if he owned the place and swung back the wainscotting. Behind it lay the huge bank-type safe they had bypassed by blowing out the rear wall. Joplin pulled out a wrench from his black coveralls and banged twice on the safe's steel door. Then he listened. Presently the reply came from inside—two sharp, distant tinkles. The Czechs were inside all right. Joplin struck the safe again—two longs, two shorts—meaning wind it up right now and get out.

Prentice opened the bottom drawer of Quincey's desk, riffling through the contents. Letters, documents, more photographs. One photograph stopped him cold. It was a color photograph of a rose bush. Prentice, a rose lover from boyhood, would have recognized that rose bush anywhere. He gazed at it with admiration. He rummaged through the drawer looking for the plans.

"We haven't time to be admiring rose bushes, Chief," said Joplin.

"That's a very special rose bush, Jop. Have you

got a canvas bag? Good. Let's take all of this." Prentice dumped the entire contents of the bottom drawer into Joplin's canvas bag. Then they departed, running down the corridor, through the empty upturned drawing room and out the window.

Prentice grasped the rope just over the large knot, lifted his face skywards, and hung on. He shot up to the roof. Joplin, on a different rope, was right behind.

"You sure you don't want it burned, Boss?" asked Joplin.

"I want them to find it just as it is, Stern and all."

The siren was getting much closer, sounding like it was in a great hurry. Prentice grasped Hasbrouck by the arm. "Come, my friend, we'll give you a lift."

He escorted him with exquisite courtesy to the helicopter and put him into the front compartment along with Joplin, the driver, and himself. The Czechs were piling their canvas bags into the back. Quincey was already stowed in the rear, his astonished eyes gleaming from the floor of the helicopter.

The black silent whirlybird lifted off and melted into the night, in the direction of the sea.

At about the same time as the Fifth Avenue clam bake was terminating, a gunman atop a telephone pole in the countryside outside Hot Springs, Arkansas, was listening intently to the quick cha cha cha of a motorcycle approaching with great swiftness. He'd have to be quicker than at rehearsal, he decided. Fifty-seven seconds later he let go of the pole and came swishing down the rope through the velvety, starlit night—lovely country nighttime smells, he thought, but then he was a Corsican and he appreciated country smells. The Robson subautomatic P-34 developed in the CIA's own ord-

have a cozy lawyer-client relationship that means anything you see or hear is entirely confidential."

"Goddamn it," barked Jacques, "you know lawyer-client confidentiality doesn't extend to rockets blowing holes in citizens' walls, killing people, or any of this."

Prentice held up the syringe. "Then I'm afraid it's this, Jacques."

Hasbrouck capitulated instantly. He really hated missing anything. "All right, all right, all right," he muttered, "anything but that damned needle."

Joplin spoke up quietly, "Okay, stop jawing both of you. We're getting there and sound carries over the water."

Prentice leaned close to Hasbrouck's ear and whispered, "Watch closely. This is a *beautiful* operation. I planned it myself."

The silent helicopter whispered silently up the gleaming river, losing altitude quickly until it was barely ten feet above the water. They were headed for a thickly wooded island in midstream. Atop the island rose the battlements of a medieval castle that looked straight out of Grimm's fairy tales—rounded towers, Teutonic, crenelated, anachronistic—with an air of definite menace.

Dead ahead on the shoreline and, in fact, actually overhanging the water, was a delicate little folly used in earlier, more sentimental times by lovers for kissing matters. Now it was a watchtower. The Jensen submachine gun with its lovely silencer shot a stream of noiseless tracers into the little folly, as the whirlybird hovered twenty feet away six feet over the water. That was all. The naked eye could see no result of this fire at all. But Joplin and Prentice watched through the ultrasonic scope, as if in daylight, the three bodies crumpled in death.

Joplin swung the copter wide around the island and approached the northern watchtower head on. Again the Jensens sent their noiseless little lights into the darkness. This time Hasbrouck watched the scope and saw the two men inside ripped up by the bullets.

He faced Prentice, grim as a judge: "Murder!" he said.

Prentice gazed back calmly: "Think of it as *war*, Jacques," he said very low. "And *shut up*—this is the tough part."

The helicopter rose swiftly to five hundred feet and Joplin rapped sharply on the cockpit door. Ed Grove poked his head into the cockpit and then climbed into the driver's seat, which made things very crowded indeed. Joplin stood at the doorway and checked his equipment, knife in its little slit in his jump suit, ropes around the waist, flash hanging on belt, silent grenades hanging on their clips, Mauser (he was very old-fashioned in some ways and scorned the CIA's fancy new guns as effeminate) in its special pocket. The bird hovered noiselessly over the topmost round tower with its pole sticking into the night sky. Joplin stepped placidly out of the whirlybird, wrapped his arms around the pole and then as Grove pulled up the helicopter sharply, Joplin slid down the pole and spread-eagled himself on the gray slate cone of the roof. He slipped the rope around the pole and then inched himself down the roof to its edge. On the edge of the slate roof, standing like a great figure of Jehovah, Joplin undid one of the grenades from its clip. Below him was one of the crenelated battlements which protected the two men there from gunfire. But not from grenades dropped on their heads.

The crump was muffled but the flash was quite bright. Seconds later, Joplin lowered himself to the parapet. From the helicopter they saw and heard the Mauser.

"Someone wasn't dead enough," said the President. "Joplin is fixing that."

Joplin's flashlight shot at them, on and off, on and off. The all clear. The helicopter settled delicately on the battlements. Three Chinese gunmen, four Czech safeblowers, and two Arab arsonists in the black jump suits poured silently out of the interior onto the gray stone parapet. Prentice hopped lightly from the pilot's cockpit and after him came Jacques in a ferment of ambivalence. He disapproved of this caper altogether, but he had no intention of missing any of it.

This was the risky bit. They had no further information on this imitation Rhine castle—no map, no plan, and no idea how many men were inside or how well armed. From here on it was ad lib. Joplin glared at the President and Prentice smiled and held up his hands submissively. He had promised not to venture off the parapet until the place was secure—if it ever was.

"What happens," he had asked Joplin, "if you all get killed in there? Even if I could fly a helicopter, where would I go?"

Joplin's answer to that was simple. "I don't get killed very often."

"There's a first time for everything," Prentice had pointed out. But Joplin wouldn't budge and Prentice had promised.

Joplin led the men through the door. Prentice and Jacques were left alone in the starlit night. It was very quiet. Far below they could hear the river sighing gently against the shore of the island. From the woods opposite came the inappropriate screech of an owl. Presently, from the north, they heard the distant sound of a freight train on the water-level tracks where the Twentieth Century once ran. Three minutes later the train flashed past on the west bank, looking in the starlight like a toy train in Gimbel's window.

From inside the fake Rhine castle there was no sound whatsoever, which was probably good news. When operations got noisy they were going wrong.

Ten minutes—a long time—after Joplin had vanished through the door, he reappeared through the same door. Over his shoulder draped casually like a cloak was one of the Arab arsonists. Joplin put him down gently on the stone parapet. Lips pursed, Prentice stared down at the handsome young Arab who had taken four submachine gun bullets in the chest.

"Any others?" said Prentice softly.

"Some scratches," said Joplin. "Come on."

The three men went down the circular stone staircase which smelled of years of Hudson River dampness and came out on to a long high-ceilinged main corridor off which the chief master bedrooms lay. Doors to the bedrooms all stood open. Prentice and Joplin strode past them without a glance. Trailing behind, Hasbrouck peered into each bedroom. In the first a man had tried to get out of bed and been gunned down still entangled in the bedclothes, on his back, eyes and mouth open. In the next room the pair looked as if they had never awakened at all. A middle-aged balding Middle European lay, eyes closed, mouth on the pillow in permanent sleep. Next to him lay a young girl snuggled into the pillow, very peacefully dead. Hasbrouck glared angrily then strode out. In the next bedroom, the largest, with a marvelous view up river—presumably the head man's bedroom—the scene was even more interesting. One man, two young girls, all naked and entwined without even a sheet over them. Caught in the middle of whatever they were doing, Hasbrouck surmised. He turned away.

Prentice was in the doorway looking at him. "We thought you'd got lost," said Prentice politely. "We haven't much time, Jacques."

"You didn't give them much chance," said Hasbrouck indicating the bodies.

Prentice shook his head: "Oh, Jacques! You innocent! Come *on*."

Prentice hauled him out of the room and down the great high-ceilinged corridor overlooking the great hall past the next two bedrooms. "No more sightseeing, Jacques. We haven't time. If you want a rundown, I'll give it to you. There were twenty-two Rhine maidens guarding the treasure. They're all dead, most of them in their sleep. What would you have us do? Subpoena them?" Prentice chuckled dryly.

From below came a crump that shook the stone castle to its foundations. "Oh good," he said, "they're blowing the thing."

Prentice started to run, his lanky frame all elbows and knees like a giraffe. Hasbrouck sped after him. Down into the main great hall, its walls hung with stag horns and cutlasses, its main window offering a splendid view of the Hudson, through the kitchen and down another steep circular stone staircase, which seemed to have no ending. Down, down, and round and round it went into the solid rock of the island's foundations. The room at the bottom, carved out of solid rock, was thick with stone dust. Through the haze, they saw the safe door, twelve feet high of twelve-inch steel. It had come from Belgium because the sale of a safe of such size in the States would have caused talk. The great door stood open, its two-foot-long plungers twisted like cornstalks; the Czechs had used a very new, very fancy explosive indeed. They were sawing through the inner steel barred gate now with their high-speed tricetylene torches, which tore the heart out of a steel bar in under twelve seconds.

Prentice was the first through the barred gate. Inside were the steel drawers, tier upon tier of them from floor to twelve-foot ceiling, lining the length of the 150-foot chamber. Prentice pulled at a drawer. Locked, of course. One of the Czechs fixed that with a lone delicate spit from his tricetylene torch. Prentice pulled open the steel drawer, which was packed neatly from bottom to top with one hundred-dollar bills. Prentice pulled the drawer out and dumped the contents casually on the floor.

The Czech's eyes glittered with amusement, not cupidity. That much money had no meaning. "A million dollars," said Prentice casually to Hasbrouck. "In each drawer."

The Czechs were busily and rapidly using their deadly little tricetylenes on the other drawers. A spit of flame and the drawer would open. The Czech would pull it out and dump the money on the floor, replace the drawer and go on to the next one. They worked silently and in great haste and the piles of money on the stone floor grew higher and higher until it was over their heads—and still the stack grew, big as a haystack, solid money.

"Have you ever seen a hundred and fifty million dollars in cash?" asked Prentice.

Hasbrouck shook his head silently. "Can't say that I have."

"Now you have. This is just a week's haul from

the northeast. It has to be recycled, poured back into the economy within two weeks or we'd be out of one hundred dollar bills," said Prentice. "This is only one of four of the Mob's main banks."

"How did you find this rock?" asked Hasbrouck.

Prentice grinned. "We found the address in Tasio's safe—which you tried very hard to keep us out of."

Hasbrouck was silent. There was nothing he could think of to say to that.

Joplin stood at Prentice's elbow. "All accounted for, Chief."

"There are no other chambers? You're sure?"

Joplin nodded. "Nothing but solid rock. The Arabs and I have checked every inch of this island."

The Arabs were already drenching the pile with kerosene and the Czechs were gathering their little toys.

"Off we go. Come on, Jacques."

They stood at the bottom of the steep stone revolving steps and watched the Arab send a stab of electronic fire into the money, which whooshed into monstrous green and yellow flame.

Hasbrouck looked at the burgeoning flames, appalled. "You're not going to burn it?"

Prentice smiled wryly: "Have you ever tried carrying a hundred and fifty million dollars with you? It would take four helicopters to carry it." He tugged at Jacques' sleeve: "Come on, it's going to get very hot in here in a few minutes. And nothing stinks like burning money."

Jacques stared at his old friend, helpless with admiration: "What do you have to do to get that casual about a hundred and fifty million?"

"Become President of the United States," said Prentice. "It's not very much money, Jacques. We spend more than that in military appropriations under *et cetera*. Come *on*.'' He yanked savagely at him.

The party fled up the stone staircase, round and round and round, the stench of burning money keeping up with them all the way.

At the top of the staircase a panting Hasbrouck faced Prentice and Joplin: "Did you know," he gasped, "that it's a federal offense to burn money?"

Prentice grasped his sleeve and hauled him up the main staircase: "Yeah, and the helicopter's illegally parked as well."

High above the Hudson, the argument raged. If argument was the word. It was a clash of principles as high as a mountain. "You could have called in the FBI," raged Hasbrouck, a lifetime of law on his head. "They have enormous powers."

"You are a child, Jacques," growled Prentice. "We'd never have found that hoard of crooked money if we hadn't killed Tasio and wrung the secret out of his own safe, quite illegally. And even after we found out where it was you goddamned lawyers would have tied us up for weeks with the First Amendment and the Fifth Amendment and the rest of that garbage, and when we got there every penny would have vanished into a Swiss bank. You are living in the seventeenth century, Jacques, and so is the English common law. You acquit the crooks and convict the innocent. The English common law is as obsolete as the horse and buggy."

Hasbrouck faced his furious friend unflinchingly: "You are talking pure tyranny, President Prentice."

"This is multinational crime, you ass, a tyranny of its own! If we hadn't blown it up, that pile of money would have been corrupting judges in the south of

France, buying up Scotland Yard—which is no longer as incorruptible as we like to believe—purchasing oil wells in the Gulf of Mexico and buying Peru outright.''

"You could have taken your case to Congress," shouted Hasbrouck.

"Case? What case?" thundered Prentice. "We didn't have a case until we broke into Bobo Schotz's safe in Grosse Point, quite illegally, and what we found there led us to Tasio's safe, also illegally, and that led us here—and also to Everett Quincey's house on Fifth Avenue and we don't yet know where *that* safe is going to lead."

"The law—" cried Hasbrouck.

Prentice shook his head: "The law, my fucking behind, my friend. Charles the First went to the scaffold protesting that no court had the authority to try him—and they didn't! Cromwell was illegal from start to finish—the whole Cromwellian age was unlawful. The Declaration of Independence was unlawful from start to finish, every last comma."

From Joplin came a low warning growl: "Cool it, you two hotheads. We're approaching target."

Ten minutes later, in the bedroom of a New Rochelle house, the three men stood over the body of the French mobster who Joplin had dispatched with his knife—which he always preferred when it was at all possible.

"What did you kill this one for?" asked Hasbrouck.

"*Everything!*" said Joplin.

Prentice said, "His name was Louis Galitzine and like Joplin says he did a bit of everything. Extortion, torture, murder, pimping, drug pushing. He was personally responsible as muscle man for the Mob for twenty-six murders and indirectly responsible for the death by drug overdose, suicide, or injury of about fifty more. We *know* all that, Jacques. *Know* it beyond the shadow of a doubt. Yet none of it can be proved in a court of law. Inadmissible evidence? What bullshit! You should be ashamed of yourself that you and your fellow lawyers have constructed such a Byzantine labyrinth of the law that scum like that can run loose, killing, corrupting, at will—protected by expensive lawyers saying 'This is the law.' You should be ashamed of yourself.''

CHAPTER
FIFTEEN

The happenings that night across the U.S.A. were to become legends of the new activists for generations to come.

In San Francisco's Chinatown, the little CIA tank charged out of a great moving van spitting fifty-caliber bullets into the second of the big Mob banks—this one stuffed with yen for payment of raw opium stocks to the Chinese (the whereabouts of the safe, like that on the Hudson, had been found locked in Tasio's safe)—mowing through the best-guarded defense of all the great treasure troves. One hundred and twelve Chinese assaulted the little tank with every form of mayhem, bullets, grenades, and fire weapons, except anti-tank rockets which they didn't have and didn't expect to need. The defenders died gallantly to the last man, trying to defend some two hundred million dollars in Chinese and Pacific currencies that was packed into the moving van and transported to an immense troop C-5 which flew the whole thing to Utah.

At the very moment of the San Francisco job, Prentice, back in the hut in Utah, was gravely pouring a very stiff drink for Hasbrouck. "You drink too much, old fellow," he was saying. "You should drink less and talk less and read more. Have you read Ramsey McMullen's *Enemies of the Roman Empire*? He writes of a period much like ours when the established order was under sustained attack not by peasants or oppressed slaves but by men of wealth and education—like him." Pointing to the recumbent and heavily-drugged Everett Quincey. He handed his friend the drink.

Dawn had long broken over the Utah woods and the glade in which Joplin's hut was so skillfully concealed was flooded with sunshine. Joplin was sleeping noisily in a rude wooden bunk.

One hundred and eighty-seven lawyers were killed across the country that night. Every last one of them had little white cards on their bodies with the words COCAINE KILLS on them. All of them had Mob associations and most of them had no other clients. But Prentice had ordered the extinction of a few part-time Mob shamuses, too. Prentice explained just why he had done that.

"I wish the idea to take root in every lawyer's mind that they are assuming responsibility for the crimes they are defending, *if* it is the profit from those crimes that is lining their pockets. That includes you, Jacques. Would you like me to tell you where the $750,000 Tasio has paid you came from?"

"Privileged information," cried Hasbrouck. "Where did you get it?"

Prentice just grinned and said, "Heroin in Harlem, white slavery in Bolivia, and I don't mean old-fashioned prostitution. I mean young Indian girls being forced to submit to a life of prostitution—that's what bought your Jaguar, Jacques—white slavery."

"How the hell do you expect every lawyer to look into the source of every penny he's paid?" cried Hasbrouck.

"I don't expect every lawyer to investigate the source of every penny he's paid. I do expect all lawyers to know what is common knowledge to every cop on the beat, every newsman, and almost every schoolboy. Where do you *think* Tasio got that $750,000 he so light-heartedly peeled off his wallet for you, Jacques—selling prayer rugs?"

"You're a criminal yourself, Harry," muttered Jacques. "President of the United States—a murderer!"

"No," said Prentice gently, helping himself to Joplin's peanuts and chewing them with relish. "A *revolutionary*—new style." He washed the peanuts down with a great draught of beer. "Every revolutionary has to violate the old moralities in order to set up the new morality—these things always scandalize the existing lawyers. As an establishment lawyer in 1861, Jacques, you would have represented the plantation owner against the runaway slave, now wouldn't you?"

One of the things that puzzled the forces of law and bemused the press about the night of the long knives was the colorful characters who threaded the tale.

Lamport of *The New York Times* wrote of Kurds—

whale-sized—who tore open the house of the celebrated Kansas City mobster Georges Terillian almost with their bare hands and dispatched the whole household the same way. The Kurds had been observed entering the estate and remarked upon simply because of their vast size.

In Dallas, Texas, the newspapers were full of tales of Chinese gunmen who had been seen just before and just after the home of a respected citizen (whose wealth had never been adequately explained) went up in smoke with all the occupants in it. In Miami, the papers reported an influx of what looked like Turks in fezzes with vast handlebar mustaches who had been seen around the day before eight prominent members of the old Chicago gang were found slain in their homes. In St. Louis, where the waterfront mob was rubbed out to the man, the talk was of Rumanian gypsies who were observed in an encampment outside the city singing their wild gypsy songs and playing their wild gypsy violins, on the night of the long knives. The same wild gypsy music was heard emanating from the lovely homes of three enormously rich and enormously mysterious citizens which went up in smoke.

Only Lamport pulled this wild mélange of nationalities into one story. "In Philadelphia, it was Hungarians, in Memphis, Poles and in Seattle an enormous Japanese who looked like a wrestler, weighing in at about three hundred and fifty pounds. None of these people appeared to know any English at all, which was why they were noticed." Later in the story he drew the conclusion that "Whoever organized this vast bloodbath had recourse to literally dozens of nationalities, but not one single American seems to have been involved."

*   *   *

In the Utah hut one of the few Americans involved was rubbing his haggard eyes. Prentice was laying now on the top bunk of the wooden doubledecker. Jacques lay in the bunk underneath, his arms under his head.

"Three things made the mob invulnerable, Jacques. The sheer naked, brute power of hundreds of killers, extortionists, arsonists, and torturers—and their vast reservoirs of money. But perhaps most important of all—the mystique, the legend of invulnerability."

Prentice yawned a vast yawn. "We're smashing all three. We've smashed the four big banks and grabbed all the loose gang money we knew of. When the Colombian hood arrives from Bogota for his money for the cocaine, there won't be any money to pay. Or anyone to meet him. They are all dead. When the cop in Tuscaloosa or the judge in Harlem goes for his quiet money, there'll be no one there to pay off."

Prentice's eyes closed. He muttered sleepily: "And the mystique. The mystique is shot to hell because the enforcers—2,109 of them from coast to coast—whose names we got . . . out of Tasio's safe and Shotzie's safe and Okrelli's safe . . . are dead. Every last one . . ."

He trailed off. He was asleep.

In the bunk below, Hasbrouck was still wide awake, eyes thoughtful.

CHAPTER
SIXTEEN

The white phone in the Oval Office had been disconnected when Prentice left the White House. Communications had been transferred to the red network altogether and linked to the white telephone securely locked in Joplin's wooden chest with its white light on top. The light was blinking now. It had been blinking uninterruptedly for four hours. The three men—Prentice, Joplin, and Hasbrouck—slept off their long night of the long knives. From 8:00 A.M. until noon (which was two hours earlier in Washington), the white light blinked patiently off on, off on, shouting Emergency! Emergency! Emergency! The men slept on, sunk in a thousand fathoms of sleep.

It was Joplin, first asleep, who was first awake. And then not very. He awoke slowly with a great rumble of throat clearing and thrashing of legs and arms and scratching of crotch and underarm, an earthquake of awakening—culminating in the opening of the eyes only after minutes of solid body convulsion. Then came the hands over face routine, the massage of the entire face by both hands, sighings and croakings emanating from the throat.

When Joplin caught the insistent blink blink blink of the white light, his feet hit the floor with a massive wallop and he jerked across the floor wide-awake, tugging at the ring of keys on his belt. He unlocked the chest and picked up the white phone inside.

"Joplin," said the voice without preamble. "Ferrier."

"Yeah?" said Joplin.

"I've been trying to get through for four hours."

Joplin yawned: "It was a long night, boss, with much merrymaking."

"I know," said Ferrier grimly. "You left the dishes in the sink."

"We were told to—by himself."

"Where's himself?"

"Asleep."

"Get him up."

"Urgent?"

"Top."

Joplin yawned another huge yawn, scratching at the stubble on his chin and crossed to Prentice's bunk. He shook the President awake with one movement. Prentice, unlike Joplin, awoke in a rush, one moment totally asleep, in seconds every nerve awake, eyes wide, mind alert.

"Ferrier on the blower. Top priority."

Prentice swung himself over the side of the double-decker and leaped to the floor with a crash that awakened Hasbrouck underneath.

"Yup," said Prentice.

"Two o'clock here," said Ferrier abruptly. "Lot of laughs in the bladders." He didn't sound like he was laughing much. "The Red Knight is bubbling." The Red Knight was McMillan, now duly sworn President of the United States. Bubbling meant questions, nasty questions.

But something else struck Prentice even more urgently than the crisis. Background noise which sounded like jet engines, many jet engines.

"Christopher?" asked Prentice. (It was a very simple-minded code. Christopher meant simply: "Going somewhere?" like Columbus.)

"Absolute zero," said Ferrier, which meant he was coming direct to Prentice at all possible speed and *that* meant B-52's at fourteen hundred miles an hour. "It's June twenty-third."

It was in fact June twenty-third that very day—but said like that with nothing but "It's" in front of it was the worst possible news. It meant Destruct! Destruct! The camp was to be vacated, the records destroyed, the whole operation to vanish like smoke—and the only reason for that was that something had gone terribly wrong, which Prentice had known the minute he had heard that McMillan got back from Northwest Africa with such unprecedented speed.

"How do you do?" said Prentice. (When was Ferrier due.)

"Minus five," said Ferrier. That meant twenty-eight minutes. Ferrier must have been trying very hard to get through before taking wing as the quickest way to communicate. "Right on, man," said Ferrier with a note of urgency no code could conceal.

Prentice grinned and whistled two sharp clear owl-like notes which meant, "I read you loud and clear and am getting on with it with all possible haste." And he hung up.

Joplin was pouring water into an old tin coffee pot which he put on the stove. He looked at the President. "It's destruct at all possible speed," said Prentice. "Something's gone wrong."

The President grinned at Hasbrouck, who was pulling himself out of his lower bunk stiffly. Prentice felt marvelous. Emergencies always concentrated his mind and emotions, even his body. Emergency, to Prentice, was what life was all about. It was why he enjoyed the Presidency so much.

"Did you sleep well?" he asked Hasbrouck politely.

"Christ, no!" said Hasbrouck sourly. "What's up?"

"Disaster!" said the President cheerily. "Crisis! Everything is going entirely wrong—and we must put it right. But first breakfast. Have you got any eggs, Joplin? I'm starved."

The B-52 put down in the long clearing slashed through the woods that was actually a fire brake no more distinguishable from any other fire brake from the air, its concrete runway mud-colored and looking from the air like a ploughed field. (The new sensors could see through this easily, but it was designed only to befuddle the airline pilots and rich private plane-flying ranchers.) The big bomber was trundled off the runway and under the dark trees to join the other B-52 and the C-5 and the fourteen Bell X-20's. Ferrier, Tupper, and Whitney got out. There was no one to greet them, but Ferrier didn't expect anyone. He strode off under the trees to the encampment.

The camp was roaring with life. Turks in fezzes

were chopping down the great replica of Everett Quincey's Fifth Avenue townhouse. Chinese gunmen were bulldozing great holes in the forest floor into which Corsican thugs were tossing the replica of the New Orleans Mafia bank they had riffled. Everywhere the camp was being restored to its prior state as an old Conservation Corps camp. The rocket range was being bulldozed back into a reasonable facsimile of a field, its great steel craters smoothed. The signs in Chinese, Turkestan, Italian, and Greek were being replaced by signs: Bird Sanctuary, Nature Study area, Land Reclamation—all earth-loving symbols of peace.

Inside the huts the men were rolling up sleeping equipment, packing away disguises and costumes, restoring the place to emptiness. Others were seated on the now unmade bunks oiling their guns. They'd need those, Joplin had told them. The Kurd was checking and counting rockets and the huge Japanese was packing grenades in great wooden crates.

Ferrier walked through this bustle, grim-faced, Tupper and Whitney trailing behind. They went straight to Joplin's cabin and entered without knocking.

A Chinese girl was filling the syringe at the table where Prentice, Hasbrouck, and Joplin had just breakfasted. The three men were watching the girl, who was in an olive drab jumpsuit just like that of the men. Prentice grasped Ferrier's hand; his face lit up with a mocking smile at the sight of Whitney and Tupper.

The CIA chief handed the President *The New York Times* and Prentice glanced at the eight-column banner headline. GANG WAR ERUPTS COAST TO COAST ON EVE OF PRESIDENTIAL FUNERAL. Prentice chuckled hollowly and tossed the paper aside. "You shouldn't read trash like that. You'll ruin your mind."

Ferrier's gaze had settled on the lower bunk where the white-maned Everett Quincey lay, a cherubic smile affixed on his face, eyes closed. The Chinese girl sat on the bunk and took out Quincey's left arm. She rolled up the sleeve of the shirt and plunged the needle into the arm. There was total silence in the room.

"Trinetelene?" asked Ferrier.

Prentice nodded, eyes somber.

"What is trinetelene?" asked Hasbrouck.

The President and Ferrier exchanged looks. "It's better than sodium pentothal," said the President, briefly. "Quicker, for one thing."

"Why doesn't everyone use it then?" demanded Hasbrouck.

Ferrier looked Hasbrouck full in the face: "Because the victim doesn't usually survive it."

The beatific smile on Quincey's face seemed to deepen and broaden until it looked as if he were bestowing blessing on all mankind.

"Get at it," said Ferrier. "We haven't much time."

"Is he ready?" asked the President.

"He's ready."

Prentice sat on the edge of the bunk and started. "What is your name?"

"Everett Hale Quincey."

All three as American as apple pie, thought Prentice. "Who is the head of the Invisible Government?"

Ferrier tensed visibly with discontent at this question. He would not have sprung it so quickly. But Prentice was a jugular man—go straight to the heart of the matter. Never give an interrogee a chance to get his feet dug in. The answer was long in coming, Quincey's beatific smile had vanished and the rubbery features were working hard—his ingrained duplicity quarreling almost audibly with the trinetelene. The drug won.

"*I* am," said the adviser of Presidents, with a look that suggested he was astonishing himself, as if the secret had been buried so deeply that he had never before admitted such a thing even to himself.

The admission sent a ripple of unspoken emotion through the room, as if Jesus and Judas had just changed places. Hasbrouck grasped Prentice by the shoulder and murmured directly into his ear, "Aren't you going to tape-record this?"

"Why?" asked Prentice bluntly. "No one would believe it. Anyway the lawyers would throw it out as obtained under duress."

He turned back to Everett Quincey, whose rubber face—now that the big admission had been made—had regained some of its serenity, this time overlaid with submission. That was the advantage of getting at the hard questions first, Prentice felt. Once they had cracked, there was no further resistance.

"Who planned the assassination?" asked Prentice almost conversationally.

"Oh, we all did," said Quincey eagerly, like a little boy telling just who won first prize in apple ducking. "Stern was of very great assistance because he knew all the details of the President's public appearances— in fact, he helped to plan just where he would stand and what time he arrived. Very important."

His old school chum, thought Prentice. He remembered Stern being very insistent on arrival and time for the diplomatic dinner, and just where he should stand and whom he should greet.

"Then Hasbrouck was useful," said Quincey.

That produced a heightening of the general silence

which was already almost complete. It was as if the listeners around the lower bunk—Joplin, Ferrier, Tupper, and Whitney—stopped breathing altogether. There was a very great avoidance of eyes, everyone avoiding everyone else's. All except Hasbrouck, who stared defiantly at the President—who did not look at him.

"Hasbrouck knew about the assassination?" asked Prentice politely.

"Oh no," said Quincey. "Hasbrouck was the President's closest friend. We told him nothing. But he told us many things without realizing it. Hasbrouck was in and out of the White House constantly. Sometimes just the President's quips at dinner were very useful in assessing the situation. Hasbrouck was our thermometer, so to speak. He took the temperature of the White House."

Hasbrouck's looks were thunderous. He didn't like his role as thermometer at all. Prentice, on the other hand, was buoyant with relief. Hasbrouck had been unwitting altogether. That was a very great weight off his mind. He resumed. "How about McMillan?"

"Oh, the Vice-President, of course," said Quincey heartily. "In fact, he suggested it."

"He suggested the assassination?"

"Well, of course, it would make him President, you see. He's not very bright, McMillan, and he won't be very easy to manage now he's in the White House. But he is our man . . ."

"Your man?" asked Prentice.

"Oh, yes. We put him there. He's ours altogether."

Ours? The Mob's? The Mafia's? That thought pierced even Prentice's normally impenetrable aplomb. He thought furiously. Where had McMillan first been involved? Who'd first suggested him as Vice-President? Oh, my God—Quincey, the good old adviser of Presidents. Of course! Quincey had suggested him as a compromise candidate—all Vice-Presidents were compromise candidates—aimed at mollifying the South and Southwestern voters.

"How did he get back from Northwest Africa so quickly?"

"Oh, he was waiting for our confirmation. He was in the air within minutes after Stern sent him the flash."

That was it, then. The whole plot. There was nothing especially surprising in it. Prentice had suspected most of it. Still, suspicion and confirmation were very different. For the moment, it took the wind out of him. He looked at Ferrier.

"Any questions, Paul?"

"Yes," said Ferrier crisply. "What are McMillan's immediate objectives?"

"To stop the killings, of course, before we are wiped out altogether," cried Quincey.

"How is he going to do that?"

"He will first call Ferrier to account." Ferrier smiled dryly because that was just what McMillan had done, summoned him to his office. That's why Ferrier was in the Utah woods at that moment. To gain a little time. "It's the CIA, of course, behind all this," said Quincey. "No one else could manage these executions so swiftly and leave so little trace. McMillan will ask for an explanation and then he'll replace Ferrier with..."

"Who?" asked Ferrier dryly.

"Me," said Quincey triumphantly. "I am always the man the nation summons in periods of emergency. It will be McMillan's most popular appointment."

An hour later the questioning was almost finished. They'd extracted all the details of what had happened and what was to come. The penetration into the federal government was fairly horrifying but, horrifying as it was, it could have been worse. They knew far too much about how the gang killings had been done and who had planned them. But they had no idea they had *not* killed the President. That left Prentice a very high card indeed.

Ferrier had one last question: "What was the rose on the White House lawn for?"

"Communications," said Quincey benevolently. "You see, at one time we thought we might have to mount an assault directly on the White House, because the President was so difficult to flush out into the open. The rose was our transmitter to give instructions to our soldiers in the White House."

They didn't need the names of the "soldiers" in the White House. They already had them. Prentice cut off Ferrier's questions on the working of the rose. "We have the plans," he told him. Prentice had one last question that had been nagging at him: "What was the function in your plans of Fenella Jones?" In his mind's eye he summoned up the picture of his pretty sub-assistant.

"Oh, she was one of our failures," said Quincey. "She was supposed to seduce the President. She never succeeded in pulling it off."

Prentice scratched his head ruefully. "She never even tried, actually. That's one of the great penalties of being President. The women are all too frightened of you to make passes."

CHAPTER SEVENTEEN

Prentice called it his Little Cabinet—Ferrier, Joplin, Hasbrouck, and Tupper and Whitney, the two White House aides. They sat around the wooden table in Joplin's hut.

"You are the President of the United States," argued Hasbrouck. "All you have to do is *appear*. Take command. The Army, Navy, Secret Service, the works! You're *it*, man. Why all this skulking in the woods in Utah?"

Prentice listened respectfully, Ferrier's face was a mask. Tupper examined his knuckles. Even Whitney, the young Yale lawyer, who six months earlier might have sided with Hasbrouck, had been too thoroughly educated by his short tenure with the hidden microphones. He suppressed a smile. Joplin couldn't suppress a sneer.

"If you'll pardon the expression, Mr. Hasbrouck,

you are being naive,'" blurted Joplin. "He'd be dead within a minute after he poked his head up. Afterwards they'd say they were sorry."

Ferrier pursed his lips: "They probably wouldn't even say that. They'd whisk away the body, substitute another—it's done all the time—make it out to be some kind of a nut. The body would disappear in a vat of acid. Nothing to it."

"McMillan isn't going to give up the seals of office lightly," said Prentice, very calm. "I'll just have to go in and take the office away from him. And he has the Army, the Navy, the Secret Service, and the FBI on his side. Any suggestions?"

Great laugh line but nobody laughed.

Silence. Six men were thinking.

"Yes," said Ferrier, briskly. "Here it is."

He outlined it on the wooden table, using Joplin's shoe as the White House, sketching the ingress path with his pen on the table top. All five of Ferrier's listeners were struck dumb by the sheer audacity of the thing. Each one waited for someone else to say "It won't work." No one did. As a consequence, no one said anything.

Finally, Ferrier threw in diffidently (only Ferrier could be diffident about his own brilliance as a tactician), "It *will* work." No one had said it wouldn't. "What's more, it is the *only* one of the sixteen methods that will work."

Prentice grinned: "The sixteen?"

"There are sixteen possible methods. Obviously you've all thought of all of them." Prentice had considered—and discarded—three. "This is the only one that will work, and I'll tell you why."

And he did. For twenty minutes he analyzed the

sixteen paths open to the President, and the reasons for discarding fifteen of them, and the reason for embracing the sixteenth—an exercise in cold, remorseless logic that awed them all. "I'm glad you're on our side, Ferrier," said Prentice. "Okay, the rest of you pick holes in it."

Joplin was the first into the breach: "It needs rehearsal—anything that elaborate needs weeks—and we haven't any time."

"It doesn't need that much rehearsal," said Ferrier quickly, "because every bit of the plan has been rehearsed. You've done it again and again. I've just adapted your . . . previous stunts . . . to the White House lawn. You can use the same men who've rehearsed these things at Tasio's place, at Quincey's town house, and all those other places. They've got identical duties— well, *almost* identical—just a new locale. You've got an hour, Jop, before we get out of here. Get your men out and explain it to them. Same duties, different place. Same timing, because any change would just confuse them. We'll just have to adjust the master plan to your earlier timing."

Joplin rubbed his jaw hard and thought about it, almost out loud.

"Cut along, Jop," commanded the President. "We haven't much time for nit-picking."

Joplin nodded and left without a word.

"Why do we have to get out of here in an hour?" demanded the President. "We're not mounting this operation until the wee hours."

"Because," said Ferrier. "McMillan has asked for an explanation of CIA operations. All of them. They're wise to us. McMillan wants everything accounted for and he's asked the Air Force—and the Army—to call in all these lovely toys—the C-5's, the B-52's, the helicopters. That's why I took to my heels—to avoid answering questions.''

"Where are you officially?" asked Prentice.

"I'm in the mountains of Yugoslavia checking operations behind the curtain. I can't be reached for three days.''

Prentice laughed: "If McMillan swallowed a story like that, he's obviously unfit to be President. How about you, Whitney? Where are you officially?''

"I resigned when you were assassinated. I'm back in private practice.''

"Good," grunted Prentice. "You, Tup?"

"I'm on official duty for President McMillan," said Tupper blank-faced.

"Well, well," said the President.

Tupper rubbed his nose quizzically: "I was summoned to the presence—twenty minutes after he got back from Northwest Africa." Tupper smiled, enjoying the sensation he was causing. "The President—if you'll pardon the expression—said he wanted a rundown on the activity of all Presidential aides in the last six months. He had some crazy idea that you, as the President of the United States, had ordered these gang executions—and that one Presidential aide was helping out. He said he knew that I would never connive in such a thing, but he commissioned me to find out who was.''

There was a total silence after this bombshell.

"Even McMillan can't be that stupid," said the President quizzically. "What was he doing?"

"Trying to panic me," said Tupper calmly. "I was supposed to take to my heels, first destroying any records I might have, thus leading him straight to them. He had men on my tail the minute I left his office.''

"Where are they now?"

"Ask him," said Tupper and he pointed to Ferrier.

Ferrier scowled. He hated bringing any of his little coups out into the open. "They had . . . accidents," he grunted.

"We all disappeared—the hunted and the hunters," said Tupper. "But McMillan has other things on his mind besides worrying about where I am."

Prentice was staring out the window, watching Joplin muster his troops. A hell of a lot of men to keep under cover, denied the protection of the Utah woods.

"Why do we have to get out of here so fast, Paul?"

"Because Soames has been on the carpet. McMillan —or more probably somebody in the brains department of the mob—has suspected that this operation had to be mounted from some place out in the wilds and that instantly suggests the Interior Department. They have got all the wilds in their hat."

"Did Soames tell him anything?"

"No, he didn't. He's scared to admit he'd loaned Utah to the CIA—and since there are no records, he thought he'd keep his mouth shut. Just the same, McMillan now has all the muscle to make a search—Air Force planes running out of his ears. And he'll do it. Or rather the brain that is running McMillan will order him to do it."

"Who is the brain running McMillan now that we have *him*?" Prentice jerked a thumb at the sleeping Quincey.

"I wish I knew, but I don't," said Ferrier grimly. "But you can bet your bottom dollar someone is at McMillan's elbow telling him what to do, because the moves have been very smart and very quick. And

McMillan is not at all smart or quick. That's why we have got to get airborne before someone tumbles this spot and takes us on the ground."

"Where are we going to kill fifteen hours before H-hour?" asked Tupper.

"Flying round and round and round and here and there, that's the nice thing about a B-52—it has enormous range. So has a C-5."

"A helicopter hasn't any range at all," said Prentice.

"Oh, the helicopters," said Ferrier, smiling one of his rare smiles. "Well, the whirlybirds have been ordered back to their base in Virginia and we have orders and routes and flight plans that are all tied up and cleared with the right people. We're all crew members—and we'd better get going."

Prentice was in the forward copter, dressed in a jumpsuit. The famous face had been enriched with a mustache, and cheapened with a lowered forehead and long curved sideburns. Plus a pair of very dark glasses.

"You could scare a fellow to death . . ." said Hasbrouck, sitting next to him in the pilot's cockpit, "in the dark. In the daylight you look just improbable. Like somebody made you up, and not very convincingly."

The President just grunted. He was amusing himself by watching his own funeral on the little Japanese Sony. On the tiny screen the cortege looked like a line of ants. The commentators, he noted with sharp irony that hurt him a little, seemed to have forgotten him altogether. They concentrated their cameras and their prose on the living Presidents and Prime Ministers who had come from all over the world to walk behind his casket. There they all were—France and Britain—even the Russians had sent the President of the Politburo who wasn't, of course, the top man but pretty important nevertheless. And the little countries, every last one, had sent their Presidents—from Escoria, Plurandi, Yescoteo, North and South Korea (not speaking, of course). Oh, he was great for international amity, all right. Would they have a party after they got him planted? he wondered.

"I feel like Tom Sawyer," said Prentice. "Remember—he and Huck went to their own funerals."

The mountains rose up beside him, almost embracing the big silent helicopter. In the bright sunshine the black as night fighting helicopter looked indecent, like a bat caught out of its cave at daybreak. They were at full power heading east, and the route had been picked to keep the little caravan of copters over mountain, forest, and river as much as possible in the daylight hours.

It was very quiet in the cockpit. Joplin was flying the bird, the creased face a study in concentration.

"What are we going to do with you, Jacques, when this thing starts?" asked the President.

"What do you mean—what are you going to do with me?" said Hasbrouck.

"Do we drop you on your front lawn? Or what?"

"Oh, come off it, Harry. I'm coming along. I've always wanted to have a look at that rabbit warren underneath the White House."

"If we get caught, we'll get it on the spot. Poof," said Prentice and snapped his fingers.

"Oh well," Hasbrouck shrugged, "I'm unmarried and Mother has independent means."

The President looked out at a mountaintop and rubbed his false mustache. "Jacques, how did you get mixed up with that bunch of crooks in the first place? McMillan, for Christ's sake!"

"It wasn't McMillan that got me into this, it was Everett Quincey. He was very persuasive, Harry. He said the rule of law was threatened in the United States."

Prentice looked thunderous: "Rule of law! The head of the Mafia talking about the rule of *law!*"

Hasbrouck smiled ruefully: "Yes. That thought kept me awake last night. That is one of the ironies of legal history—as you so unkindly pointed out—that the most vocal supporters of law are the lawless, *after* they get established. Anyhow, *I* didn't know any of this. Everett Quincey is one of the most respected figures in the United States. He wanted to set up a group of secret vigilantes like the group in Chicago that ultimately got Capone in the twenties—well, that's what he said, and it sounded good. I was to head the legal side and give free legal advice. Hell, Harry, how was I to know you were mixed up in this?"

"If you had known, I'd have been seriously re-miss," said Prentice grimly. "My operation was a thousand feet underground. I don't know how Quincey and his mob stumbled onto me at all. There must have been a chink somewhere."

There was silence in the helicopter as it climbed to two thousand feet to get over the Colorado mountain peaks.

"Harry," said Hasbrouck tentatively, "I don't want you throwing me out of this helicopter, but may I suggest something you won't like?"

Prentice nodded bleakly.

"It might have been Rosemary who, quite inadver-tently, gave them a clue."

Prentice's brows beetled ominously. The lower lip thrust itself out. He said nothing.

"Harry, I'm only throwing this out as a suggestion—because she said something to me."

"What?"

"She said she thought you knew more about these gang killings than you were letting on because of the way you listened and the way your shoulders moved. That's what she said, Harry, the way your shoulders moved. She said that wives knew things about the way their husbands thought about things and *felt* about things just by the way they moved. She said she knew you were emotionally involved in this gang war by the way your eyes went dead when it was brought up. She said that to me—and what she said to me, she might have said to Quincey. He sat next to her at the dinner that night."

The silent copter in the glittering sunshine was passing over the Republican River into that most republican of states, Kansas. The endless prairie stretched out brown and dry as prohibition underneath. There was a long silence in the Bell X-20.

Hasbrouck broke it. "Rosemary is the most loyal person in the world, Harry. We all know that. But she isn't always . . ." He didn't quite dare finish it.

"The brightest?" suggested Prentice ironically.

"I was going to suggest she wasn't always the most *discreet* person in the world. You didn't tell her anything?"

"It might have been better if I had," said Prentice sadly. "I could have told her to keep her mouth shut. I'm being penalized for *not* telling her anything. Oh Christ, Jacques, people like me shouldn't have wives. They get in the way of the decision-making process. It'll come to that one day, you wait and see. The President will have to shed his wife, as he has to get rid of his stocks in corporations as bringing a baleful influence into the White House. It's a lousy job, Jacques. Don't every let me catch you running for President, old buddy.''

Twilight began to dim the glorious spring day as they passed over the Mississippi. They could see the haze of St. Louis far to the south of them. Then they were in Illinois and the gaggle of black copters had to put down for the third time to refuel at the little Army and Air Force base near Decatur. Prentice stayed in the copter, hunched over maps to keep his face from view.

When they took off half an hour later night had fallen and the silent copters began to look more at home in the pitch blackness they had been designed for. They still had almost a thousand miles to go.

CHAPTER
EIGHTEEN

Ferrier and the electronics man—one of the four safe-blowing Czechs to whom telephones were like candy—passed the long trip hunched over the plans for the White House rose they'd found in Quincey's safe. It was vital to the exercise. In the back of their helicopter, Everett Quincey slept heavily, the Chinese nurse checking his pulse from time to time. He, too, was vital to the exercise.

Ferrier's flight path worked like magic—*too* well, really. It made him nervous when things went too well in the early stages. He needn't have worried about that. Trouble struck in the Shenandoah Valley. The copters were flying single file now, loaded—overloaded actually—with the full complement of over four hundred men. They flew low under the very rim of the Blue Ridge Mountains, evading radar, their silence cutting down the chances of any other kind of detection. But detected they were.

The loud hailer cut through the early morning silence like an obscenity at a church picnic. "Halt and identify! Halt and identify!" It echoed through the wooded slopes of the Blue Ridge like a sound effect in a horror movie.

Ferrier snatched up his loud hailer: "Identify yourself!" he barked.

"National Park Police," echoed up the valley.

National Park Police! Ferrier shot an exasperated look at Tupper sitting next to him. Ferrier had planned on Army, Navy, Air Force, Secret Service, and FBI, but National Park Police had not entered his calculations. It was news to him that they had helicopters.

"Okay, National Park Police," snapped Ferrier coldly, "this is Special Force 62, operating on Flight Plan 992, cleared by CAB, operating under special authorization of the National Security Council. Request permission to proceed."

There was a silence. All fourteen helicopters were hovering now at two hundred feet. Ferrier turned his radio dial to the red circuit, bouncing the message off a satellite. Long way to deliver a message to a copter barely two hundred yards away, but it couldn't be intercepted. "Jop, do you read me?"

"Loud and clear."

"Where is he? I can't see him."

"He's right under you, that's why."

"How big? What kind?"

"Little Fairweather-12. Seats only two."

The National Park Police hailer was booming forth now: "Sorry, your flight plan superseded by new National Security Order 26, issued midnight. You'll have to ground for clearance.''

"Ground *where*?'' barked Ferrier. Into the mike, he muttered, "Jop, I'll do the talking. But he's your pigeon. Take him out.''

The National Park Police copter said, "Follow me.'' Light blazing, the little Fairweather led the fourteen black heavily-armed copters to a clearing and settled on a grassy park which nestled along a broad curve of the Shenandoah River.

"No bloodshed,'' said Prentice. He was reiterating a rule he'd laid down at the briefing, to the dismay of Joplin and Ferrier. They couldn't, said Prentice firmly, leave a trail of innocent dead behind them as they had left a litter of dead mobsters. There was no point in regaining the White House with that kind of blood on his hands.

Joplin handed over his controls to Ed Grove and reached for the little nerve rifle. It shot the same kind of pellets as those used on wild animals in the game parks, but worked faster. It put the victims to sleep, but not permanently. It wasn't very accurate over forty yards.

The Park copter, lights blazing, was on the ground now, surrounded by black CIA machines. Inside the Park copter they could see the two policemen. One got out and Ferrier leaped out to meet him. The other policeman stayed in his whirlybird. He had a rifle and he was clearly covering his companion.

"We'll have to take 'em both at once, Chief,'' muttered Joplin. "Grove, how are you on a rifle?''

"Terrible,'' whispered Grove. "I couldn't even pass basic in the Army.''

"I can't hit 'em both at once,'' said Joplin.

There was a flutter of looks among the four men in

the front seat—Prentice, Hasbrouck, Joplin, Grove. Then the President reached for the other little nerve rifle. "Hasbrouck," he said wryly under his breath, "couldn't hit Central Park with a cannon."

He took aim. He'd been a very good shot since boyhood.

"I'll take the moving man," said Joplin. "You take the copter target. Aim for the breast."

Prentice nodded.

"Ready," said Joplin calmly. "Squeeze."

The two National Park policemen were like men in slow motion. The one walking toward Ferrier became a sort of clown, lifting his leg experimentally as if he'd forgotten how to walk. The leg stayed lifted, the body swung around and down—in slow motion. The man in the copter simply keeled forward as if he'd decided to take a nap.

Prentice and Joplin leaped down and joined Ferrier kneeling over the National Park policeman. "Where's the Chinese girl?" said Ferrier. "Tell her to bring her needles."

The Chinese girl was fetched.

"No trinetelene," commanded Prentice. "They look like nice boys."

Ferrier sniffed coldly. "Okay, sodium pentothal," he grunted savagely. To Prentice he added, "If we're following the Geneva Convention all the way I'm only permitted to ask his name and serial number."

Prentice just grinned at his CIA chief and asked the questions himself, talking very politely, very conversationally as if he was just passing the time of day. "Tell us about this new National Council Order 26. We've been on the way all day and we hadn't heard about it."

The recumbent park policeman told him all about

National Security Council Order 26—at least what he knew of it—which provided quite enough food for thought in itself.

"Obviously they're expecting us," said Prentice. "Or they're expecting something."

Ferrier was thinking furiously, mouth pursed.

"How long does that stuff knock them out for?" Prentice asked the Chinese girl.

"Four hours," she said.

"Wrap a couple of blankets around him," commanded Prentice. "He'll catch his death of cold lying on that damp ground." He felt only elation. Emergencies were the greatest wine of life. Improvisation in the middle of a crisis—what could be headier? He slapped Ferrier on the back, grinning a great grin.

Ferrier had already examined the new situation from beginning to end and modified his plans. "Running into them could be the best break we've had. We know a bit what to expect. It would have been calamitous if we hadn't found out they're waiting."

"What do you suggest?" asked Prentice.

"We use the rose on the White House lawn—a bit earlier than I'd planned. Otherwise, same plan. Only you're going to have to be a little more adjustable about bullets. This isn't a taffy pull."

Prentice sighed. "As few as possible."

Ferrier said coldly, "I always *plan* the fewest possible bullets. Sometimes only one."

Joplin put on the Park Police helmet and with the Czech electronics man took the Park Police helicopter. They stowed the sleeping Quincey in the back, knees under his chin. Then Joplin quizzed the sodium pentothaled Park Police for ten minutes before take-off—both of

National Park policeman was considered suspicious. HQ, thought Joplin, had a hot potato and didn't know how to handle it. He grinned hugely, not daring to chuckle. They might hear a chuckle.

There was another pause, then HQ rapped out an order: "Proceed at all possible speed to Green 22. Land at exactly 45 stroke 62." Joplin looked at his chart. That put him down between the great south fountain and the White House tennis courts just south of Grover Cleveland's maples.

"Follow procedure *precisely* every foot of the way," rapped out the voice of HQ.

"Yes, sir," sang out Joplin, grinning, and snapped off his transmitter. "Keep feeding them their little colored pills, Jan, baby," he said to the Czech sitting next to him. He gunned the little copter full out. On the red circuit he sang to Ferrier, "Move 'em, boss. We're taking the Big Man right to the front doorstep."

The black mass of heavily loaded Bell helicopters lurched forward under the shelter of the Maryland trees. At four miles the Czech fed the tecticon another code, this one white, and at three miles another one, this time orange. At that exact moment the little copter had swung sharp right from the center of the broad Potomac and into President's Park. Following procedure, Joplin dropped the copter down to one hundred feet.

HQ crackled out a message: "You'll be floodlit in exactly one minute. You won't be able to see in the glare. We'll guide you in. Follow instructions to the letter."

Joplin turned on the transmitter: "Roger and over." He snapped it off and flipped on the red circuit to Ferrier. "They're floodlighting me in under a minute. Splendid cover for the rest of you."

The one thing about a searchlight is that you can't see anything else anywhere near it.

"Read you," said Ferrier. "Silence from now on unless very urgent."

"Yeah, man," said Joplin, impertinently. He was grinning now. This was the big one and he felt the tremendous adrenalin charge of the professional adventurer when he got to the core of the action, a heightening of every level of consciousness—which was what the business was all about. In that way he and Prentice understood each other thoroughly. They both lived for emergency; it was the heart of their being.

The searchlight hit the little copter like a fist. Both men shut their eyes for a moment, the flash of light was so bright.

A new voice, very professional, much more at ease, came on from HQ. "Adjust course five degrees right. Hold level."

"Roger," muttered Joplin.

"Reduce speed by half. You are now directly on course." Joplin sheltered his eyes to be able to see his instrument panel. He nodded to the Czech, who held up the last of the discs. The Czech slipped it into the tecticon.

"Reduce speed again by half. And again by half," said HQ.

The little copter was over the White House ground now, traveling at barely twenty miles an hour.

"Okay, hover," drawled the voice. "Bring it down right there."

Joplin brought the copter down light as a feather and killed the engine. He sat, awaiting instructions. The light was painful. There seemed to be searchlights boring in from north, southeast, and southwest. They weren't taking any chances. He couldn't see a thing, but he felt there were a lot of men out there.

Suddenly from out of the glare a rifle was armed directly at his middle. A Mossman-333, he thought professionally. Very last word in sniper rifles. What was this one doing on the White House lawn?

Aloud he said coldly, "What's *that* all about."

"Identification," said a voice.

Joplin handed him the ID card he'd taken off the Park policeman. The photograph on it was his own, Ferrier's men having done a bit of instant forgery. "Touchy, aren't you?" he said flippantly. It was always best to carry these things off with a high hand.

"Okay, where is he?" The voice handed back his ID card. The rifle disappeared into the pool of light.

"May I get out?" asked Joplin coolly.

"Please do," said the voice, also coolly.

Joplin hopped to the ground.

"Kill the torches," came a voice from far away. The searchlights went out instantly and they were back in the starlight, blinded by darkness. Joplin fumbled for the luggage compartment and lifted the lid.

Inside, squatting on his haunches, and still wearing the drug-induced smile and radiating idiotic benevolence, was Everett Quincey.

"I'm afraid that's the condition we found him in in Shenandoah Park," said Joplin calmly. "Comatose. He muttered his name over and over again and he told us his code name. He said it was urgent that he be brought to the White House immediately. Here he is."

Men came out of the blackness now and lifted Quincey to the ground.

"Get the President," said a voice, the same voice that had ordered Joplin out of the copter. "He wanted to be awakened immediately if we got any news of Quincey.''

Joplin's face was a mask. He was wondering if the other copters were on target and what, if any, trouble they were running into.

CHAPTER
NINETEEN

Prentice was flying in a copter piloted by a madcap gypsy who liked to sing silently to himself in moments of stress, and was shrieking a Romany lullaby soundlessly as he pushed his machine up the Potomac. The President's eyes were fixed on Joplin's brightly lit Park Police copter swinging up South Executive Drive as it was hit by the glare of searchlights.

"Split," commanded Ferrier, seated next to Prentice.

The covey of fourteen helicopters split into two groups and shot across the Potomac at full power, only ten feet from the water. As Joplin's machine monopolized the full attention both by sight and by radar of the security screen, the silent Bells sped into the Washington shore just outside the perimeters of President's Park—one group to the east, the other to the west.

Prentice and Ferrier were in the west group, headed for the West Wing, where the most dangerous action loomed. Also the least predictable. Prentice and Ferrier knew from experience that the West Wing teemed with Secret Service men. What they *didn't* know was how much the drill had changed. If they were expected—and it looked as if they were—there might be surprises. The copter lifted over the line of trees at the edge of President's Park and dropped to the lawn as close to the great sheltering oaks as safety permitted. Two Arabs hit the grass, silent as smoke, and sped on rubber soles to the guard house concealed in the trees at the entrance gate. There was no one there. The guards had been lured by all the excitement to the center of the White House lawn far south and west of their post.

Two of the west group copters were hovering now inches off the West Wing roof. Two of the Chinese landed in silence on the roof, laden with scaling equipment; the copter left them instantly and dropped two more Chinese gunmen farther down the colonnaded West Wing roof, two more farther on. They bypassed the President's Oval Office altogether. There were other plans for that.

Seated in his copter, the President could see in the starlight the glimmer of white of the colonnaded porch outside his office; he could hear nothing of that operation. Too much racket was going on around Joplin, the perfect cover.

Ferrier was hunched over the code box they'd found in Everett Quincey's safe. His lips formed the words "Here goes." He pushed the coded card into the slot. In a fourteen-millionth of a second it shot its instructions to the rose bush on the lawn—beaming into two of the Pentagon's highly secret heterodynes and thereby activating its most complex and thorough local defense operations.

*   *   *

The east wing of Ferrier's invasion force was commanded by the lighthearted Jerry Patch, who was humming to himself as he brought his seven-copter force swinging wide around the east perimeter of President's Park. One of his copters dove quickly to the East Wing roof and discharged two-man teams at forty-foot intervals. Another, silent as a plunging hawk, plummeted straight down onto the White House roof itself. This was the most split-second operation of all because the roof would have its guards. The copter never touched down—it was too much of a jar—but hovered inches away as three Hungarians, a huge Japanese wrestler, and two other Japanese jumped out on silent feet. Their task was easier than expected, again thanks to Joplin attracting all that attention on the lawn. The four roof guards, every last one, were facing south down the lawn, their backs to the trouble. They hardly knew what hit them. Arms encircled their necks, needles plunged into their arms, and they dropped like stones, out of play for at least four hours. Where possible, pretend they were wild animals in a game park, Prentice had said.

Jerry Patch had a far tougher drill to perform to take out all six of the guard houses—four of them on the gates, one of them on East Executive Drive, the other very large one on Pennsylvania Avenue itself. He used all six copters, holding out only his own—one for each post. Again using the copters' silence, he came straight down on each guard post, the gunmen dangling beneath on hanging ropes. The first inkling the guards got was when a gunman of some very interesting nationality, face set in a ferocious scowl, appeared at his window, usually inches from his face with a huge pistol in hand which fired right into his chest—with a sort of apologetic cough—a needle heavily impregnated with viazene, which worked very quickly indeed.

Patch himself hovered over the Pennsylvania Avenue gatepost where he expected trouble—and got it. Ozone gunmen dangled from ropes on all four sides of the copter—one for each corner—but even that wasn't enough. Normally only two men would have been awake at the gatepost at that hour, but these were not normal times. Four Ozone gunmen rushed the gatepost—flailing down the man at the door before one of them pumped him with viazene—and gained the inside before the defenders knew anything was afoot. One Secret Service man got out his gun before the needle hit him, but he got no farther. Another leaped at a Polish gunman and grappled before he sank to the floor. Two others went quietly, too startled to draw or to do anything. The trouble was that there were four others who had been counted upon to be asleep—but weren't. They were off duty, only one of them armed. The Polish gunman, his drug pistol empty, leaped at the armed man with his knife, and blood flowed for the first time in the operation. The man was dead before he struck the carpet.

The Kurd and the Cossack took on the three others with their pistol butts, but not before one of them had landed his fist on the emergency button which set off alarms and lit lights and activated emergency procedures all over the White House from the East Wing to the West Wing, from the North Portico to the southernmost tip of President's Park.

The Pole, leader of the group, took out his transmitter and sent a message bounding off a satellite: "Condition red," he said. Ferrier heard it in his copter with pursed lips. "The party's getting wild," he said to the President. "I wish Jop would hurry."

Joplin *was* hurrying. After the searchlights went out, it took a minute or two to get his vision back. During that spell, he'd been occupied with Everett Quincey, whose drugged presence shifted the attention away from him altogether, prize of all prizes that he was. It wouldn't last, but while it did, Joplin took a quick reconnaissance to be sure he was where he thought he was—just east of the tennis courts which he knew were completely screened by trees. He judged the distance. Thirty yards. He'd need five seconds. He reached for Jan's hand and gave it two quick squeezes. The two men edged to the other side of the helicopter, then broke for the tennis court where a copter was waiting.

Things were not going to work out quite that smoothly. From behind him Joplin heard the voice of the man who'd stuck the gun in his ribs. "Hey," said the voice, "where are you going?" Joplin sprinted for the protection of the trees, the Czech behind and to his left. "Hold it right there!" came the voice in a tone of icy rage.

Joplin was already fumbling with the wire door to the tennis court, praying it wasn't locked. It wasn't. He half expected a burst of gunfire, but they were too befuddled for that. Instead he heard them order on the searchlights. The two men threw themselves into the copter, which rose directly into a glare of the searchlights.

"Take out those lights," roared Joplin.

He grabbed the nearest machine pistol away from its owner and took out one light personally. Cossack sharpshooters took out the other two.

But of course the game plan was out the window.

Joplin poked his head into the cockpit. "Come down hard, right on their heads," he commanded.

The helicopter plummeted straight down the White House lawn and charged on the group near the fountain. Joplin heard the voice of the same man who seemed to be in charge. Then came a burst of automatic fire which rattled off the copter's bulletproof windshield. One burst was all the defenders had time for. Then the copter was upon them sending men scurrying for cover in all directions.

"Automatic fire!" roared Joplin. "We're blown! Fire! Fire! Fire!"

He aimed the machine pistol he'd requisitioned at a fleeing man and brought him down with a burst.

Prentice and Ferrier heard the gunfire on the copter. "Looks like the party's over," said Prentice scowling. He didn't like that gunfire. Ferrier didn't either, for different reasons. "Come on," he said. The two men dropped to the lawn and sped for the President's Oval Office, one hundred yards away. Hasbrouck sped after them. Their copter rose straight up and headed down the lawn to join the battle.

Prentice had never felt so nakedly exposed as he was in the fourteen seconds it took him to get across the wide sweep of the lawn. Blessed relief engulfed him when he reached the lovely sheltering darkness of the Presidential porch. Hasbrouck, panting hard, was behind him. Ferrier, in better condition than either of them, pulled up the rear. If a shot had dropped the President, someone had to pick him up. And that someone would have been Ferrier.

The Oval Office was black as tragedy. If there was any sound on the inside, it was lost in the crackle of gunfire on the lawn. Just the same, Prentice listened hard at the french doors that led directly to his office before inserting the intricate Cholmondsley key with its bewildering filigree of design, one of only two in existence. McMillan may have had the lock changed but Prentice doubted it. He'd only been in office seventy-two hours and he had many things on his mind. Prentice uttered a silent prayer and turned the key. It turned easily and Prentice smiled.

He would have entered but Ferrier elbowed him aside and slipped into the Oval Office ahead of him. Black as the inside of owls. Ferrier sent his flashlight licking around the walls. The American flag, the Presidential flag. The Great Eagle crest on the carpet, which Prentice loathed. The Vermont barn red walls. The three-quarter-length portrait of George Washington. At the far end of the oval was the gilt chair sometimes occupied by a Marine when the President was in residence but not in his office. It was empty. Finally, the flash lit up the immense limewood desk that Prentice had designed himself. Empty.

"Come," whispered Ferrier.

Hasbrouck and Prentice slipped into the Oval Office. Ferrier turned off the flash and the room was lit now only by stars.

There was a pause in the firing outside. In the silence Ferrier was conscious for the first time of the bell resounding through the pavilion that Thomas Jefferson had designed—but not for purposes such as this. Just outside in the long corridor the other side of his secretary's office, the three men heard pounding footsteps headed in their direction.

"No lights," said Ferrier. "Come on." In the not-quite darkness of the room he looked fiercely at

Hasbrouck. "You are to forget everything we are about to show you."

The pounding footsteps were getting uncomfortably close. Prentice sat in his black leather armchair facing Hasbrouck with a quizzical smile and pushed the concealed button underneath his desk, disappearing into the floor. Twelve seconds later the empty chair reappeared through the floor.

"Your turn," said Ferrier politely.

Hasbrouck sat, gingerly, and a second later vanished into the floor. The chair reappeared and the footsteps now slowed to a walk out in the President's appointments office. Ferrier sat in the black leather armchair, pushed the button, and vanished into the floor—just as the great double doors leading into the President's Oval Office opened.

The lights in the office switched on. The room was empty, the great leather chair back in its place.

Spence was at the door, surveying the place with narrowed eyes, examining the room inch by inch. McMillan, blowing like an asthmatic whale, was standing next to him. "It looks . . . all right to me . . ." puffed McMillan. "What was all the hurry?"

"Shut up," said Spence.

He crossed the room quickly and tried the outside door the three men had just entered. It opened to his touch. Spence examined it for signs of force. There were none. Spence looked wild.

"There are only two keys to this door," he said harshly, "and I have one of them."

"Who has the other one?"

"Prentice had it. He's in the building."

"Prentice is dead," said McMillan, smiling the

blubbery smile that had got him the nickname of Happy Walrus.

"Oh God, I hope so," said Spence.

Just before the firing broke out on the lawn, a Magyar gunman named Wenceslas slipped down a black nylon rope from the roof—looking as if he were suspended on nothing at all—and swung into the window outside Lincoln's sitting room, the room least likely to have anyone at all in it or near it. The window wasn't even locked and he stepped into the little room once used as an office by nineteenth-century Presidents, sliding over the Empire desk at the window and stepping down on the red plush Victorian chair next to it and onto the green carpet. Without a pause he slipped out into the little antechamber that led to the Queen's Bedroom where five Queens had slept and listened at the door. Not a sound. Then he listened again at the door to the Lincoln Bedroom. A long time. There was almost certainly someone in there, asleep or awake.

The Magyar turned the doorknob as gently as a lover caressing his beloved. The door opened soundlessly and the Magyar stole like a cat into the room where Lincoln had signed the proclamation freeing the slaves. The oak bed's great, heavily carved headboard shone dully in the starlit room. Next to it on one of the green plush Victorian chairs was a Marine in his full-dress reds quite shamelessly asleep.

He was not to sleep long. The first burst of automatic fire on the lawn—the one that bounced off the windscreen of Joplin's helicopter—made him snap erect, eyes wide open, just as the Magyar's gun, with an apologetic cough, put him to sleep again for four hours. The Magyar stepped to the window, unlocked it, and helped in his two Hungarian friends. The gunfire was lighting up the lawn with its long flashes now, and one wild shot from the helicopter whistled past Wenceslas's head and smashed the great square gilt mirror over the Lincoln fireplace.

The three Hungarians ran into the corridor, guns drawn. There should have been two Marines there keeping each other company. There weren't. They had run into the Yellow Oval Room when the firing started and were looking out of the lovely curved windows down the south lawn to see what was going on. In the uproar of shooting the three Hungarians were on their backs before they were aware they had company—three Marines. One went off quietly on the viazene, while the other two powerful young Marines fought a splendid battle under the disapproving glare of the Rembrandt Peale portrait of George Washington over the mantelpiece. One Marine sent Wenceslas reeling into the same mantelpiece, smashing two priceless gold and alabaster candlesticks. The other Hungarian was rolling across the yellow carpet, sending another pair of ormolu candlesticks to the floor. The Marine was drawing his revolver when Wenceslas stunned him with a yellow Louis XVI chair, much too delicate for that line of work. Then he shot him with viazene and the Marine toppled like a stone.

The third Marine was astride one of the Hungarians, his pistol poised to smash his skull in, when Wenceslas splintered one of the French vases purchased by President Monroe in 1817 over his head. It distracted him just enough to slip a little more viazene into him. He gave a huge sigh and rolled over.

The three Hungarians departed running for the West Wing of the top floor of the White House where the President's wife still resided. She was their whole responsibility. It was just at that moment that the Secret Service man at the Pennsylvania Avenue gate hit the alarm button.

All hell broke loose. Sirens rose and fell throughout the White House. The three Hungarians sprinted down the corridor, guns at the ready, and dove at the door of the President's bedroom. It was securely locked from the inside.

CHAPTER
TWENTY

The alarm bell going off prematurely had thrown the game plan into chaos, nowhere more so than in the West Executive Wing where four Chinese had lowered themselves from the roof into the upper story. A detachment of Marines no one had counted upon, alerted by the alarm bell, came charging out of the basement. The Chinese under young Hsu Chin retreated prudently back to the roof where Hsu messaged on the red circuit TTTT—for Trouble, Big Trouble.

With Ferrier deep in the sub-sub-sub-basement Joplin had taken command. He broke off the lawn engagement and directed his copter to land on the roof. "Jerry," he said on the red circuit, "do you read me?"

"I've always read you, Belasco," said Patch, irretrievably flippant. "Even the fine print."

"The Chinese are in the soup in the Executive

Wing. Have you got any troops? More trouble than we'd counted on."

Patch just whistled at that news: "We're blown, baby, blown," said Patch gaily. "The news has traveled clear to Cincinnati by now. Here come the gendarmes." Patch was hovering just inside the iron fence barely off ground level, where he could see the action most clearly.

"D.C. police!" spat out Joplin. There seemed no end to the forces they had to contend with—Secret Service, Marines, Army, Navy—and now the District police. "For God's sake, don't shoot the District police," grunted Joplin.

"No bullets," said Patch. "Tupper is handling."

From his copter, Patch watched Tupper as he sauntered out of the gatepost to meet the shrieking police car hurtling up Pennsylvania Avenue. "I'll send some soldiers to help the Chinese. Do we go ahead with the North Portico as planned?"

"Instantly," snapped Joplin.

Patch sent four of his copter loads to the Executive West Wing, where they discharged one hundred fifty men on the squat square roof. At that very moment, Joplin was getting very bad news from Wenceslas who used his laser transmitter to get through: "Door locked, boss," he said. "Do we break it down?"

It was a decision he never had to make. Joplin heard a crack of the Jasper-363 as clearly as if it had been shot on the roof. Wenceslas uttered a sort of whoof of departing air and departing life. Joplin had heard it many times before. Two more cracks of the Jaspers downed the other two Hungarians as well.

"Damn," said Joplin, which was as far into sentimentality as he ever descended. Wenceslas was one of the best, the most experienced, and the most lighthearted killers he had. It was difficult to find truly lighthearted killers these days; the young ones were sobersides who didn't enjoy the work.

"Over the sides, men!" he roared. There was no particular point in silence anymore. Suspended from the balustraded rooftop, one hundred men worked down the sides of the great white palace of the Presidents. This was the force intended to storm the first floor where most of the state rooms were located and where, Ferrier hoped, security forces would be the thinnest. Cossacks burst simultaneously into the three enormous windows of the East Room as three Romanies flung themselves with a shattering of glass through the three windows facing Pennsylvania Avenue. It was the biggest room in the White House and, until they arrived, the emptiest.

Directly opposite, Ozone troops of six nationalities were shattering the glass of the State Dining Room windows, entering through the gold damask curtains shrouding the two immense windows facing west and the three other great pilastered windows facing south.

The strongest force of all—because Joplin smelled trouble at that source—poured off the South Portico roof and lowered themselves onto Harry Truman's controversial balcony and from there, simply opened the tall windows and stepped through. Forty Ozone men had gathered in the Blue Room, when the Marine detachment on the ground floor charged down the great Cross Hall and into the room lit only by the light from the Cross Hall. The Ozones opened up with their little drug pistols as they had been ordered, but it was a bitter mistake. The Marines sprayed the room with automatic fire, reducing the Ozones by one third. The burst also smashed the great crystal chandelier and stitched a line clear across the chest of President Washington in yet another portrait.

Joplin deployed the rest of his force through the windows of the third floor. Twenty of his men invaded the Queen's Bedroom, the Lincoln Sitting Room, the Lincoln Bedroom, and the Treaty Room. The others went into the private quarters at the west of the house. Joplin reserved himself the President's bedchamber. Prentice had given him the key to the window, the only thing that could open the bulletproof windows from the outside, but with the instruction not to use it except in an extreme emergency. It had been planned from the very first to get Rosemary out of the line of fire as quickly as possible. Ferrier had a horror of the First Lady being used as a hostage at the height of operations, which would cook the business altogether. But Prentice had insisted the rescuers come in through the door. Men in black suits with blackened faces shooting into her window would scare her half to death, he said. But with Wenceslas dead in the corridor there was no other way.

Joplin unlocked the big window, pushed it up, and stepped into the room. Close behind, covering him with his machine pistol, came Kyptos, his Greek second in command. There was a terrified female shriek. Joplin had fully expected that. The trouble was, it was the wrong shriek. Joplin's torch caught the woman in bed, hand over her breast, clutching the bedclothes in a caricature of female terror. The woman wasn't Rosemary Prentice. It was Angela McMillan, a lady almost as blubbery in body and soul as her husband—yelling the house down.

"Jesus Christ," rasped Joplin, "nothing at all is going right in this fucking operation."

He picked up the screaming woman with one hand, held her high above his head, and stuck a needle, very hard, into her buttocks. The screaming stopped abruptly.

Joplin flung the drugged body on the bed and picked up the telephone by the bedside. He got a dial tone, then he dialed W. From the phone came a single rising and falling tone. From his breast pocket he pulled out a cube the size of a cigarette packet. It had six square buttons on it. Joplin pushed the lower right button and the box emitted a tone, 2893 cycles into the phone. From far below him in the sub-sub-sub-basement of the West Executive Wing—a room to be used only in nuclear bomb attack and in emergencies such as these—Prentice answered the phone.

"We got the wrong First Lady," drawled Joplin. "Mrs. McMillan, not Mrs. Prentice. What do we do now?"

Tupper sauntered—no other word for it—to the curb where the District police car pulled up. A burst of gunfire from the great house shattered the morning air but not Tupper's calm, which always became gradually more glacial the greater the emergency.

"Is something bothering you?" he inquired.

Another burst of gunfire split the air.

"I could swear I heard gunfire," said the District cop apologetically.

"President McMillan is very high-spirited," said Tupper enigmatically.

Another burst of automatic fire.

"You mean he fires off tommy guns at four in the morning?" asked the cop, a shade less deferentially.

"That's not for us to say, is it?" said Tupper frostily. "Ours to do and die, and no questions asked."

Belligerence, never far from any cop's outer skin, surfaced. "And just what is your rank in the White House hierarchy?"

Tupper was waiting for that one. He flashed his Presidential aide card. You couldn't get any higher than that, short of The Man himself. It was not his President Prentice card; it was his President McMillan aide card, the very last word in aide cards.

The cop looked at it, nonplussed. Another burst of rapid fire came from the big house. The cop looked in that direction, just dying to bust in. "What do you expect me to do about that?" he asked bitterly.

"Nothing," said Tupper. He drew a line with his toe on the top of the curb. "Your authority stops right there."

He sauntered back to the gatehouse without a second glance and entered the door.

That was the whole point. The thing had no precedent, and whenever precedent-shattering events, like Pearl Harbor, occur, the defense forces who should handle it are in chaos. No one had told them what to do because no one had anticipated that particular thing. All armed forces from the police to the Army are superbly trained to deal only with what has happened, not with what has *not* happened. Pearl Harbor is magnificently equipped and trained now to handle the second Pearl Harbor, which will never come. The first one caught them in a state of total unpreparedness and left them in a state of total shock. The normal situation for the military.

The 126th Infantry—which was supposed to deal with any such wildly unlikely eventuality as the one actually occurring at the White House—was at that very moment rumbling in their trucks exactly the opposite direction from the White House southward down the Potomac where the phony alert Ferrier had fed the Pentagon computer said the trouble was. At the same time a Navy task force of three destroyers and the mini-carrier *Guam* were headed out from their moorings in Norfolk. Fighters from their base at Hampton Roads were taking off in the early morning darkness to rendez-vous in a magnificent exercise in split-second timing, with the Navy in the middle of Chesapeake Bay, where nothing at all was happening.

Down in the sub-sub-sub-basement the President face his slim, dazzlingly brilliant CIA chief who for once was dumbfounded.

"Where is Rosemary?" asked Prentice.

They were seated in the chillingly bare, grayish, cream-colored Operations Room designed to run nuclear wars from. At Prentice's side was a telephone. In front of him was a TV monitor screen, and it was monitoring the scene in the Oval Office. Spence was seated in the black leather chair, deep in thought. McMillan was leaning against the desk watching Spence, almost waiting for him to make up his mind, a reversal of roles which the men in the sub-sub-sub-basement would have found deeply intriguing if they hadn't had Rosemary on their minds.

Ferrier lifted his hands, for him an eloquent gesture, in bafflement: "She was in your room. I talked to her there. She said she wasn't leaving the White House until Thursday and she would stay right in that room."

"McMillan has moved her," said Prentice.

"Spence has moved her," said Hasbrouck, his eyes on the monitor. "He seems to be in charge."

The three men were surrounded by TV monitor screens. At the end of the room was an immense glass war map of the world—including the North and South Poles—all magnificently inappropriate to the tiny war they were fighting inside the grounds of the great house itself. Next to the map stretching tier on tier was a quarter acre of electronic wizardry designed to communicate instantly to the Arctic, the Antarctic, Europe, Africa, South America, Southeast Asia—in fact, everywhere except someplace in the private quarters of the White House where Rosemary was.

"We've got to find Rosemary," said the President calmly. "There are bullets flying up there."

He still held the phone in his hand, and said into the receiver, "Jop, take Mrs. McMillan up to the roof. We may need her as a bargaining counter. How are things going?"

"I don't know," said Joplin. "I'm here on the second floor and the battle is down on the first floor."

The fighting on the first floor had become very confused. Decimated by the first burst of automatic fire, the Ozones in the Blue Room were hugging the floor and holding on, just barely. The Marines had turned on the lights from the wall sconces and the Ozone forces shot them out, bringing down the enormous French gilt bronze crystal chandelier at the center of the room. The beleaguered Ozones were reinforced by Joplin's Cossacks —outflanking the Marines from the East Room—and minutes later the other Ozone force which had come in the State Dining Room windows rushed in to help. The trouble was that just as they attacked the rear of the

Marines in the Blue Room, their own rear was attacked by a fresh force of young Marines coming up from the first basement. In an operation Joplin would have been proud of, if he'd been there to see it, the Cossacks and Bulgarians wheeled on their heels, and drove the new Marine force back into the Cross Hall, bullets ricocheting off the marble columns. The Ozones shot down the two great eighteenth-century English cut glass chandeliers, extinguishing their blazing light in a shower of cut glass, and in the darkness forced the Marine force back into the gilt wilderness of the State Dining Room.

Down in the sub-basement, something happening on the TV monitor took the minds of the three men off the First Lady. They watched as the porch door of the Oval Office opened. Two men carried in Everett Quincey, and sat him in an armchair. A third man, obviously in charge of the operation, followed the others into the office. He waved the other two men out and faced Spence.

"Well, well," said Prentice far below in the sub-sub-sub-basement. "My long lost gardener. Meet Mr. Canozzi, Paul."

"Mr. Fitts," corrected Ferrier.

On the screen, Spence was leaning negligently on one elbow on the desk, his chin cupped in one hand, scowling at Everett Quincey. "It would have been much better for all concerned, Mr. Quincey, if you had been killed," said Spence. "As it is, you have screwed up our defense arrangements to a fare-thee-well."

Everett Quincey smiled his idiotic drugged smile.

"How much did you tell them?" asked Spence quietly.

"Everything," shrilled the drugged man, aglow with benevolence for all humanity.

"Oh, my God," quavered McMillan, who looked a very unhappy walrus.

"Shut up," said Spence. "Canozzi, is it sodium pentothal?"

"No," said Canozzi, the sometime Fitts.

"You see," said the President to Ferrier, "he calls himself Canozzi. A Wasp trying to pass as a Wop. A new switch."

Canozzi was saying: "A man like Quincey wouldn't tell too much under sodium pentothal. He's under something stronger. And if it's something very much stronger he's not likely to come out of it at all. So if you got anything to ask him, you better ask it now."

Spence set his square, all-American jaw. "Everett, who did you tell it all to?"

"To President Prentice," said Quincey eagerly. "Personally."

"Oh, my God," said McMillan, blubber-voiced. "Is he alive?"

"Oh, quite alive."

Far below in the sub-sub-sub-basement, Prentice uttered a deep sigh. "There goes our trump card," he said quietly. "They know I'm alive."

As if echoing his thought, Spence on the TV screen said, "He's in the building—somewhere."

Canozzi spoke up and for the first time the men in the deep basement shelter got a glimpse of him, a handsome ruthless face with eyes like holes. (He'd make a good member of our team, thought Prentice.)

"There are a lot more men besides him in the building. You got any idea how big this operation is, General?"

General? The three men in the sub-basement were a study in dismay, their minds changing gears almost audibly. The word *General* changed a lot of things.

"General?" said Prentice, looking at Ferrier accusingly. "In whose Army?"

Ferrier shook his head slowly, eyes never leaving the screen, biting his lower lip, his mind racing in all directions. *General?*

On the screen, Spence was also thinking, rubbing his lower lip, the eyes hooded. He radiated power and authority now. Spence. He'd never had this kind of authority before. His must have been a great performance indeed. Spence, the slow-witted, stolid bureaucrat. Transformed into the Leader of Men. For the first time in this exceedingly dangerous operation, Prentice felt a thrill of fear. Because Spence knew all about this rabbit warren directly underneath him; in fact, Spence had shown it all to him—minus a few refinements Ferrier had added, refinements that now seemed dangerously inadequate.

On the TV screen Spence appeared to have made up his mind. "Bring Mrs. Prentice to this room, Canozzi," he said.

"If I can get her through the gunfire alive," said Canozzi lazily.

"Afraid, Canozzi?" asked Spence.

"Not of you, General," said the former White House gardener. He was baiting the other one. Bad blood there, obviously. "I thought Mrs. Prentice was important to your operation."

"She is," said Spence. He was looking holes into Canozzi. Abruptly he laid his fingers on his lips and said "*Ummi*." The word seemed to hit Canozzi like a slap in the face. The lazy impudent look gave way to one of sullen quietude.

Spence leaned back in the armchair and contemplated the ceiling, which he then addressed as follows: "Prentice, wherever you are—down in the sub-basement, I expect, in the operations room—I feel strongly you're listening. Now hear this. We're going to bring Mrs. Prentice to this room through corridors which are at the moment under fire. Would you like to ask your forces to lay down their arms?"

Prentice leaned back in his chair in the deep sub-basement, his eyes unseeing. To Ferrier he said tonelessly, "Get him on the phone." Ferrier took out his little minivox from his breast pocket and pushed a button. He held the minivox up to the transmitter on the telephone. Instantly the telephone at Spence's elbow on the President's desk rang. Spence picked it up. Prentice, watching him with narrowed eyes, took the telephone from Ferrier's hand.

"Spence," said the President. "We have Mrs. McMillan. You have Mrs. Prentice. I suggest we trade wives."

Spence smiled and scratched his ear at this naivete. "Prentice, you may—with my full permission—drop Mrs. McMillan from the White House roof into a vat of boiling lard."

McMillan gave a squeal of anguish clearly audible, though unseen, to the watchers below.

"Mr. McMillan wouldn't like it much, but Mr. McMillan's feelings have no influnce whatsoever in our decisions," said Spence—and there was no mistaking the sincerity of that utterance at all. McMillan, President of the United States in the opinion of two hundred million Americans, appeared to have no say whatsoever in the business at hand.

"*Now* will you order your men to lay down their arms?"

Prentice didn't hesitate: "Certainly not. We might, however, arrange a cease fire." Then, watching the man closely, he added very casually, "General."

Spence didn't like it. He glared at Canozzi, angry at the man for having spilled it. This was an important glance and it wasn't lost on Ferrier. If there'd been any doubts that the word General was a real title and not just a soubriquet, they were banished by that look.

Spence hesitated and Prentice dove headlong into that hesitation with the expertise of an executive who had been Governor and President for twenty years. "That offer is final, General, and I won't bargain with you any further until I *hear* Mrs. Prentice on *this* telephone."

Both the words *hear* and *this* were subtly underlined in his voice for a very good reason. Prentice strongly suspected, because Spence had used the word *listening* rather than *watching*, that Spence didn't know he was being watched as well as overheard. It was a small trump in his hand and he was going to need it. The emphasis on *this* was for another reason. It was central to his thought that he get his wife on that phone in Spence's hand, and no other.

Spence made up his mind. "Agreed. Tell your men to cease firing and we shall do the same."

Prentice nodded to Ferrier, who messaged through to Joplin on the White House roof.

"I'm hanging up now, General," said Prentice politely. "I'll call you back when I hear my wife's voice"—again the emphasis on hearing rather than seeing—"in that room."

He hung up.

"RASD," said Ferrier and uttered a deep sigh. "They've come a long way."

"Rasd?" said the President. It struck a dim chord. No, not Rasd. RASD—all capitals. The intelligence wing of Al Fatah.

"Oh, for Christ's sake," he exploded. "I don't believe it! Are you trying to tell me Spence is an Arab?"

"No, obviously he's not," said Ferrier, toneless. "RASD trains all nationalities now. The IRA is learning their tricks at the RASD training camp near Damascus in Syria. So is the Red Army of Japan. So is—hold on to your hat—the Mafia. In fact, RASD has a lot in common with the Mafia. It's strong on family, it's elitist, and it's very, very rich. It has at least one hundred million dollars stashed away in Italian and Swiss banks—the profits from hijackings, kidnappings, bank robberies, and hashish smuggling. The Mafia is undoubtedly trying to infiltrate it to keep an eye on it."

"Do they have *Generals*?" asked Prentice.

Ferrier smiled one of his unamused smiles. "Even Field Marshals. Terror is getting to be very big business, and very international. RASD was both the brains and the operations of the massacre of Israeli athletes at Munich, the murder of Jordanian Prime Minister in Cairo in 1971, blowing up an oil refinery at Rotterdam the same year, and the massacre at Lydda airport in Israel in 1972.

"The RASD training camp is at Deraa near Damascus with at least twenty-six nationalities there, some of them trained by old Nazi SS men. Just to show you how international RASD is, the massacre at Lydda was carried out by Jap terrorists with Czech weapons they'd been given by Italian fellow terrorists of the Red Brigade. They carried documents forged by German terrorist friends. They might have called in help from a dozen affiliated outfits including the Tupamaros of Uruguay, the Turkish People's Liberation Army, or the Naxalites of India. The International office is in Zurich, the organizational methods are taught in China, and the intellectual center is the American University in Beirut—which is full of disaffected Europeans and Americans.''

There was a pause.

''I will lay you eight to five,'' said Ferrier negligently, ''that Spence spent some time at the American University in Beirut.''

The President nodded, speechless at Ferrier's prescience. Spence had spent two years at Beirut studying international relations according to his pink file. ''How did you spot him?'' asked Prentice.

''*Ummi*,'' said the CIA head, making it two distinct musical syllables. ''It's an Arab word you'll find in the Koran. In the Koran it signified that Mohammed couldn't read or write. Now it's used as a code word on the secret RASD radio in Damascus which issues instructions to RASD outfits all over the world. In the sense it's used now, it's the closest word the Arabs have to the Mafia's *omerta*. It means more than silence. It means loyalty to death, all that. Spence was not only trying to shut Canozzi up—he was furious at him for blowing the General bit—but also reminding him of his loyalties and obligations. You saw how fast it worked.''

Silence hung in the room. Then the President spoke up: ''Well, we know something Spence wishes we didn't know. Does it give us an opening anywhere?

CHAPTER TWENTY-TWO

When he had ordered Ferrier to build the new secret elevator Prentice had only the vaguest idea as to what he wanted it for. He already had an emergency exit in the chair. But, a politician to the fingertips, he wanted another option. No President can have too many of those. His mind dwelt much on assassination when he ordered the elevator and he thought a second escape hatch might be useful. But like many another good idea, its usefulness was now quite opposite to its original purpose—as a means of ingress to the Oval Room, not the other way around. It was also, Prentice suddenly perceived, a superb *trompe d'oeil*.

It was a stainless steel cylinder just big enough to admit one man, hidden away among the electronic gadgetry of the Operations Room. As he folded his tall ungainly form into the elevator, his mind working furiously, he had another powerful thought, and he stepped out of the elevator to communicate it to Ferrier.

"Look, Paul, if Spence is truly a general in RASD, he is our savior—my savior, especially. I need him, oh God, do I need him, alive and well. I want you to put Joplin in personal charge of his safekeeping."

Ferrier nodded. He'd already had the same idea, but of course for entirely different reasons than the President, whose ideas were solely political. He wanted a live RASD general to question. He helped fold Prentice back into the elevator—and closed the curved steel door. The elevator moved upward at a snail's pace.

It gave Prentice plenty of time for thought—it stopped nowhere but the sub-sub-sub-basement and the Oval Office—and Prentice's mind was racing ahead. It did not dwell for an instant on the encounter in front of him. He'd already decided precisely what he was going to do in the Oval Room when he got there. The plan would work—or it wouldn't. And that was that. No point at all in tightening up one's reflexes with worries about that.

No, his mind was shooting forward into the political and legal aftermath of it all. Because the fact was, and it had bothered him ever since Utah, that he was blown sky high. The original plan, brilliant in its simplicity, was to swallow the Mafia in its own *omerta*. Their tradition of saying nothing, explaining nothing, was to strangle them. They were to vanish in the black hole of their own silence, as black as the hole the astrophysicists had discovered in the skies where the whole stars were swallowed and vanished into nothingness. That was to be the fate of the syndicate and up to a point it had worked.

Now, as the elevator inched its way to the Oval

Room, Prentice was constructing out of the ruins of the original plan, the outlines and hard foundations of a new plan—all of it centering around Spence, who praise God, was the representative of a foreign power. For the fact was that the American people were not very much exercised by the syndicate; they had never been or they would never have let it take over the country as it had. The Mafia was a sort of folk legend in a way—even as villains, the Mafioso were always seen as sinister in only the most romantic sense.

But if a foreign power was behind them, or at least beside them, then any measures taken by the President would not only be forgiven but applauded. And if the foreign power was Arab—which had the advantage of not even having a sizable minority in the U.S., and which was the perfect villain because hadn't one of their number assassinated Bobby Kennedy?—then the applause would be deafening. He, Prentice, would be in grave danger of sainthood. And for the legend-makers, what couldn't they do with this scene—a President in a secret elevator charging to the rescue of his First Lady? Wryly, Prentice recognized that he was occupied more with the legend than with Rosemary.

Prentice was thinking furiously: a trial. We'll have a huge public trial of Spence that will eclipse anything the Soviets ever pulled, in which we will accuse the Arab countries of everything from nuclear blackmail to poisoning wells. Before the United States Supreme Court itself! No, we can't do that. Unconstitutional. But perhaps I can get old Chief Justice Wright to resign—just to preside over the trial—with a promise of instant reappointment. We might even televise the trial. In the public interest, of course . . .

The elevator, black as the ace of spades, had

stopped. Prentice shook his head quickly to banish all this bright wishful thinking, to focus his mind on the urgency of right now.

The door curved silently round the back of the elevator and Prentice put his eye to the hole, which he'd ordered personally. For what he was looking through was the eye of George Washington in the three-quarter length portrait by Charles Willson Peale from its commanding position over the mantel.

The first thing that struck his eye was Rosemary, seated in his chair at the desk. Behind her, so close he was actually touching the chair, was Canozzi. In the center of the Oval Office was Spence. Stationed in a curve around the walls of the Oval Office were Spence's men—grimly Prentice recognized at least six of them as members of his personal bodyguard. Well, well, he thought. One was one of the men who had ridden the running board of the Presidential limousine. Very interesting.

Every face was turned toward the big double doors. Expecting him to come through there, were they? He smiled. No President since Franklin D. Roosevelt so enjoyed doing the unexpected as Harry Prentice. He pushed the small white button on the frame of the painting. It slid noiselessly to the left vanishing right into the wall. Prentice stood on the mantelpiece, imitating exactly the negligent pose of the Father of His Country.

So quietly had this little bit of legerdemain taken place that no one noticed, and for seconds Prentice stood there, savoring his little joke. It was Rosemary who first noticed him.

"Harry!" she cried. She rose from the seat, and instantly Canozzi wrapped both arms around her.

Immediately, he was the cynosure. Not only of all eyes, but of all guns. He smiled, in spite of a moment of freezing terror. He'd never had a gun pointed at him before. Then he leaped to the floor, landing with a heavy thud, instantly putting his hand to the small of his back with a grimace of pain.

To Spence he said, almost apologetically, "I'm not really young enough for these Errol Flynn entrances, you know."

There was no expression at all in Spence's black eyes. He lifted his 38-caliber Mossman to shoulder level, aiming right at Prentice's eyes.

"Surely," said Prentice, "you will allow me to kiss my wife." For an instant, he thought: it's not going to work. This is a real professional who doesn't allow these little exercises in gallantry.

There was a long silence while the gun pointed straight at his eyes. Then Spence said, "You have seven seconds." There was a hissing sibilance in every S.

Prentice leaped gaily to Rosemary's side. She flung her arms around his neck, fortunately leaving both his arms free for other purposes. He needed them both. With one hand—his left—he reached under the desk and pushed the square of wood. The bulletproof plastic oval shot up from the floor, surrounding the desk and protecting the people behind it—Prentice, Rosemary, and Canozzi.

With his right hand Prentice put the little pistol right to Canozzi's forehead and shot him dead.

Spence's bullet hit the plastic shield, ricocheted off and tore a gaping hole in George Washington's midriff.

"Hang on, dear," said Prentice to his wife. He pulled her into the big black leather armchair and pushed the little square of wood under his desk. President and First Lady vanished through the floor.

In the sub-sub-sub-basement, Ferrier watching the whole operation, said into his microphone: "Now, Joplin! Now!"

Joplin's men hit the Oval Office, rockets splintering the bulletproof windows as if they were made of tissue paper. Joplin was first man through the splintered door, hurtling himself directly at Spence. In the dust and dim crazy light after the rockets Spence squeezed off only one shot, which caught Joplin in the shoulder. The force of the charge overturned Spence and Joplin fell on him heavily and pinned him down as the bullets careened around him, protecting the man underneath with his vast bulk for other later purposes.

It was 5:00 A.M., at broad daylight, an hour after they'd first arrived over the White House lawn. Ferrier, Hasbrouck, and Prentice soberly walked through the wreckage of the White House. Prentice stared sadly at the remnants of the Sheraton break-front cabinet in the ground floor corridor, torn to ribbons by automatic fire. It had been one of his favorite pieces of furniture. A pile of bodies lay at the entrance of the East Room, young Marines caught in a crossfire from front and back. The East Room itself was a shambles of torn gilt furniture. The two enormous cut-glass chandeliers hung crazily askew, their glass mostly on the floor. The enormous concert grand piano, with gilt eagles for legs, had been overturned and used as a shield. It was riddled with gunfire. The great gilt mirror over the marble fireplace was shattered and the two tall gilt candelabra by Pierre-Philippe Thomire lay on the parquet floor, miraculously unhurt. Prentice picked them both up tenderly and put them back on the chipped mantel.

"Can your electronics wizards handle the television equipment in my office?" asked Prentice suddenly.

"They can handle anything," said Ferrier.

"We'll have a broadcast right now," said the President. "I must get my point of view on the record before anyone else puts *his* point of view on it."

"For God's sake, Mr. President, it's five o'clock in the morning. Nobody will be watching."

"Oh, somebody will," said Prentice cheerfully. "There is never a time when *nobody* is watching television. Anyway, you can tape it and the networks can play it all day long. It's always important to get your message across first. We are going to have a great public trial and you, Hasbrouck, are going to be Special Prosecutor."

An hour later Prentice delivered his special emergency message to the people across the sleeping land—a bit of statesmanship that was to be analyzed, praised, denounced, and thoroughly misunderstood for decades to come.

For what Prentice was doing—as he usually did in all his more important actions—was about eight things simultaneously. He wanted to explain, of course. He wanted to cover up, of course. He wanted to strike, to accuse the whole Middle East with special brimstone for Tripoli and Teheran, Ghaddafi and Khomeini (and in a lower key because he knew the electorate didn't give a damn—the Mafia). He wanted to attack because it was always the best defense. He wanted to make a dramatic gesture with his dawn special message. But above all he wanted once again to take charge. He wanted to obliterate any tiny imprint McMillan might have made on the people as President of the United States, and take back the reins of power into his own hands.

From the shattered Oval Office—and he specially forbade any attempt to clean anything up—the steel frames of the windows twisted in their frames, the chairs overturned, the Peale portrait hanging from its frame like a rag—Prentice faced the three television cameras.

"This is the President," he said. "Our nation has been the victim of a conspiracy so vast, so evil, so subtle, and so monstrous that it is almost impossible for the average American to grasp. Let me try to explain..."

About the Author

JOHN CROSBY is the author of ten novels, mostly thrillers like this one, and two non-fiction books. Before taking up novel-writing he was for many years a reporter and later a columnist for the *New York Herald Tribune*. He was born in Milwaukee and has lived at various times in New York, San Francisco, Paris, London and Santa Fe. Currently, he lives on a farm near Charlottesville, Virginia, where he raises horses, goats and children.

There's an epidemic with 27 million victims. And no visible symptoms.

It's an epidemic of people who can't read.

Believe it or not, 27 million Americans are functionally illiterate, about one adult in five.

The solution to this problem is you...when you join the fight against illiteracy. So call the Coalition for Literacy at toll-free **1-800-228-8813** and volunteer.

Volunteer Against Illiteracy. The only degree you need is a degree of caring.

Ad Council Coalition for Literacy

Warner Books is proud to be an active supporter of the Coalition for Literacy.